I0757667

Book 2: LOW COUNTRY BLOOD

Silver Falchion Award Finalist--Best Thriller

—Killer Nashville 2020

This novel is hard to put down.

—Kirkus Reviews

This story is a thrilling adventure from the first page to the last. Author Sue Hinkin's compelling work, Low Country Blood: A Vega & Middleton Novel, embodies an exciting story with memorable characters – not to be missed!

—Readersfavorite.com 5/5-STARS

Published by small but mighty Literary Wanderlust in Colorado, "Low Country Blood" measures up with mainstream mysteries from major publishing houses.

—Mark Stevens writes the award-winning Allison Coil Mystery Series-*Antler Dust*, *Buried by the Roan*, *Trapline*, *Lake of Fire*, *The Melancholy Howl* and others.

Author Sue Hinkin has either done her research or has a cop in the family, as her descriptions of police procedure and communication seem spot-on.

—Colorado Book Review

Book 3: THE BURN PATIENT
WINNER Colorado Book Award 2020 Best Thriller
WINNER Foreword Indies 2020 Best Mystery

This is a fast-paced, intelligently plotted, and deftly written story that will have readers on the edge of their seats. The Burn Patient: A Vega and Middleton Novel is a page-turner that is balanced and filled with adventure and humanity; a riveting narrative with strong conflict.

—Readers Favorite 5/5 stars

With likable heroines, depraved villains, and a cast of interesting supporting characters, Hinkin proves she is more than just a writer of thrillers, her writing is a thrill to read as well.

—Colorado Book Review

This is an action-packed tale that will keep readers on the edges of their seats. It was gripping from the first page, and the breathless suspense was maintained throughout the story.

—OnlineBookClub.org 4/4-STARS

This is a crackerjack high voltage mystery from beginning to end. Once you read this, you'll want to read the rest of Sue Hinkin's novels. Great!!

—Ted Elrick is the co-screenwriter of the feature motion picture, "Home Sweet Hell," he has been the longtime editor of the Directors Guild of America Magazine and his mystery and science fiction short stories have appeared in numerous publications.

Book 4: THE MERMAID BROKER

The Mermaid Broker has made it clear that Sue Hinkin has the chops to become as big a fish as she wants in whatever waters she likes.

—Colorado Book Review

A frothy thriller set on the Southern California coast that will leave you gasping for air as it dives into the terrifying underworld of sex trafficking.

—BestThrillers.com

Sue Hinkin does a fantastic job of building a story. The heart of this plot though is a fast and firm thriller that begs to question Hinkin's artfully chilling dialogue, "Who knows what evil lurks in the hearts of men?" Very highly recommended.

—Readers Choice, 5/5 STARS

The Rx For Murder

A Vega & Middleton Novel

Sue Hinkin

Literary Wanderlust | Denver, Colorado

Published in the United States by Literary Wanderlust LLC, Denver, Colorado. www.LiteraryWanderlust.com

ISBN print: 978-1-956615-04-3
ISBN digital: 978-1-956615-05-0

Cover design: Pozu Mitsuma
Printed in the United States of America

1

"We can't just walk away from this, chief." Veteran newspaper reporter David Pine, early fifties with the nervous energy of a chihuahua, paced the floor in front of News Director Lance Ludlow's desk. Its surface was as empty and untouched as a piece of showroom furniture. This unsettling display of workplace vacuousness stoked Pine's niggling paranoia about the guy. Dude came out of nowhere to manage a significant LA news outlet, but he had zero understanding of journalism.

Ludlow adjusted his cuff links.

Pine hadn't seen cuff links since he'd viewed his grandfather's open casket.

The news director cleared his throat. "I don't find anything viable in the direction you're suggesting, Mr. Pine."

Pine jammed his hands into the pockets of his rumpled khakis. Two of his fingers almost ripped through the seam. "Not sure how you can say that," he said. "We've got a reliable informant who'll implicate Brandon Doyle—emails, texts, bank accounts in the Caymans—the *Full Monty*, literally. Got photos of him bare-assed, breast-stroking underage girls."

Ludlow pursed his lips as if tasting something sour. "Old news. Attorney Doyle's been exonerated on sexual abuse of minors. It's over. They're just trying to drum up bad press to thwart his run for Congress."

"It's not over." Pine felt his unfortunate pale complexion begin to flush. "And who the hell is *they*? It's *us* reporting the story, and we're telling the truth, giving the facts, not trying to sabotage the election. Give me a fuckin' break, Ludlow."

The news director winced and checked his fingernails. "No need to be crass."

The reporter gritted his teeth so hard he thought his molars would crack. Ludlow was a complete Luddite. "Okay, sorry, but I've known this asshole, I mean this, uh, fellow, Doyle, since we were roommates at Berkeley. He doesn't give up until he wins, no matter the cost. And now, since he's after the Senate seat, all the more reason the people need to know who this sleazeball really is."

Starched shirt and pricey suit, Lance Ludlow's round, black glasses rested on his Pinocchio-like nose. He was a younger version of one of former President Trump's old cronies, Roger Stone. Pine knew that Ludlow had come into the LA paper's top news position from the *San Francisco Evening Monitor*—an unimpressive rag where he'd been head accountant with a law degree from a third-rate school on the side. Pine took a deep breath and struggled to keep his cool. An award-winning journalist himself, he felt a psychic shop vac begin to suck hard at his gray matter because of this job.

Ludlow seemed oblivious. "Doyle's been fully acquitted on sex crime charges," he said. "We're not going to get him on anything else. Be realistic, Mr. Pine."

"He's neck-deep in the swamp with Big Pharma. Been dealing since he was sixteen. This time, it's generic drugs. We have to tell the story. It's what we promise the public to do—you know, the Fourth Estate."

Ludlow looked confused.

Pine tried not to roll his eyes. "You know—the political system:

executive, judicial, legislative, and the press. The idea is often attributed to the British politician Edmund Burke—"

"Please, stop. I understand the concept. Just slipped my mind for a second."

"Okay, sorry." Why was Ludlow stonewalling him? Something wasn't right. Pine's journalistic antennae buzzed like mad bees.

Ludlow tapped his manicured fingers on the shiny desktop. "Regardless of your history lesson, Mr. Pine, the Doyle thing sounds like fake news to me. Move on."

Pine stopped pacing and jerked to a dead stop like a dog who'd hit the end of his leash. "Fake news? Did you really say that?" He leaned toward the news director and truly considered punching him hard in his smug face. "Are you accusing me of falsifying information for a story?"

Ludlow drew back, held up his hands in protest, or maybe protection. "Of course not. I'm told you have an impeccable reputation. A bad choice of words."

"Choosing words is what we do, sir. I take that task very seriously."

"Yes, of course."

The reporter let out a long breath. "I get pretty touchy when my profession, *our* profession, gets trash-talked. Sick of being beat up for telling the facts."

"Yes, I understand." Nodding sagely, Ludlow steepled his eerily long fingers. "Why don't you bring me everything you have on this Doyle story? I'll review it all carefully." His thin eyebrows were drawn in a slash. He looked up from his desk, watery peepers the color of weak tea. He blinked through trifocals. "Have you shared this information with anyone else?"

"Not yet. I knew you'd want to be the first to vet it and give the okay."

Puckering his lips into a donut hole, Ludlow nodded again. "Okay, good. I'll take another look. This information is completely confidential and off-the-record until I get back with you. Agreed?"

"You got it, boss." But was it smart, Pine wondered, to keep the story exclusive to the *Daily News*? Would this bean counter develop the piece or kill it? His gut said don't trust the son of a bitch, but the dude was still signing the reporter's paychecks.

He tightened a fist. What the hell had this organization come to? The group that just bought the *Angeles Daily News*, where Pine had been onboard for a decade, clearly had a hard-on for Ludlow's uniformed, conspiratorial-type views. They recently canned the paper's long-time exec, a woman with more centrist leanings and a respectable portfolio of professional experience. Lance Ludlow's journalistic credentials were sketchy at best.

Pine felt a rush of anxiety dampen the edges of his thinning hairline. He rubbed at his short, graying beard. If he were ten years younger, he'd hustle up a new job someplace with integrity, if such places still existed. Times had changed.

Ludlow adjusted his eyeglasses. "Can you get me your notes by tomorrow morning?"

Pine's cheerless mood brightened just a flicker. "Yeah, sure. In fact, I can give you my files on a thumb drive right now."

"Excellent. I like your initiative."

Pine squeezed out a scant smile. The asshole was definitely bullshitting him. Guy probably hated any kind of initiative. Pine, however, knew from bitter experience that former LA County Prosecutor and Senate candidate, Brandon Doyle, was a charismatic, sociopathic, drug-dealing predator who'd only sharpened his hunting knives over the years. But Pine had sharpened his weapons, too. Information was his blade, and if he went down, it would be fighting.

His angry stomach began to rage in its usual noxious way, and he excused himself from the news director's office in search of a Pepcid.

Back at his cube, David Pine popped a couple antacids and copied the majority of the Doyle information onto a flash drive for Ludlow. But Pine would be damned if he'd give the son of a bitch everything— he'd hold back certain documents for now. And as insurance, he dropped a drive containing the entire file into an envelope addressed to a friend and veteran reporter, Beatrice Middleton.

2

Bea Middleton was an intense, early forties, African-American woman with the head-turning good looks that could give any Hollywood luminary competition. She stared at the computer screen in her office at the Cable News Network's West Coast Bureau high above Sunset Boulevard. She was absently twisting a paper clip into a knot.

A throat cleared nearby. She glanced up and froze.

A wild-looking woman with explosive curly hair the color of copper shell casings and a face bleak with fatigue slumped in the doorway. Savannah, Georgia Detective Mary O'Hanlon gripped the jamb like it would save her from drowning.

"Oh, my God, Mary, what are you doing here?" Leaping from her desk, Bea stumbled over a pile of folders she'd stacked on the floor.

Pulling the surprise visitor into her arms, she hugged her tightly. A triathlete and karate black belt, Detective O'Hanlon felt frail as a bird. Something was seriously wrong.

Bea released the embrace and grabbed Mary's hand, led her into the office, and shut the door. Cleared off a chair and motioned for her to sit. "Sweet Jesus, what is going on, girl? When did you get into LA?"

Mary pushed her hair out of her face. "About an hour ago. Sorry for barging in like this, but I don't know where else to turn. I'm desperate, and I don't trust anybody in this godforsaken town."

Bea studied her friend's face. Usually rosy with ginger freckles that matched her hair, Mary was now as pale and bloodless as skim milk. There was only one answer to the unhealthy transformation. "This's about Brandon Doyle, your asshole ex, isn't it?"

"How'd you guess?" Mary's lips trembled.

"I know your history with him, sweet pea. Why else would y'all show up in Tinseltown looking like hell and skinny as a stem of salt-marsh grass?"

The detective squirmed in her chair. Clenching and unclenching her fingers, her green eyes were glassy and feverish. Her breath came in little gasps.

"Panic attack?" Bea asked.

Mary nodded. "I'll be okay." She pulled a water bottle from her bag and took a long drink. "He has everybody in his pocket. You have no idea."

"I think I have a pretty good idea." Bea opened a desk drawer and lifted out a bottle of Baileys Irish Cream and two paper cups.

"Oh, yes, much better." Mary's mouth pressed into a wan smile. "Didn't know this was your stress beverage of choice."

Bea smiled and poured them each two fingers. The scent of whiskey, cocoa, and vanilla was soothing. They tapped cups and drank, paused, and let the warmth take hold.

Bea held up the bottle. Mary refused the offer for more, but Bea poured herself another splash. "So, I was pretty damn sure ol' Brandon Doyle was going to be off the street for a decade, at least, on that sex crimes thing." Bea shook her head. "I was shocked at the ruling."

"Acquitted. Unbelievable." Mary uttered a strangled cry. "No disbarment. Lots of sympathy for what he's *gone through.*"

Bea gazed out toward the Hollywood sign, tinged yellow in the acidic air. "It's a travesty."

"And in the meantime, he showed up unannounced in Savannah

and took our daughter!"

"What?" The air whooshed from Bea's lungs. Less than two years ago, Detective Mary O'Hanlon risked her life to help find Bea's son, Dexter, who'd been abducted by a sadistic psychopath. The screaming panic still lived in Bea's brain like a latent virus ready to erupt given the right trigger. And triggers lurked everywhere. "Tell me."

"He flew into Savannah-Hilton Head on a private jet and stole Molly when I was at work. He told her I was okay with it! Bribed her with a hot little Mini convertible, a no-limit Black Mastercard, and God only knows what else."

"Molly's twenty-one, isn't she? Of consent age?"

Mary nodded. "It's why I can't do anything. And since the car accident that almost killed her, residual brain trauma has really screwed up her cognition. You talk to her. She seems twelve in a hot woman's body."

"Sounds like Doyle's wet dream." Bea threw back the Baileys and gritted her teeth.

"But she's walking again, barely limps anymore." Mary's pride shone in a blush that suddenly colored her complexion. "Was living with me, doing well, going to school part-time at Armstrong Atlantic. She also worked with a local pet rescue. Then, *he* shows up. I knew it would come to this. Nobody leaves Brandon Doyle without getting sliced to the bone."

She broke into fresh tears. Laid her head on Bea's desk and wept. "He won't let me see her. His security man almost broke my arm when I tried to push past him. And then suddenly, two intimidating black vans nearly ran me over. Brandon's blocked her social media, too. Molly must have absolutely no idea what is going on."

Bea pushed a box of Kleenex toward her friend.

Mary straightened up with great effort, pulled out a wad, and blew her nose. A tear-wet Post-it from the pile of memos she'd been drizzling on stuck to her cheek.

"Girlfriend, you're a hot mess." Bea reached over and peeled off the note. "Listen to me. He'll let you see her, or I'll have my new investigative unit all over his ugly ass." She wouldn't mention that *the unit* was just two rookie kids and an intern.

"I appreciate that." Mary yanked out another clump of tissue and blew her nose again. "But he has so many media connections—and I found out he just made a significant investment in one of your local newspapers."

"Newspaper, snooze-paper. I have a few connections, too, honeybun. And a whole bunch of us would like to see Brandon Doyle burn in hell. He's a scourge on this community."

Mary laughed with a touch of hysteria, then started to cry again.

Bea patted her shoulder. "Where're you staying? You need some rest. And some deep-fried Southern food."

"I'm at an Airbnb in Culver City."

"You're now at my place, *Casa de Middleton* in Santa Monica. Let's get your stuff. We'll order in some barbecue tonight and plan how we're gonna get to your daughter."

Mary dragged her sleeve across wet eyes. "He's dangerous, Bea, homicidally dangerous. Has no boundaries, no sense of decency. It's all about getting whatever the hell he wants at any cost. Our daughter is just another tool for his personal use."

A dark question formed in the air like a miasma. Bea hesitated, then asked it. "Do you think he sexually abuses her?"

Mary groaned as if she had been punched in the stomach. "Molly says no, but there are things unsaid. And he'll be the first to tell you he was completely cleared of sex crime allegations not too long ago."

Anger and outrage clawed at Bea's insides. She'd been in this space with her own daughter when the girl had been kidnapped by a psychopath and almost trafficked into the porn industry. Bea folded her arms and looked intently at her friend. A strong, gifted police officer had been brought to her knees by the son of a bitch, Doyle. Soul-sucking fear for one's children can do that. But she knew Mary O'Hanlon, and the woman would rise up.

"Detective, we've taken on hideous excuses for human beings before."

"He's up there vying for the grand prize. And guess what? He'll be announcing that he's running for the US Senate. Has a bundle of money-people all lined up."

"Really? Senate? Ballsy son of a bitch." Bea poured a few more drops of Baileys and drank up.

"He presents himself as an innocent casualty of the Me Too movement gone wild," Mary said.

"He was supposedly victimizing children, not adults. That's not Me Too, that's pedophilia—something insanely twisted."

"Whatever you call it, he has a lot of sympathy in this town. Scratch LA's shiny liberal surface, and you'll find a shit show of frustration, misogyny, and hate festering just below the rhetoric. I grew up here. I know this place. Brandon Doyle'll come out unscathed. Hell, it's ultimately all about power."

"I hear ya, but we can play that game, too." Bea hauled her briefcase from a nearby chair and loaded in manila files, unopened mail, and other workday detritus. She paused to glance at a mailing envelope from a fellow reporter, then tossed it in with the rest.

"My house will be command central. Doyle, you piece of crapola, two pissed-off mamas gon' take you down."

3

The next morning at her office desk, Bea was downing a second cup of black coffee when her cell phone rang. She checked the caller ID and smiled. Hit the *Accept* button.

"So, darlin', you heard the news already?" she asked.

Her friend and lover, Los Angeles County Sheriff Detective Pete Anthony, was on the line. "Lucy filled me in. How's Detective O'Hanlon?"

"She's a wreck, but we'll talk about that later." Bea had left Mary sound asleep in the guest room, exhausted from worry about her daughter, Molly. "Only got a minute, Pete, honey. My newbie fledglings are waiting in the conference room to hear from Yoda."

Bea checked her watch. Could barely make out the digital numbers. Where had she put the damn reading glasses she resented?

He chuckled. "Yoda, being you? Dollface, you don't look a thing like that pointy-eared, fuzz-haired...although first thing in the morning..."

"Yeah, you should talk, boy toy." Bea smiled over the phone at her on-again, off-again honey. A Cajun Italian with a remoulade recipe to die for and a secretly thoughtful and gentle nature beneath his gruff, take-no-shit cop exterior, they'd been exclusive for over a year. Guess that indicated on-again.

"What're you doing with those poor, clueless baby reporters, besides sharing questionable advice?" he asked.

Bea heard him bite into something crunchy.

"My junior journalist flock? Actually," she explained, "the bureau chief tapped me to help amp up the network's appeal to younger generations on the rise. Millennials, but mostly Xs, Ys, and Zs."

Pete snorted. "X, Y, and Z—whatever the hell those are. Do we expect the world to end after Z hits thirty?"

"I dunno, but the brass wants to create something similar to Canada's *Vice News* with punchy short-form stories focusing on Southern California."

"So, you got yourself a bunch of naive lefties who're gonna have their idealism crushed by the end of the summer."

"You're so cynical. It's gonna be cool. The format's set up so we do an opening with several two-minute pieces, then three longer segments, and end with a hot sheet of up-and-coming stuff. Our program's called statNEWS."

"Stat? Like the medical term that says the vic's gonna bite the big one at any second? Fire up the defib, young correspondents—stat!"

"Yeah, just like that, Sarge. Not. We focus on the concept of immediate action rather than impending death. Homicide's your territory, bud."

Bea heard Pete's cop radio squawk in the background. A horn honked. He was probably parked near the breakfast burrito truck on Topanga Canyon.

"Sounds interesting," he said, "but probably too bleeding-heart liberal for my, uh, unevolved, unwoke sensibilities."

"That's why you and I never talk politics, hot sauce."

"Why talk at all when there's so much other stuff to enjoy?"

Bea groaned. Pete had many issues, some downright infuriating, but no more charming lover existed between the sheets.

The voice over the garbled radio sounded more insistent.

"Gotta boogie," he said.

Bea wondered who was found dead behind a dumpster in LA County today. "Okay, baby. Be careful out there," she said.

"Roger that. Love you, woman."

"Love you, too, Pete." That phrase made her twinge just a tad, maybe more, if she was being honest. She knew she loved Pete Anthony but often struggled with whether she really *loved* him in a way that was enduring. She already had two exes, and so did he.

Bea sighed and compartmentalized. The next gen of news professionals awaited, and they weren't interested in producing bad versions of Romance Theater.

—

Seven floors above Hollywood Boulevard in the West Coast Bureau conference room, Bea looked around at the fresh, eager faces of her two newly hired cub reporters and the intern, her son Dexter, who'd just completed his first year at Emory University. She felt a touch guilty at the appearance of nepotism, in which Hollywood was notoriously awash, but he'd been the best qualified candidate by far. She'd recused herself from the selection and let her bureau chief, Winfrey Chambers, make the final call.

Dexter, tall and dark with a high-rise Afro, projected passion for the news business and perhaps a hint of mania in his bright eyes. He'd be onboard only for the summer, with the primary task of providing social media research support to the newbie reporters. It was going to be a challenge to keep the kid cuffed behind a desk for long—he'd want to be out in the field rattling cages. Before Bea had given him the approval to take this gig, he'd sworn he wouldn't push the margins of his job description.

In her gut, however, Mama knew she might have some challenges with the kid. Chambers, the tall, professorish black man who was her boss, promised to provide her backup.

Sitting at the far end of the small conference table was the oldest of the group, Tito Luna. A former Marine and double amputee para-athlete, he'd just completed his degree online at the University of San Diego. Aja Kapoor, attractive, with long straight hair hanging in a braid over her shoulder, was a recent Occidental College grad who'd started her own successful lifestyle blog when she was still in high school.

Bea smiled. They were a promising crew. "And with us for this pilot project," she said, "will be photographer Lucia 'Lucy' Vega. She has a couple Emmys to her name, as well as an Oscar for Best Documentary Film a couple years back on the Guerrero black tar heroin cartel. She teaches Photojournalism at Santa Monica High School in her nonexistent spare time. And did I mention she's the mother of a toddler who doesn't understand the concept of sleep?"

Lucy, bleary-eyed, took a long slug of Diet Cola and nodded acknowledgment. She was Bea's closest friend. The woman was a force of nature, with icy sharp facial features and fjord-blue eyes inherited from her Norwegian father, and a fiery, impulsive nature passed on from her Mexican mother. Lucy carried a wariness in her demeanor that expected the unexpected.

"Ms. Vega has a lot of experience helping rookies launch their careers, so use her as a mentor."

"Best teacher ever," Dexter said. "Had her for two years."

Bea tapped on the table for attention. "The clock is ticking, y'all. We have a six-month window of opportunity to prove to the network that our smart, ambitious little group here can generate something fresh and edgy for the viewing public. I asked you to come in with ideas. So, let's get started."

Embracing his peon intern status, Dexter rose and dragged a whiteboard closer to the table. He cracked open a fresh box of dry-erase markers.

Aja snatched a marker and prepared to be the scribe. "I've got good handwriting, actually learned cursive. I'll take this job."

Bea nodded consent. The young woman was either a real go-getter or an annoying takeover artist. Time would tell. The other newbie, Tito, mustachioed with a full sleeve of tattoo art on his left arm, had his network-issued laptop fired up.

Bea had to admit she was a tad intimidated by this youthful drive and energy. She hoped she could provide an environment that was smart, disciplined, and creative. All too soon, these rough gems had to shine. Tito had a degree and some fine writing samples, and her son was a loose cannon who'd been party to his mom's roller-coaster news career all of his life. Only Aja had more than two years in the business—a whopping twenty-six months as a popular blogger on the local Hindu youth scene. Bea shook her head—she hadn't even known the Hindu youth scene was a *thing*. Initially thrilled at the new aspect of her job assignment, the reality was beginning to hit home. At forty-three, she was feeling a hundred years old—what had she gotten herself into?

She turned to Tito to begin, but before he could speak, the conference room door banged open. Assignment Editor Elliott Katz, burst into the room. Mid-thirties with wire-rimmed glasses and curly black hair in a ponytail, his grim expression said, bad news.

"Lucy. I need your help. Got a breaking story. Another school shooting going down—North Hollywood."

Lucy caught her breath, and her blue eyes narrowed. Bea sensed her friend's struggle for composure.

Lucy frowned. "I'm not a stringer anymore, Elliott. I'm contracted to work with Bea, and only on this project."

"Consider your contract extended—I need an experienced photog immediately."

Bea's anxiety began to spike. Lucy was not ready to deal with anything acutely stressful. Certainly not dead children. It was barely a year ago that she gave birth to a preemie son in the high desert wilderness by the light of an exploding car, next to a grave that had just been dug for them both. Lucy and the baby barely survived. Bea shuddered, recalling the scents of creosote bush, gasoline, and blood.

Bea leaned toward Elliott. "There are plenty of other people you can call in."

Tall and lean, he twitched like bacon on a skillet. "Jill broke her foot this morning, Tom's wife is in labor, everybody's booked or out on assignment for the next couple hours, at least." He looked both desperate and pathetic and joined his hands in prayerful supplication. "Lucy, please."

Lucy asked, "At a high school? What is it?"

"An elementary school, near the mall off Laurel Canyon. Please, Lucy."

Bea saw her friend's face fade to a corpse-like pallor. Elliott needed to stand down. Before Bea could say anything, Lucy spoke.

"No, man, I won't do it. Just can't. Have to set my limits."

He clutched his fists, insistence turning to acute frustration. "Gimme a break, Lucy, this is huge. You gotta step up. Set your damn boundaries tomorrow."

Bea bristled. "Back off, Elliott."

Lucy's jaw set tight.

Bea held her breath, picturing the tiny, blue newborn in Lucy's arms as the medevac helicopter had hoisted them up into the cold, black night.

Lucy stood and gathered her belongings. "Elliott, I said, *no*."

The room went dead quiet.

"I can't deal with stories about dead children. Won't bring that down on myself. Understand?"

Elliott's shoulders slumped. "Okay, I get it, I wasn't thinking. I'm sorry, Lucy." The man who usually knew how to make everything hum in the newsroom couldn't make this happen.

Aja, face stricken, looked like she was about to cry.

"I'll do it." Dexter rose.

The Assignment Editor rubbed his whiskery chin like it was on fire. "Thanks, but I can't use an intern. Liability and all that shit."

"I'm good with the camera." Tito snapped his laptop closed, stood, and headed toward the door. "Got 4.0s in digital production classes. Let's go."

Bea nodded approval. "His demo reel is excellent."

"Okay, we'll get you geared up." Elliott scurried out of the room. Tito, at his heels, was slightly off-balance with his prosthetic legs.

Watching Tito disappear around the corner, Aja pulled at her braid. "A school shooting. And little ones. He'll never be the same after this. Never."

"No, he won't," Bea said. "Folks in this job carry a heavy load sometimes."

"I have to leave," Lucy said, trembling. "We'll reschedule. I'll call you this afternoon, Bea. I'm sorry if I upset everybody."

Bea's heart flooded with pain and empathy. And guilt. "Lucy, I pushed too hard to get you back in the saddle. This is my fault."

"No, Bea. I pushed myself too hard. It has nothing to do with you."

Bea was additionally dismayed when Aja got up and closed her laptop, too. Tucked it under her arm. "I don't think I can do this, Ms. Middleton." She brushed dampness from her eyes and edged away. "I knew you covered hard news, crime and stuff, but I thought I was hired as an influencer, a general interest lifestyle reporter, not this."

"Wait, Aja, let's talk." Bea stood and moved around the table toward the young woman.

"Thank you for the opportunity. Sorry." Aja bolted out the door.

Bea's chest tightened. In less than five minutes, her group had gone from optimistic youngies to rats abandoning a sinking ship.

Dexter followed. He said over his shoulder to his mom, "I'll talk to her."

"No, wait, Dex," Bea called.

Winfrey Chambers stepped into the conference room, face dour. "What is happening? Where's your team?"

Bea blew out a long sigh. "I think I may be the wrong person for this assignment, Win. Looks like statNEWS may be DOA before it even gets started." She rushed through the warren of cubicles after Aja and Dexter.

4

Rounding the copier near the exit, Bea spotted her son standing in the hall by the door to the women's restroom. His tense body language implied he was about to go in.

She jogged up next to him. "I got this, Dexter. Go finish your work."

He didn't move.

"I'm gonna talk to her. It's okay, baby. She just got a little freaked out, overwhelmed on a first day. It happens. Now, go." She squeezed his arm reassuringly. "This is my job, sweet pea, not yours. You have enough on your plate."

He nodded, shuffling his feet. Scrubbed at his clean-shaven face, then took a deep breath and let the air out slowly.

"But thanks for going after her, honey. You're a good man."

"Okay, take care of her, Mom." Dexter turned toward his workspace, face downcast, eyes haunted.

"I love you, Dex."

He winced and stepped away like he had when he was twelve and didn't want the other kids to see his mama loving on him. Since then, he'd been through some very tough times. Bea's heart ached for her child. Dexter could sense another's suffering from a mile away and would always rush to the rescue. The wounded helping the wounded. He had to stop letting other's pain become his own.

A sob sounded from the restroom. Bea went inside.

Two of the three stalls were empty. Aja had barricaded herself in the third. Bea walked to the door and leaned against the cool tile wall next to it. The smell of disinfectant was strong. "You okay, girl?"

Sniffles. A nose blew. "Yeah. I guess." A long pause. "I mean, no." The crying started up again.

Bea sighed. Sometimes life was too much. She wished she had comforting pearls of wisdom ready to roll from her tongue. She didn't. All she could do was share her truth.

"Aja, we all get freaked out by school shootings. And with little kids—can't help but think of Sandy Hook. Hideous, sick stuff. No rhyme nor reason. Impossible to understand." Tears rose in Bea's eyes, too. "But we fight back by telling the story, asking the hard questions, showing the need to not look away. As journalists, we can do more than most. That's our consolation, what keeps us going. At least, that's how it is for me."

The stall door slowly opened. A tear-stained brown face looked out.

"It's horrendous, but it's not just that, Ms. Middleton."

"What do you mean?"

"I feel like I'm losing my mind."

Bea took Aja's hand and led her to the sinks. She moistened a paper towel and offered it to the young woman. Aja pressed it to her eyes. "Something is happening to me. I have, you know, like, anxiety issues."

"A lot of us do, honey. No shame in that."

"In my culture, there's so much judgement, all negative, but I refuse to buy into it. I try not to not be a victim to other people's ignorance on mental health stuff, but sometimes, like now..." More tears, shoulders shaking. Bea pulled Aja into a hug.

Aja's body stiffened. "I'm not a hugger." She stepped away. "But thank you."

"Sorry. Should've asked."

"No, no, it's fine." She mopped her eyes and dropped the paper towel into the trash. "I'm feeling better now."

Bea sighed. "May I ask, have you been seeing a therapist or taking any medication? Can sometimes be real helpful. I've certainly benefitted at times in my life."

Aja paused, hesitated, and appeared to be struggling with how much to tell.

Bea felt the need to reassure. "I know this is uncomfortable to talk about, and I'm your boss and all. But I'm also here for you as your mentor and friend, Aja. I want to see you happy and successful in this new job."

Standing up tall, Aja squared her shoulders and gulped. "Okay, I've been in therapy and on medication for a year. It was working fine, but recently, I started going downhill." Her voice cracked.

"What changed? Was there a trigger of some kind?"

Aja's dark brows crinkled in thought.

"The only thing I can think of was that my insurance company switched me from a name-brand antidepressant to a generic about six weeks ago."

Recollection of a recent article on generics and quality control niggled in Bea's brain. She chewed at her lip. Was it about antidepressants or cholesterol-lowering drugs? Problems with active ingredients or time-release?

"Aja, when you get home, check the country of origin on your new meds, would you?"

"I have them right here." The young woman reached into her purse and pulled out a brown, plastic prescription bottle. Rattled the pills. Squinted to make out the tiny writing. "Somewhere in China, Xingtai." She looked at Bea, confused. "What are you saying?"

"Can you give me a pill I can send to the crime lab? There's an issue going on right now about generic drugs produced in countries like China, India, Thailand. They may not have the same or as much active ingredients as the name-brand produced in the US. Your pills may be just fine, probably are, but let's check. Can't hurt. Sound okay?"

"My pharmacist said there's no difference."

"I hope he or she's correct. Let's find out. It's what we do, right? Suss out truth from lies. And then, I want you to dig into some research on this topic."

A glimmer of hope lit Aja's dark, wet eyes. She wrapped a pill in a tissue and handed it to Bea. "Okay. Thank you, Ms. Middleton."

"It's Bea."

"Maybe it's the meds, Bea. Maybe I'm not going crazy, or crazier." She smiled. "Can you hug me now?"

"I got 'ya girl." Bea chuckled and pulled Aja into her arms for a quick, reassuring embrace.

5

In the secure room attached to his home office, Brandon Doyle sat at a console inspecting a huge, multi-screen monitor featuring an array of thumbnails from the twelve cameras providing protection for his Brentwood mansion, plus his four special cameras.

Tall and handsome with a thick shock of salt-and-pepper hair, Brandon Doyle had the look any politician would dream of—one of authority, control, and magnetism. The image on which he was currently fixated was of his twenty-one-year-old daughter, Molly, stepping out of the shower. His head of security and general fixer and bodyguard, Price Burgess, leaned over his shoulder in the dimness.

Paunch-bellied and perpetually in a light sweat, Burgess squinted his piggish eyes. "I'd give her a nine, only because of all the scarring. A ten, otherwise. How do you get anything done with that bouncing around your house all day?"

Doyle's nostrils flared. "She's my daughter, not my plaything."

Burgess laughed. "I guess they lose their appeal for you once they hit, what? Twelve? Thirteen? You're a sick fuck."

"I never had sex with her, just taught her the ways of sensuality."

"What the hell does that mean? Sounds like sex to me." Burgess snickered. "Kinda like, '*I smoked marijuana but didn't inhale.*'"

"I'm not a pervert—I was completely vindicated in the courts." He cleared his throat. "Anyhow, better she learns from a mature man who loves her than from some pimply-faced, STD-ridden adolescent boy. I was helping her, teaching her about life."

"*Prima nocte*? Right of the Lord to—what do they call it— *deflower* his female subserviates." He giggled soundlessly, jowls shaking like gelatin. "You seduce the budding bloom, eh, boss? Once the *fleur* bursts forth, it loses its attraction, *mais oui*?" He took a swig from his bottle of imported beer.

Brandon smirked. "Very poetic. You're a real Nabokov on the tutoring of young females."

"Nabok—who?" Price's shoulders sagged. He liked sounding smart, but Doyle always ruined it.

"Never mind. And since when are you learning fucking French?" Doyle pushed his chair back from the console desk.

"Almost got my GED. Take my last final on Thursday. Started it ten years ago when I was in the pen up in Victorville."

"A degree?" Doyle's eyebrows raised. "You saying I don't pay you enough?"

"I ain't sayin' that, boss. You pay me fine."

"Then why care about a meaningless piece of paper? Is it that librarian bitch you've been banging?"

Price Burgess looked away from Doyle's daughter getting dressed. "Don't talk about her that way. Marcia's a nice lady. I've asked her to marry me." He pressed a beefy hand to his heart. "She said yes."

Doyle rolled his eyes. "No shit? Good for you." *You poor fuck.*

"And I'm sick of thinking of myself as a high school dropout."

"Well, don't start getting all uppity on me, professor." With one last glance at the screen, Doyle rose and exited the safe room. When shut, the entry transformed into a built-in bookcase. Crossing the hallway into his airy, white family room, Burgess followed.

A row of open French doors framed the Pacific in the distance, and original artwork hung on gallery-like walls. Palm fronds gently tapped against the house's stucco exterior, a fountain burbled, and star jasmine perfumed the air. Doyle plunked down onto one of the wide, creamy sofas.

Burgess sat across from his boss in a matching club chair. Dressed in jeans and a vintage Johnny Cash concert T-shirt with a fraying collar, the loyal fixer refused to take off his pricey, cool, black leather jacket despite the heat. "Your daughter could be a real plus to your campaign. I hope you were right in bringing her back here."

"Indeed, I'm confident in my decision." Doyle, in sand-colored silk lounging pajamas, grabbed a handblown Venetian glass tumbler and poured himself sparkling water from a copper pitcher. "Got a stylist, makeup people, a manicurist, the whole squad coming over to get her ready tomorrow morning. Think about the transformation of Sandra Bullock in *Miss Congeniality*."

"That the one where she's a butch federal agent, and they make her into a beauty queen to go undercover?"

"Bingo, my man."

Burgess kneaded a throw pillow with his big hands. "I don't think your girl's gonna like having these beauty people all over her. You said she's real shy about her appearance, especially since the accident."

"I'll give her a little something to take the edge off. She'll be fine. And you'll be in charge of her."

"Oh, no. Not me." Burgess scooted back in his chair. The pillow dropped to the floor. "I ain't no babysitter."

"Yeah, you are. I trust you with my Molly. She won't have to say a word at the announcement of my candidacy. Just remind her to smile and clap at the appropriate times. Show her videos of Ivanka Trump. That's who she should look like. We want voters to get the idea that as a struggling single father I raised a beaming example of young womanhood."

Burgess huffed, face devoid of enthusiasm but ever the obedient soldier. "Roger that, boss." He wiped his damp forehead. "Anything to worry about with her maybe, uh, blabbing about, you know, what you did to her? Supposedly did."

Doyle fingered the plush fabric of his shirtsleeve. "She remembers nothing except for residual feelings of my fondness and warmth. All very positive impressions."

Burgess nodded, sucking in his ample midsection.

Doyle continued. "You'll make sure nobody gets close to her, and absolutely no interviews. No access. *Capiche*? I may be a weak man in some aspects of my life, but I'm a careful weak man."

"Good, boss, 'cause another slipup in the sex crimes department could do you in permanently."

"No worries. Molly's a sweet, obedient puppy who adores me." Doyle raised his glass, then drank. "The sex crimes chapter is closed. Has become quite boring, actually. Onto the next adventure. Speaking of that—" He checked his smart watch "—Pang's arriving as we speak. Much to discuss." He stood, signaling Burgess's dismissal.

The bodyguard, his usual smiling face now cold as a grave, raised his beer and finished it off. A round puddle of condensation pocked the tabletop where the bottle had rested. He stood and adjusted his jacket. It didn't fit quite right over his shoulder holster. He headed toward the archway into the foyer.

Doyle's phone buzzed. He took a quick look at the caller ID. "It's Lance Ludlow, my man over at the newspaper." He held up a hand to halt Burgess's retreat.

"Hello, Lance. What is it?"

Doyle listened, said nothing, then clicked off and turned to his man. "Along with my daughter, I have something else you'll need to handle, either you or the new guy."

"I hope it's something more in my line of work. A lot easier to take out an asshole, even one wavin' a hot-loaded AK, than chaperone a chick."

Doyle sighed as if frustrated with a small child. "*Zàijiàn*, Burgess."

"Huh?" Price felt a flicker of resentment burn. Doyle was doing it again, making him feel small and stupid.

"Means goodbye in Mandarin. Forget French, old boy. They got Chinese with that GED?"

6

Having just texted her credit card information to Honey's Kettle-Fried Chicken for takeout, Bea tossed her sweater onto a chair, kicked off her shoes, and shuffled into the kitchen of her pretty Mediterranean-style bungalow. Small by Santa Monica standards, it was a cozy family home, even though these days, with one child in college in Atlanta and the other living with her father and his new family in nearby Brentwood, it was an empty nest. Not a situation she chose, but like a winding river, life took its own course.

Mary O'Hanlon sat at the kitchen island hunched over her laptop with a mug of coffee. A small pile of used Keurig K-cups said it was far from her first. She looked up; her pretty face was less haggard than when she'd collapsed into bed the previous night. Her green eyes glittered with a caffeine buzz, and her rusty hair was loose and leonine.

"I slept thirteen hours, had a little breakfast, then crashed again for another two." Mary stretched and yawned. "Your big brother called, gave me a pep talk that kicked me sufficiently in the butt."

Bea's sheriff brother, Luther Middleton, from Shellman County, Georgia was Mary's lover. "Luther's good at motivation." Bea smiled and rested her hands on the countertop. Her perfect nails were painted a slate color called Urban Asphalt.

"Yep, he is." Mary rose from her chair. "And I'm ready to roll right over Doyle's ass."

"Glad to hear it." Bea gave her a hug. "Gotta have your wits sharp to take on *he-who-cannot-be-named.*"

"Frickin' Voldemort's a choirboy compared to Doyle." Mary sighed. "You look a smidge wasted yourself, sweetie. How was your day?"

"Except for another horrific school shooting where no one died, thanks be to the Lord, and one of my newbie reporters freaking out and almost bailing on me—it was another sunny day in paradise."

Mary shut her laptop. "I purposely kept the news off. Can't take it."

"Me either—too bad it's my job. But Southern fried chicken, sweet potato fries, collards, and a slab of red velvet cake should arrive any second. Does miracles for the attitude."

"Thank you, from the bottom of my heart, for everything, Bea."

"No thanks necessary, my sister. It's what we Southern gals do for family."

Mary blinked away welling tears. "This morning, your son left me a note sweeter than Georgia peach pie. Thanked me for helping rescue him during the whole Savannah fiasco and swore he'd do whatever he could to help bring down Doyle. I'm feeling some concern. We know how gung ho that kid can be. Thinks he has to personally right every wrong. Kinda like his mama."

Bea held out her arms and feigned an *I'm innocent* stance with as much believability as an NBA star who'd just elbowed an opponent in the head. "Kid knows I'd personally strangle him if he got himself in another mess like that one."

Pulling out a fresh bottle of merlot from the wine rack, Bea uncorked it and offered a glass to Mary, who gratefully accepted. Bea poured herself the same, then slid onto the stool at the kitchen island and pressed her palms to her eyes, sighing hard before she looked back up. "I'd hoped Dex would take a job coaching youth basketball this summer, but he insisted on an internship in journalism. Seems to be emerging as his passion. He's already been tapped to be assistant editor of the Emory student paper next fall."

"Impressive."

"Yeah, but potentially dangerous for a mere sophomore with an impulsive nature and a sensitive soul. Wish there was something I could do to guide him in another direction."

"Like toward accounting or insurance sales?" Mary chuckled and fingered the stem of her wineglass.

"Exactly! Something behind a big ol' desk. Maybe a bank teller—I like the bulletproof glass idea." Bea groaned. "Do I really have to accept who the kid is?"

"Yup. And you adore who that kid is, even when it's driving you nuts."

"Not sure at all about the *adore* part." Bea made a face. "At least he's at my TV station this summer, and the bureau chief is supportive."

Mary's gaze drifted out the window to the darkening street beyond. "I wish I knew what my baby girl was up to. I have the terrible feeling Brandon told her I'm too busy and don't want to see her. Something along those lines. She's blocked my phone number and defriended me on social media. She would *not* do that. Never. It's all his doing—the heartless, calculating bastard.

"Sounds like he's reading from the brainwashing 101 playbook. Got himself a vulnerable victim in Molly who he's been inundating with cool stuff that she naïvely sees as expressions of love. Now he's isolating her—all steps in classic abuse scenarios."

Mary moaned as if in physical pain. "You're right. That's just what he's doing."

Bea saw Mary's rush of positive energy vanish. The detective sagged over her laptop.

"No, no, O'Hanlon. We don't collapse. We stand strong, get angry, take Molly back." Bea gulped down her wine and tried not to think about rescuing her own daughter from a potentially lethal situation only a year ago. Her fingers itched at the recollection of almost pulling the trigger and ending the perpetrator's life.

Dexter appeared in the kitchen toting an armload of Honey's Kettle Fried Chicken containers. "We feeding an army, Ma?" He plopped the boxes onto the island.

Bea smiled. "Smells like comfy hometown eats for three hungry warriors." She passed out paper plates and napkins.

Dexter planted a quick peck on his mother's cheek, then gave their visitor a hug. "Hey, Mary. Did I hear 'ya talking 'bout Molly? Somebody at the station say she gonna be with Doyle when he announces for Senate tomorrow downtown at the Biltmore."

Like a puppeteer had yanked her strings, Mary lurched up, back rigid.

Bea patted her friend's hand. "Could just be gossip—we don't know what Doyle's plans are."

"Winfrey Chambers was talking about it to Elliott when I left," Dexter said. He opened the box of chicken and passed it to Mary. She didn't respond. Nudged it toward his mom. Bea stared at the array of food like it was cardboard cutouts. Her son shrugged and dug in.

Turning to her friend, Bea said, "Chambers and Elliott are both highly reliable sources. But if your daughter's actually there with your ex-husband tomorrow, you can bet he isn't going to let anyone get close. And Mary, if he spots you, his people will whisk her away faster than you can say *fake news*."

Dexter began to wolf down the deep-fried fare. "Not sure I told y'all this before, but after Molly's car accident, I stopped in to see her a couple times when she was at Emory Med in rehab."

He stuffed sweet potato fries into his mouth. "I was staying in Atlanta with our friend, Rio Deakins." He turned to Mary. "My gram adopted Rio when he was a kid in Savannah, so he's like family."

"Mary knows him real well. I mean, he's your Uncle Luther's best friend," Bea said. "And Mary and Luther..."

"Yeah, of course. Sorry. So anyhow," Dexter continued, "Molly and I had really nice talks at the hospital about coming back from being, you know, kinda wrecked."

Bea frowned. "How come you never mentioned that you kids had crossed paths? When was this?" She'd been the last to know details of her children's lives for a couple years now and didn't like it one damn bit.

Dexter pensively waved a drumstick in the air. "Hmm, like in the spring, last year." He took a bite.

"I had no idea you two kids knew each other." Mary cocked her head as if trying to more clearly process this new information. "But that's good. I'm glad to hear it."

"And, by the way," Dexter said, "Mr. Chambers assigned me to go with the reporter tomorrow morning to Doyle's Senate announcement thing. Maybe I can get a message to Molly."

"They're not gonna let you anywhere near her, son." Bea finally went for a plate and dug into the collards. "An edgy-looking young black man from nasty CNN, the Satan of the cable networks? Not happening."

"I'll use my Emory press creds."

"Your offer's very kind, Dex, but I won't let you get involved in my family drama." Mary rubbed her neck, fingers digging deep. "Having your mother's help frightens me enough. Doyle's not just a major son of a bitch. He's dangerous. Wouldn't think twice about hurting you if he decided you were aggravating him."

Dexter smirked. "What's he gonna do? Kill me if I talk to your daughter?"

Mary pushed away her untouched plate. "If he ever thought you could be any kind of threat, yes, he would."

For an instant, Dexter stopped chewing.

7

Reporter David Pine sat in the living room of his modest Santa Clarita condo, watching the Golden State Warriors hammer the Lakers. Fifteen points down at halftime, today he barely seemed to care.

Brown-haired and pretty, Claire Thompson, his thirtysomething girlfriend of barely three months who lived in the unit across the hall, snuggled next to him on the cozy chenille couch. Pine had been divorced for a decade, and the comfort of this wonderful creature's company still amazed him. It had truly been love at first sight for them both.

He pulled her close.

The timer on Claire's iPhone beeped. "Pizza's ready, hon. Be right back."

"I don't know why you don't bake it here." Pine reluctantly let her slip from his embrace.

"I told you, I make it from scratch, and all my cooking equipment is in *my* kitchen." She rolled her eyes. "Plus, your oven is so mis-calibrated, the same dish can be raw on one side and overdone on the other." Claire gave Pine a playful smooch and moved toward the door.

He jumped up and followed her. Overwhelmed by a sudden feeling that he couldn't live without her, he grabbed her hand. "Claire Thompson, why don't we move in together? I love you; you love me. We'd have a much nicer place; we'd get the oven of your dreams. Life is short—what the hell are we waiting for?"

She raised an eyebrow. "How many beers have you had?"

"One, barely one! I swear I've never been more sober." Emotions had been building for some time, and he finally knew he couldn't live without her. Work was turning to quicksand, his two children lived on the East Coast, and he wasn't getting any younger. Claire was his rock.

Her hazel eyes filled with tears. "Oh, David. You've always been so hesitant to discuss—"

Pine gathered her tightly into his arms. "I even miss you when you leave the room." He stroked Claire's soft, straight hair, then pushed her back and gripped her shoulders. "I've been an idiot, scared to commit, but I'm through with that. You make me so damn happy. Just hanging together, having dinner, watching some stupid TV show—it's heaven." He laughed out loud.

"I'm so glad you think so, too." Claire sniffed. "But speaking of dinner—the pizza's burning, sweetheart." She gave him a deep, soulful kiss, then reluctantly drew away and stumbled toward the door, eyes glossy with joy. "We'll talk in a minute." She practically skipped across the breezeway.

His whole being radiated with warm certainty as he collapsed back onto the couch, smiling. Hell, he even loved how practical she was, so concerned with the little things like oven calibration. He was one lucky dude.

This time, he wasn't going to blow it.

—

The next morning, Bea brought Mary O'Hanlon into work and set the detective up at a small round table in the corner of her office. Dexter had been off early as usual, stoked about helping to cover Doyle's Senate announcement. Bea and Mary were anxious to get his take on

Molly's quasi-hostage situation.

"Thanks for letting me come to work with you," Mary said. "Nice to be around other people. Got a bunch of Savannah PD paperwork to finish or they're going to fire me." Her smile was grim.

Bea nodded. "Good to have you here."

Winfrey Chambers, with the uncharacteristically rumpled look of a long day's end rather than the beginning, stepped in and approached Bea's desk. His head swiveled, and he hesitated for an instant, surprised to see an attractive redhead in the corner clacking busily on her keyboard.

"Hey, Win—this is my friend from Savannah, Detective Mary O'Hanlon. Just giving her a little workspace today."

"Pleased to meet you, Detective." He nodded. "Welcome to LA."

Mary rose and stepped forward to shake his hand. "Thanks, sir. Bea speaks very highly of you."

Winfrey turned to Bea and winked. "I hope that's true, at least some of the time."

"It is true, most of the time." Bea smiled back at him. "So, what's up, Win?"

Mary returned to her temporary corner spot and shifted attention back to her work.

Winfrey's face suddenly lost its animation. "Got some bad news about one of our colleagues at the Daily News."

Bea moved from behind her desk and joined him in the doorway. At the same time, David Pine's face came up on a big screen above the warren of office cubicles.

Win followed Bea's gaze to the bank of monitors. "I know you were a friend, I was, too," he said. "David was murdered last night."

Bea felt suddenly light-headed. "Murdered? David?" She pressed back against the door jamb to steady herself. "Who would hurt him—he's a teddy bear."

"Looks like a hit. Killed in his living room while his girlfriend was across the hall taking dinner out of the oven. Crime scene says the killer used a silencer—9mm to the base of the skull. That won't be public information."

Bea'd heard Pine mention his new girlfriend a couple months previously at a press club mixer. She was a chemist or something like that. He seemed ecstatically happy with their relationship, but Bea posed the obvious question. "Anyone think she did it?"

Win shook his head. "Your LAPD contact, Detective Marlene Simon, says the girlfriend's not a suspect. But I want you to check it out, like today. I emailed you the specifics, including Thompson's contact info. That's the girlfriend's name—Claire Thompson."

Bea's brain went to the contents of the envelope from David Pine that she hadn't taken the time to review. She wasn't ready yet to share that fact with her bureau chief.

"Let me take a quick glance at my emails and then I'll get over to Pine's condo and see if I can talk to Thompson. Sound okay? My two statNEWS reporters are with the social media team this morning. They'll be doing the usual rotation through the various departments for the next two days."

Win nodded. "And if you finish with the girlfriend early, swing down to Doyle's Senate rally, and see if you can help out, snag a few extra interviews with the crowd. We'll have to talk about your newbies soon, like first thing tomorrow morning."

"Yes, sir." Bea gulped. "Got off to a rocky start, but I'm still totally confident that it's going to work out." *That assessment was a bit of a stretch.*

Win smirked. "Okay, until then, keep me posted on all things David Pine."

"You got it."

The bureau chief headed out into the cubicle farm to touch bases with other staffers.

Bea leaped toward her briefcase and rustled through the contents, searching for the thumb drive Pine had sent. She pulled it from a ripped-open padded envelope and slipped it into the USB port on her laptop. The information immediately came on the monitor. There were three files on the drive: *1. Chinese Drug Companies and US Formulary/Generics, 2. Offshore Networks, and 3. B. D. Keeter Organization.*

"Holy shit." Bea's stomach tightened. What was this about? She clicked on number three. A photo of an org chart with numerous sub-files listed under each name filled the screen. Much was redacted.

"Mary, could you come over here for a minute? I may be wrong, but I think my friend Pine may have left me something significant." Bea clicked on the Offshore Networks file, and it popped open.

"I overheard. So sorry about his death. And murdered? Awful." The detective stood and leaned over Bea's shoulder, studying the file. "What've you got here?" She squinted her eyes. "Is that Chinese?"

Bea scrolled down. "Appears to be the English translation next to it. It's a contract between something called Keeter Enterprises LLC and—"

Mary drew in a quick breath. "Wait, B. D. Keeter Enterprises? Holy shit, that's Brandon."

"What?"

"It's the name of his deceased uncle, Keeter Doyle. I only met him once before he died, at our wedding. Brandon insisted I dance with him, but the old guy could hardly move."

"Was he a lawyer like your ex?"

"No, he was a pharmacist in Boston's Back Bay where Brandon worked as a kid. Kind of a spooky dude, looked a thousand years old with these crazy dead eyes. Smelled like formaldehyde. That's the thing I remember about him, and his gnarled, snaky fingers." She shuddered. "But what's this you're showing me?"

"Looks like an agreement between Keeter and some Chinese pharmaceutical company." Had this been Pine's death warrant? She reviewed the other files—most were in Chinese.

Bea shut down the laptop and pulled out the drive, dropped it in her purse. "I've got to get over and talk with Pine's girlfriend. She could be in danger, too."

"You want me to come with you?" Mary asked.

"No, I'm good. But if you have the time, see what you can find on Keeter Enterprises." Bea grabbed her purse and flew out the door while tapping a phone number into her cell.

—

Soon to be celebrating its one-hundred-year anniversary, the historic Millennium Biltmore Los Angeles Hotel overlooked the five-acre Pershing Square—a concrete stamp of a park ringed by high-rises. An iconic downtown destination, the beaux arts style Biltmore had been chosen for Doyle's big announcement.

Pulling into a parking lot just off Olive Street, the network's West Coast Bureau had crammed quite a crew into the broadcast truck for the live coverage. Lucy and Dexter were the last out onto the sidewalk amid a forest of antennae and satellite dishes raised by competing news outlets.

"Stay with me, Dexter," reporter Jamison Earl ordered. Long-faced, slim, and rigid as a screwdriver, Earl motioned for his beleaguered assistant, Adam Baker, to straighten his necktie.

Lucy thought Earl's tie, a strip of paisley cloth, probably cost as much as a week in the hotel's penthouse.

He turned to Lucy. "Vega, you pick up the establishing shots and cutaways. Adam's going to set up for the live interviews just north of the podium." Earl bustled away toward the stage with Dexter and a gaggle of production folks in his wake. The guy was an asshole but came across really well on camera. Dexter waved Lucy a quick goodbye.

Lucy grabbed her Sony HDR camera and dashed off to collect images of the local scene. When Win called last-minute needing a second photog for the Doyle event, Lucy was eager to jump back in after her meltdown from the previous day. When the story was completed, she'd sit with the new reporters and Dexter to review and edit the visuals.

This going-back-to-work thing, after months of mothering her tiny, high-risk infant, was turning out to be a whole lot more complicated than she'd envisioned. After endless days and nights of wondering if little Henry's next breath would be his last, Lucy kept reminding herself the kid was now healthy, happy, and in good hands with Elsa and her young niece from Norway, Carolina Olson. The eighteen-year-old was in heaven about coming to Malibu, California on a gap year between high school and college back in Oslo.

Lucy took a deep breath, shouldered her camera, and got to work. Images of storied faces, gestures, and details gathered like colorful pebbles on a beach always chased away uncomfortable thoughts and put Lucy fully in the moment. She ambled through the roil of passionate Angelinos who shouted, sang, and waved placards—both supportive of Doyle's candidacy and damning.

Today, the candidate had the PR machine running in high gear. When his acolytes took the stage—local politicos, business leaders, sports idols, and Hollywood *glitterati*—the paparazzi were all over themselves vying for photos. Her press credentials granted Lucy access to a roped-off area near the main attraction.

After high-energy music from a Beach Boys cover band and enthusiastic endorsement speeches from a Vietnam veteran, a Hispanic firefighter, and the political party chair—the man himself, Brandon J. Doyle, Esquire, made his way to the podium. Amid the applause, he shook hands, clapped, and pointed at random people in the crowd. His daughter, Molly, auburn hair shining like new pennies, clutched his arm. They made a stunning duo. She pulled at the tight, white sheath dress she'd been poured into.

Doyle was movie-star handsome with classic features and wavy gray-flecked hair. He was expertly groomed with just enough hint of dishevelment to say—I'm one helluva professional who'll fight for you, and by the way, I just got out of bed with a babe so hot I'm still smoldering.

Lucy chuckled. Doyle was a full-on work of fiction. She knew him from way back when she and Bea were young newsies covering local politics together. It was soon apparent to both that he was a narcissistic sociopath who had only one concern, and it sure as hell wasn't serving the people.

A beefy, balding bodyguard type with a feigned smile pried Molly's grip from her father's arm and ushered her to a chair. She sat and gracefully crossed her legs at the ankles like an English royal. She struggled to project demure confidence. Through her telephoto lens, Lucy pulled the girl into a close-up. The facial scars were barely visible but rapidly blinking eyes glinting with fragility was a giveaway as to what was likely going on beneath Molly Doyle's expertly crafted exterior.

Next to Molly sat a good-looking, but not as good-looking as Doyle, star of a current sitcom. Gently, he took possession of her hand and appeared to whisper encouraging words and pretend like they were old friends. Lucy could see the young woman breathe deeply and feel her struggle for emotional balance by fixing her gaze to the back of her daddy's head as he charmed, cajoled, and made impossible promises to the supportive throng. Cued by the actor at her side, Molly clapped her hands robotically and smiled at all the right times—playing the perfect ornament for Senate candidate Doyle.

For a moment, the beefy bodyguard stepped away to talk on his radio. Molly's eyes swept the crowd at her father's feet and caught on something that grabbed her attention. A sliver of openness flashed from her protective shell and almost brought her to her feet. The sitcom star pulled her back down. The young woman's attention remained with someone in the crowd.

Turning her camera to find the object of Molly's momentary switch from obedient bauble to live human, Lucy's long lens captured a familiar face. Dexter pressed against the stage sporting an Emory University ball cap, grinning.

8

Thirty-five minutes later when the rally ended, Doyle was hustled off into the horde of reporters panting for their breaking news interviews. With barely a nod at Molly, the sitcom star disappeared into a swarm of his own fans. The beefy guard reached for Molly's arm, ignoring the media who shouted out questions for the candidate's statuesque daughter. Before Doyle's post-event security posse could reposition themselves at the stage's exit, Molly bolted toward Dexter.

Lucy saw the girl's face transition from "Bambi on the ice" to "woman on the run." Hoisting her camera, Lucy moved up to the edge of the stage, close to Molly and Dexter.

"Dexter, oh, my God. I can't believe you're here," Molly cried.

Cameras from all the stations swiveled as the girl practically leaped off the riser into the embrace of a tall, hipster-looking, young black man who hugged her like a long-lost, but very hot, cousin. They both looked stunned to find themselves in each other's arms.

The beefy guard tried to slide down from the stage in pursuit of his out-of-control charge, but his shoulder holster snagged on an electrical hookup. He let out a string of profanities as he fought to disentangle from the spaghetti of cords. Lucy chuckled, continued recording the scene, and pushed her way toward Dexter.

Dex was seconds away from experiencing major blowback from Doyle's security team, but he ignored the threat and focused only on Molly.

"Look at you, girl, all stylin' in that dress."

"I feel like a total freak, Dexter. Haven't worn anything but sweats and T-shirts in, like, forever. What are you *doing* here?" She let go of him for a moment and fingered his press credential.

"Interning at the network. And your mom's staying at our place in Santa Monica. She been tryin' to get hold of you."

"Mom's here?" Molly's eyes popped round as golf balls. "Oh my God!"

"Hell, yeah. Crying all over the place that your old man practically kidnapped you. She wants to see her baby girl real bad."

When the beefy guard—Lucy heard Doyle call him Burgess—finally extricated himself from the wires, his face was an apoplectic balloon ready to pop. "Arrest that motherfucker," he bellowed, a fat finger pointed at Dexter. "Stand away from the girl." He made it onto the grass in front of the stage, wrenched away Lucy's camera, then shoved Dexter hard. Molly slipped and fell.

In nanoseconds, Dexter was all over the bodyguard. Molly, in her white Dior dress and red-soled Louboutin heels, struggled upright and joined in, kicking Burgess repeatedly in the shins.

Lucy snatched back her camera, still rolling, from his grip.

"Leave Dexter alone!" Molly screamed as more security piled into the fray. An LAPD officer rushed up, gun drawn, and aimed at Dexter. Molly screamed and threw herself between them. Tears ran down her cheeks, taking the mascara with it. She clutched Dexter's shirt, not willing to let him go.

"If anything happens to that boy—" Lucy shrieked at the cop who looked dangerously young and unsure, "—your fuckin' face is gonna be all over the network and across the goddamn *world*! You can kiss your life goodbye!"

The deputy hesitated, then holstered his weapon.

Molly shrieked, "Dexter's my friend! Daddy, where are you? Help us!"

Lucy spotted Doyle cowering with his minions next to a dumpster.

Then, suddenly, Bea appeared. She knocked Doyle's security dog, Burgess, to the ground with a right hook and pinned him beneath her. Cursing, he squirmed away but lost his pistol. It spun across the sidewalk. Molly broke free from the melee. She and a homeless-looking bystander pushing a Vons shopping cart filled with crushed soda cans struggled for possession of the SIG Sauer. The cart overturned, and they scrambled for the firearm amid the flood of aluminum debris. Molly crawled away with it in her hand, dirt streaking her designer dress, one pricey shoe missing. When LAPD backup arrived, Doyle suddenly found his balls and got on the mic, calling for civility.

Three hours later, the skirmish had been sorted and the perpetrators released. Dexter, Lucy, Molly, Doyle, Bea, reporter Jamison Earl, Doyle's bodyguard Price Burgess, a couple of security guys, and the shopping cart owner named Pookie, were ushered onto the pavement in front of the county jail. No charges were filed.

And thus, Doyle's run for Senate had been launched.

—

Bea sat across from her boss, both letting their coffee go cold. "They called it a minor altercation started by a college student interning with a local media outlet," she said. "Molly, who heroically nabbed Burgess's loose gun, was immediately seized back into Doyle's clutches, with his camp demanding Dexter be fired. The nerve of those assholes."

"Hell, Bea, this ludicrous brawl could have been a real disaster—somebody could've been shot."

Bea shuddered at the thought of anybody, but especially her baby boy getting killed—a black kid with his hands on shiny, white Molly. Sweet Jesus, she hated and resented that fear. It was always there.

Win rested his elbows on his desk and steepled his fingers, eyes fixed on Bea. "We're going to put Dexter on suspension this week. He was out of line pounding on the guard."

"Come on, Win. Is that really necessary?"

"Listen, he's getting a huge break by keeping his internship at all, but I hate to see a promising young journalist fired his first week out on the job."

Bea frowned, eyes blazing. "But that Price Burgess bastard stole Lucy's camera and shoved Dexter, knocking Molly over in the process. My son was just defending both of them."

"Come on, Bea. Don't argue with me on this. If you can't stand back and see he made the wrong choice, a choice that could've gotten him hurt bad or even killed, then I'm wondering why I even considered letting him work here this summer."

That comment hit her hard. Bea flushed with guilt. Win was completely correct. And if it hadn't been her son involved, she'd never have leaped into the scrum. It deeply pained her to admit that she was off base on this one.

"Okay, boss." She grimaced at having to swallow the bitter medicine. "You're correct. He was out of line; I was out of line. The whole thing was a fiasco that won't happen again. Ever. Was completely inane. I'm sorry."

Win sighed and scratched at his short, gray hair. "Apology accepted. You're lucky you're not getting suspended as well. HR has been pressing me hard." Then, he laughed out loud.

"What's so funny?" Bea felt ready to cry.

"Lucy showed me the footage this morning, and over all my years in the news business, I never saw anything like it! You'd make a helluva linebacker, girl. Guy was twice your size. Thought I might send a clip of that move over to the Rams scouting department."

Scowling, Bea rose and grabbed her coffee cup. "Yeah, well, seeing myself on the local news is enough humiliation for a lifetime. And my hip and shoulder are killing me, so I don't want to hear another comment."

9

When Bea limped back into her office, Detective Pete Anthony was studying her laptop screen, his eyes narrowed. Lucy was perched on the edge of the desk.

"Thought you were going to visit Pine's girlfriend, Claire Thompson, today," he said.

"She couldn't meet. Too upset. Needs a little time. I'm stopping in tomorrow. Win sent me to Doyle's Senate announcement instead."

"I heard you were the life of the party," Pete said.

"No snide comments, please. I've had all I can handle today."

Pete leaned over the computer screen.

Bea joined her longtime boyfriend at the workstation. He gave her a wink, and she pressed in for a quick, reassuring hug. Pete Anthony always made her smile and was the perfect person to take her mind off the fiasco. "What's caught your interest there, Sheriff Peety-Pie?"

"Peety Pie?" He groaned. "Jesus, Bea, can't you behave professionally?"

"Evidently not." The Doyle melee proved she'd missed that bus. "Sorry, sweet cheeks."

He turned to Lucy. "Sweet cheeks? See what I have to deal with day in, day out?"

She smiled. "Looks pretty good to me."

Wrinkling her nose, Bea put on a pair of chunky, blue-framed reading glasses and leaned in. Figured if she was going blind, she might as well do it in style. "Seriously, Pete, what're y'all finding that's so absorbing?"

"It's a close-up Lucy snagged of the bodyguard's 9mm SIG Sauer, enhanced and enlarged. Gonna email it to the crime lab. Shows part of the serial number. And check this out." Pete moved over to give Bea a better viewing space. He picked up a pen from the desktop and pointed it at the firearm. "Has a threaded barrel and a suppressor sight."

"Like for a silencer?" Bea asked.

"Exactly."

Lucy picked up the Styrofoam cup of gas station coffee next to her and took a swig. "You're thinking Doyle's bodyguard might be a suspect in the David Pine murder?"

"No idea," Pete said, "but maybe. Sure as hell gonna check him out." He pressed *PRINT* to make a copy of the screenshot. "We gotta get a good look at that gun and need a slug to compare with the one from Pine's skull." He grabbed the hard copy from the printer. "I'll look at his registration, see if there are any issues."

"Sounds good, Detective." Bea took off her specs and stuffed them in the pocket of her pink silk shirt.

"That said, I'm outta here, ladies." Pete gave Bea a quick kiss, saluted Lucy, and exited the office.

Bea was grateful for every kiss. The man was, after all, a homicide detective. Their love affair could end at a dead stop anytime. Mostly, Bea could bury that fear. After the crazy fight and a loose gun almost in the possession of a homeless man who, it turned out, had been booked multiple times for assault, she was again reminded that every day was a gift.

Lucy lifted the camera from her lap and placed it on the credenza next to Bea's desk. "When're you going to fill me in on the thumb drive Pine sent you? Mary wouldn't say a thing, indicated the info could put

Molly at risk. Is that true?"

"I hope not, but I don't know. Doyle may be involved in some kind of generic drug racket."

"That sounds nasty."

Bea nodded and rubbed her eyes. "Mary's doing some research on it, but right now she's having breakfast with her daughter. Trying to figure out what to do next. If Molly won't go back to Savannah, then I'm sure Mary won't let the girl stay here alone with her father. She has this bizarre fantasy that he'd stage his daughter's suicide if Molly ever stumbled onto anything that could disrupt his voracious ambition. Probably a baseless fear, but she's scared."

"Probably baseless is not definitely baseless." Lucy moved to the window. Gazed out across Sunset toward Beverly Hills. "That inch of possibility would be enough for me to give up everything and stay with my child."

"Yeah, me, too. Motherhood adds a major note of caution to everything. Keeping our babies safe is paramount."

Lucy's eyes narrowed. "Tough when you're in a business where risk is part of the job description."

"We're always walking the line, Lucy. Never quite knowing if we made the right decision. We can only do our best, sweet pea."

Lucy sighed. "All new territory for me." She checked her iPhone and smiled. She held up a photo of her baby, Henry, back at the ranch, harassing Maddie, their golden lab mix.

Bea pulled her friend into a quick hug. "It's all so hard. I'm always here for you, girl, to share my bad choices and lousy advice."

Lucy laughed. "Couldn't ask for more support than that. So, Beebs, what's this illicit enterprise David Pine thought Doyle was involved in? I'm photog for Pine's funeral tomorrow morning, by the way. I'll have eyes out for anything iffy."

Bea shut her office door, then returned to her desk.

The two women sat together on leather chairs. She edged closer to Lucy. "Okay, let me fill you in on the thumb drive. First, I'll give you the thirty-thousand-foot summary. Three-quarters of it is written in Chinese, so I've got to find a translator I can trust to get anything more."

Lucy perked up. "I got somebody. David Lee, my lawyer friend at the talent agency. I've known him since elementary school. Speaks Mandarin and Cantonese. I trust him, but I'm not sure he'd want to get involved."

Bea nodded. "We'll check him out, but let me continue. Do you remember the scandal a couple years ago around a generic version of a top-selling drug for depression?" She considered telling Lucy about the same possibility with Aja's meds but decided that was Aja's to share, unless it blew up into something bigger.

Lucy thought for a moment, then nodded. "When the medicine became a generic, the FDA never tested it correctly, right?"

"Good memory. Mine's shit. I had to look all this stuff up. Anyhow, people got sicker and sicker because they weren't getting their proper medication. Patients complained that they were doing poorly with the generic, but the FDA said it was all in their heads."

Lucy frowned. "How many times has the medical establishment used that old ploy to shut people up?"

"Yeah, it's cruel. Makes sick people feel like their observations are worthless. Hell, if you weren't already depressed, being given a shit drug and having your experience denigrated could put you right over the edge."

Lucy nodded. "Along with the active ingredients, generics have fillers, too, don't they? To make the actual pill."

"Yup, and they weren't being effectively monitored either. The fillers are supposed to include only harmless, inert materials. Turns out they contained everything from drywall dust to ground glass, especially when the product was out of unregulated labs in China, India, or Thailand. Whatever was on hand was fair game."

Lucy opened and closed her fists as if ready to grab something and do damage. "So, it was like—hey, we got a pile of plastic soda bottles— let's grind 'em up and toss 'em in the generic blood pressure med?"

Bea shrugged. "Afraid so."

"Holy crap, that makes me really nervous. I take generics." Lucy pulled a brown plastic prescription container from her backpack and frowned.

"Ninety percent of us do," Bea said. "But they're not identical to the brand-name medication, they're *bioequivalent*."

"What's the difference?"

"As I understand it, the generic, supposedly, has almost the same active ingredients and produces similar wellness outcomes. In other words, the generic version does just about the same thing as the brand name, thus, they're bioequivalent. And responsibly-made under top-notch supervision, they're totally safe, and you can't beat the cheaper prices."

"Got it. But to parse words again, *almost the same* is not *identical*." Lucy paled. "Don't we share like 99.9% of our DNA with worms or dinosaurs? Would they be considered generic humans since they have 'almost the same' chemical makeup?"

Bea laughed. "Chill, dino-girl. You sure like to go from zero to a hundred at light speed."

"Sorry. Seems like everything's freaking me out these days. I get the equivalency thing, but what does all this have to do with Doyle?"

"Here's the deal." Bea cut a glance to the window in her door, waving as the sports guy walked by. She leaned closer to Lucy. "At some of these offshore drug manufacturing companies, looks like the amount of active ingredients and general pharmaceutical safety correlates with the market."

"What does that mean?" Lucy asked.

"It means impoverished countries with sketchy pharma regulations and oversight, places like Uganda, Ethiopia, Uzbekistan, for example, are sent the worst merchandise. Sometimes there's no active ingredients at all. Places like North America and Europe, with stricter oversight, get more of the good stuff."

"You saying that Doyle is getting onboard with the Chinese to sell crap meds to the poorest countries?"

"Pine thought they were using this same distribution model but here in the US. They're targeting the states, cities, and counties with the weakest oversight."

"Oh, great, fucking with our own citizens. Poor people of color will especially get screwed again."

Bea nodded and Lucy continued. "Would it be like what the supposedly legit Big Pharma companies did with opioids? A tiny drugstore in Bumpucky, West Virginia, population fifty, sells a half-a-million oxy prescriptions in a month."

"Precisely." Bea's mouth pinched in disgust. "Also looks like Doyle's setting up online distribution through untraceable IP sites. Pine said they've been doing it for months. They're getting ready for something."

Lucy rolled her eyes and sunk back into the chair cushion. She paused and grabbed her abandoned cup of cold coffee. Took a gulp and grimaced. "Can you imagine if he wins the Senate seat? And it's clear he's growing an activist base that wants to catapult him into the presidency. A drug lord president. Once again, the almighty dollar trumps integrity. God bless the unfettered free enterprise system."

Bea smiled. "Cynical, aren't we?"

Lucy ruffled her hands through her short wavy hair. "Happy thoughts, happy thoughts..."

10

David Pine's funeral was scheduled for 11:00 a.m. at the Valley of Eternal Peace Cemetery in Santa Clarita. Lucy hit the gas and sped onto the busy US 101, heading northwest to the I-5 for the hour trip. Going against the worst traffic, she hoped to arrive early enough to find a comfortable spot where she could discreetly watch and record the attendees. Many of her colleagues from various news venues would be present, and she didn't want to be sucked into conversation and miss the visual details that might reveal subtle clues worth following.

The wrought iron gate to the cemetery, anchored by impressive stone pillars, looked more like an entrance to one of Southern California's many high-end subdivision communities with exclusive-sounding names like Falconcrest Trace or Viewpointe at Chateau Springs. The only difference was an American flag, the size of a typical suburban garage, hanging from a crane above the un-staffed gatehouse. Valley of Eternal Peace was known for its huge military component. David Pine had been an army ranger.

Lucy joined the half-dozen vehicles parked in a lot closest to the main building. A low-slung, rambling, faux Mediterranean affair, it housed the administrative offices, including the casket showroom, an event room, and the chapel. She'd printed out a map of the place's three hundred, hilly acres before leaving home. Tucking the map and a small Nikon camera into the pocket of her loose black dress, Lucy headed uphill toward an old-growth stand of eucalyptus adjoining an area called the Tanzina Ramirez Peace Garden. Sprinklers sounded nearby and birds chirped. A sign said Stay on Trail, but Lucy sought the cover of the grove. She brushed past the sign.

With the Santa Clarita hills in the near distance, the day was uncharacteristically overcast, lending a pallor of despondency around the already tragic occasion. It had been two years since her murdered uncle had been buried at a similar place. Lucy tamped down the persistent fluttery wings of caged recollection.

As she entered the grove, the minty menthol aroma of eucalyptus was comforting. Dry leaves crinkled underfoot. She leaned against one of the tall, elegant trees and ran her hand over its gray-green bark. Long, flaking swaths like woody strips of paper revealed an underside as smooth as skin. A shadow in the distance caught her eye, then disappeared. A gardener? A coyote? The spirit of the dead? Or nothing at all.

Through her mini-telephoto lens, Lucy could easily watch the comings and goings at the building below. One of the first people to arrive was Pete Anthony. A niggle of guilt tightened in her chest. She should have coordinated more closely with the detective. It drove him to distraction when she and Bea didn't keep him in their investigative loop, especially when it was *his* case. Pulling out her phone, she texted him.

I'm nearby recording the crowd. Talk later.

Pete texted back a thumbs-up. He didn't go directly into the facility but slowly circled the building, likely checking out the entries and exits. Soon, he disappeared around the chapel past a dense bed of azaleas with a border of small American flags stabbed into the ground.

As cars began to arrive, dark-clad mourners, including many journalists whom Lucy knew well, disembarked and filed into the building. Two men in somber suits handed out programs at the door.

A shiny black limo arrived and pulled into a handicapped spot. Lucy aimed her camera. A female driver in a tuxedo hopped from the front seat and opened the rear door. A well-dressed middle-aged man stepped onto the sidewalk, followed by Pine's girlfriend, Claire Thompson. She was flanked by a slim woman with lanky blonde hair. No one looked handicapped.

Through the camera's viewfinder, Lucy adjusted the lens to get a close-up. Claire's eyes were red-rimmed. The other two accompanying her averted their faces and hastily turned toward the entrance, leaving her behind. It felt to Lucy like they just wanted to get this obligation done and be gone as soon as possible.

It began to rain. The sound of drops pinged softly on leaves far above. The earthy smell of dust and resin intensified with the dampness. A scent memory brought Lucy back home to the Malibu ranch where she'd grown up and recently inherited from her uncle—a place where she found her only solace. Being at a funeral resurrected buried feelings of loss from the deaths of her parents, little brother, and her uncle who had stepped in to raise her when the others were no more. The grief would never end. It just lay in wait to grab her in its death cold grip. She wiped tears from her eyes with the back of her hand. She must focus on the work, take the pictures. It was always what saved her.

Twigs and undergrowth crunched behind her. A crow clicked and rattled nearby.

"Lady, what're you doing up here?" The voice was low and menacing.

Lucy spun around, stunned by the intrusion. "What the..."

The man was compact, muscular, and twice her size.

"You spying on people?" he snarled. "You paparazzi?"

"No way!" Lucy's heart hammered. "But what I'm doing is none of your damn business."

She dropped the camera into her pocket. Would he try to take it? How had she let someone sneak up on her like that?

Square-jawed in his late thirties, the dude wore black trousers and a white shirt with a skinny black tie channeling the Blues Brothers or the Geek Squad. He stepped so close that Lucy could smell his hair gel. Her angry face reflected in his aviators. Why sunglasses? It was practically dusk-like. "And who the hell are you? Some kind of security?"

His lips curled in an insulting sneer. He seemed to take pleasure in intimidation and invading her space.

"Move away from me." Lucy put a hand on his chest and pressed him back. "I'm a friend of the deceased, and I can hang out anywhere I want to."

He stiffened but stepped away. "The family doesn't want any photographs."

"I happen to know the family. Photography is what I do— David would be appreciative."

A radio on the man's belt cackled. He turned to take the call. Lucy immediately scurried down the hill toward the building, almost losing her sandals in the process. The rain had turned the soft ground to slippery adobe mud. Glancing over her shoulder, the guy had, thankfully, disappeared. She grabbed an offered memorial brochure from an usher and rushed inside. The service would be starting any minute. The organ began to play a familiar hymn.

Trailing in late beside a few stragglers, Lucy found a seat at the rear so when it was over, she could be among the first to exit and situate herself on the far edge of the gathering during the procession to the gravesite. Always on the periphery, watching and recording is what she did well.

Lucy peered around to see if the jerk in the eucalyptus grove had followed her in, but she didn't see him. She wished she'd snapped a photo of the asshole, but the effort might have cost her the camera. Maybe he'd show up again at the burial.

Spotting Pete in the same back row on the far end, Lucy texted him the limo shot of Claire Thompson and the two people with her. She added a question mark and pressed *send*.

The detective texted right back. *Lance Ludlow, Pine's boss. No ID on the woman with Thompson.*

So intent on surveilling the audience, the minister's words of consolation and the tributes to Pine from family and colleagues barely registered. Finally, the lonely sound of Taps was played honoring his military service.

When the service concluded, Lucy hustled to the door, trying not to hyperventilate. Pete was at her side. He put his arm around her shoulders and gave her a wordless hug. He knew her history. His act of comfort was enough to let Lucy compartmentalize her pain and refocus on finding David Pine's murderer.

"I'm gonna mingle through the crowd, Luce. You take the sidelines. Get shots of every face and license plate you can."

"Roger that, Sergeant. And thank you." She sped ahead, following the signs to the burial site. Pete lagged behind until he was swallowed by the crowd.

—

The intruder sat hunched inside a landscape maintenance truck a few hundred yards from the hole in the ground that would hold David Pine's remains for eternity. It had been a relatively easy hit. Now the photo chick, Lucy Vega, was coming his way, clearly taking license plate numbers with her teeny camera. He should have grabbed it, but she probably had her phone camera anyway. Firing the ignition, he pulled away from the curb before she could get close. Was he going to have to take out the Vega bitch, too?

11

The Century City penthouse offices of Creative Talent Associates International, or C-TAI as it was called in the industry, was impressive. From its wide windows, all of Los Angeles looked like the promised land.

As Lucy walked across the foyer, she checked her buzzing phone. It was a text from Pete Anthony. The photos of funeral attendees and license plates from the previous day had led nowhere. He'd sent her snapshots of the cemetery's security detail from their Human Resources files earlier, and the creepy bully in the reflective shades didn't appear among them. Maybe he was just a concerned family friend who was being protective. Her gut told her he was something else much more dangerous.

In the airy reception space, Lucy was greeted by a beautiful young black man wearing a stunning pink suit, white silk shirt, and a lavender bow tie. He led her along a sunny hallway. "Ms. Vega, I'm Chester, Mr. Lee's assistant. He's way busy but says he's happy to see a special friend."

Lucy's longtime pal David Lee was the supervising attorney for all of C-TAI's international contracts. Besides Spanish, German, and French, he was fluent in Mandarin, Cantonese, and Farsi. BFA in Painting from the Art Institute, an MBA from Berkeley, and Juris Doctorate in International Business Law from Stanford. Was nice to have a genius on your list of friends. She hoped and prayed David would be willing to translate Pine's files. "We've known each other since we were kids."

Chester smiled. "Sweet. He has about ten minutes for you, Miss Vega, then he's scheduled for a conference call with Bey's people. Can I bring you something to drink? We have everything."

Lucy noted Chester said *everything* like he meant it. He ushered her into a small anteroom with a view across the city to the ocean. Original Ed Ruscha prints depicting Southern California iconography hung on the walls. Lucy sat down in a Bauhaus leather-and-chrome chair that was probably worth more than most people's monthly salary.

"Everything, huh? Baileys Irish Cream?"

"Neat or in our exclusive Costa Rican blend coffee? Cold or hot, with or without whip, and 85% dark chocolate sprinkles, peppermint, or—"

"Maybe I'd rather have a splash of *Veuve Cliquot* Yellow." A bottle of that was definitely beyond Lucy's monthly income. She smiled at the man.

"Whatever you want, darling. In a flute, coupe, or a tulip-style glass?"

"Whoa. You got me on that one. I'm a simple horse trainer's daughter. Water's fine, thanks."

He pranced to a built-in wall fridge and grabbed a bottle from a quaintly named mineral springs and poured it into a crystal tumbler. Placed it on the table next to her.

"Your service is amazing, Chester. Thank you."

"My pleasure, Ms. Vega. Mr. Lee will be with you in a moment."

He did a little two-step as he turned and pranced back down the glassed-in hall, chatting on his Bluetooth. His thick-soled white trainers were immaculate. She couldn't have kept them that pristine if she'd left them unworn in the box.

Less than five minutes later, the frosted glass door across from the Bauhaus seating opened, and David appeared. Late thirties, jeans, crisp white shirt, warm smile, and a full head of thick black hair tied in a man-bun with a red, varnished chopstick securing it. He opened his arms and scooped Lucy in.

"It's so good to see you, woman!" Lee's smile had always been incredible. Had he not announced he was gay at their junior high school spring musical after-party a million years ago, Lucy'd have asked him out.

After a bit of small talk and a quick show of baby Henry photos, Lucy brought up the reason for her visit. She pulled a dupe of David Pine's thumb drive from her pocket and placed it in his hand.

"So, you said you needed documents translated from Chinese. What've we got here?" Lee asked.

"We're not sure, thus the need to read the contents. To my untrained eye, looks like Mandarin rather than Cantonese. At this point, consider all contents highly sensitive."

A young woman wearing a black pencil skirt so tight she could barely walk toddled past them from Lee's inner office, pulling a cart of refreshments. Inside, several men and women chatted around a conference table. The door swung shut.

"Thank you, Mallory," Lee said.

"My pleasure, Mr. Lee." She disappeared down the hall.

Lee turned his attention again to Lucy. "What do you mean by *sensitive*?" His forehead wrinkled.

She glanced at the empty doorway and lowered her voice. "The stuff in English may link a prominent local politician to some kind of generic drug manufacturing and distribution scheme. I expect the documents we need translated hold greater detail."

Lee's brows raised, and he eyed the object in his hand as if it could bite him. "Sounds like serious shit."

Lucy nodded. "I don't know who else to go to, Davy. Until we understand what we have, secrecy is paramount. Only Bea Middleton and two detectives—one with the LA county sheriff and one from the

Savannah, Georgia Police Department—know the drive exists. I trust these people with my life."

"Fill me in. Where did this intel come from?"

"David Pine, the *Daily News* reporter. Sent it to Bea on the down-low."

"I know Pine. Decent man. A fine journalist."

"Yeah, he is...was." Lucy breathed out a long sigh.

"Was?"

"Pine was murdered last week, just a couple days after Bea received the drive in the mail."

"Holy hell, Lulu, what are you getting me involved in?" Lee frowned at the innocuous data stick in his palm. He hadn't closed his fingers around it. "C-TAI has a hard-won reputation, clients to protect. I can't get involved in anything, even peripherally, that could be damaging or scandalous."

Lucy sat back down. She pulled him into the chair next to her. "I wouldn't ask you if it wasn't critical. But I need somebody I trust. That's you, my dear friend. We go back to what? Third grade?"

"Second—Miss Colburn's class." Lee chewed at his lip, checking his smartwatch. "This goes against my better judgement."

"Potentially, you could be helping the world take down despicable criminals. We always stood for that."

He took her hand. "Always. One of the reasons I love you."

"Ditto. But you're right, it could be dangerous, can't deny it. This isn't a movie starring one of your clients. This is the real deal. No theme music, no popcorn, just messy possibilities."

"Sounds like it could open up a shit-show." He gritted his perfect teeth and gazed out toward the silver slash of ocean glimmering on the western horizon. "I have a company to think about."

"I appreciate that, I truly do, but I have to get this done and need to move fast." Lucy bounced her leg impatiently. "Are you in or not? Either way, we're good."

His chin dropped to his chest, and he closed his eyes in Zen-like contemplation, resignation, or maybe in prayer. "All right. I'm in." He closed his fingers over the thumb drive.

"Thank you." Lucy draped her arm around Lee's shoulder and leaned over to smooch his cheek. Deeply relieved that he was onboard, she was equally anxious about what the drive might reveal.

Lee stuck the ominous, shiny object into his jeans pocket. "I may not be able to get to it for a couple days."

"No problem. Thank you so much, David. When you're done, please call me. Here's the number for my burner phone. We're trying to avoid any kind of info leak." She handed him a mangled Post-it. "And again, thank you from the bottom of my heart."

Lee shrugged, a faint smile on his lips.

Lucy felt mildly nauseous. "I wish there was another way to do this."

Chester reappeared with warnings to Lee that the conference call was about to start.

Lucy hugged her friend goodbye and hustled out the door.

12

Traffic clipped along at the speed limit as Bea drove her silver Beemer toward David Pine's condo in suburban Santa Clarita, thirty-five miles northwest of LA. She exited the I-5 freeway just past Six Flags Magic Mountain. Bea thought its tower jumps and roller coasters were terrifying just to look at, let alone actually ride. Much of the public appeared to disagree with her, given the perpetually packed parking lots.

Several miles down McBean Parkway, Pine lived in an area of rolling golden hills just beyond the CalArts campus. Turning into the Valley Vista Townhome Community, Bea followed the arrow toward visitor parking. She pulled into a space near a semicircle of benches where a pale, lank-haired woman sat alone beneath a shroud of fiery orange bougainvillea. Claire Thompson looked like an old black-and-white tintype grafted into the center of a full-color Southern California postcard.

Channeling an elderly woman, Pine's girlfriend struggled to rise. Bea moved quickly in her direction. Claire hoisted herself up and pressed a hand to the small of her back. "Miss Middleton? Bea?"

"Yes. Hello, Ms. Thompson. Thank you for meeting with me."

"It's Claire, please."

Although they did not know each other, they immediately shared a warm hug.

"I'm so sorry," Bea said, releasing her. "What a terrible loss."

Claire replied, voice thin as the breeze, "I'm so out of my depth with this. I don't know what to do."

"Let's chat a bit. You okay with that?"

She nodded. "It will be good to talk to someone besides the police. And you said our discussion is off the record."

"Completely," Bea promised.

"David spoke of you a few weeks ago. Said you were 'one of the good ones.'"

"So was he, for sure." Bea followed the woman through a garden of roses that would do the Rose Bowl proud. They mounted a stairway up to a second-floor unit. As they passed in front of Pine's condo, yellow crime scene tape sagged across the door. Claire choked down a cry at the distressing sight.

"Let's get rid of this stuff." Bea ripped down the plastic tape and stuffed it into her purse. "I'll drop it in the dumpster. Don't need this crapola flapping in your face every time you walk by."

Tears slid down Claire's wan cheeks. "Police say they're done with it anyway. Some special cleaning crew is coming tomorrow to erase it all. As if that's even remotely possible."

"Come on," Bea said. "Let's have a glass of something and toast to a good man, a good journalist."

"And he was the love of my life."

"And most of all," Bea said, "we'll toast to that."

They continued past the site of Pine's murder to Claire's condo which was just across the breezeway. Her casa was devoid of frou-frou and whimsy. Strong clean lines, white walls, and high-quality furniture accented with bright, tribal print pillows—all neat and uncluttered, almost magazine-worthy. The kitchen contained an herb garden worthy of a five-star eatery. Clay pots filled with wildly flourishing basil, oregano, and other herbs dominated an entire counter. Bea inhaled a deep, delicious scent.

"Please, make yourself comfortable." Claire pointed to the living area and a Pottery Barn-style couch. A big white cat lay semi-comatose across a footstool. Opening one green eye, he gave Bea a bored glance, then stretched and slinked away. "That's Polar Bear. He hates everybody but me. I'm his personal servant." She smiled. "Can I get you a glass of chardonnay?" She pulled a bottle from her fridge. "I also have a lovely pinot and Dreaming Tree red blend, David's favorite."

"Chardonnay is perfect." Bea sat down and admired a photo on the coffee table of the couple at the Santa Monica pier in happy times.

Claire emerged from the open, high-ceilinged kitchen with two glasses, a bottle of wine, and a tray she'd likely prepared for the visit. With much appreciation, Bea eyed the cheeses, crostini, and sliced pears. Lunchtime had flown by without her.

"David could be happy with burgers and burritos twenty-four seven, but I'd make us something special at least a couple times a week."

"This looks beautiful. Thank you." The two women raised glasses and toasted David Pine. Then, Bea's reporter mode turned to the thumb drive.

"May I ask a couple questions about your last few weeks with David?"

"Yes, of course." Claire sipped her wine and dabbed her eyes with a tissue. "Not sure if I can tell you anything more than what I already told the police."

Bea nodded. "I read their report, but maybe you'll think of something else. New details can sometimes pop into your mind as the days pass. Do you know if David was interested in a particular story lately? Anything he might have mentioned to you?"

"I know he had something he was excited about, but it got shot down by his new boss."

"A new boss? Do you know the guy's name?"

"Yeah, Lance Ludlow. Just came to LA from a Bay Area paper that David disparaged as a 'tattler-type piece of crap.' His words, not mine. Mr. Ludlow and the newsroom sent me those lovely white roses. He included a personal note—invited me to join him going to the funeral. We drove in his friend's corporate limo."

"That was nice. Do you know which corporation it was?"

"No, sorry. I don't remember the company." She paused, as if wondering how much she should share. Then she seemed to make a decision. "I think Ludlow's friend's name is Sandra Kellogg. Like in the cereal company. We only talked a little bit, mostly about David. I think they'd gone to college together or something like that." She placed her half-empty glass on the coffee table and sighed. "I was kind of out of it during the whole funeral. So surreal."

Bea glanced over at a big vase containing several dozen, pricey-looking blooms. Positioned at the end of Claire's dining table, Polar Bear lurked a few feet away, assessing the bouquet. Was it food, friend, or foe?

Claire waved him away. He gave her a side-eye that seemed to say "I'll be back."

"Anyhow," she continued, "David did not like Ludlow, didn't trust him, but I'm not sure why. The man was very kind to me."

"Did David leave any materials with you? Papers, articles, jump drives, anything that might be related to his work?"

She sat for a moment in thought, then shrugged. "No, afraid not. The cops searched his place. Nothing much there besides his laptop, which they seized." Claire retrieved her wineglass, took a long gulp, and tilted her head toward Bea. "You saying there might be something David was investigating that got him killed?" Her voice sharpened with alarm.

"No, that's not what I'm saying." Bea wanted to avoid going down that mine-filled road with his girlfriend right now. "Just covering the bases. He was a dear friend, a brother journalist, and we want to be sure that every angle is thoroughly explored. He'd do the same for any of us."

Polar Bear made himself comfortable on the couch between the two women. His long, bushy tail slapped slowly against Bea's black-clad thigh, which was soon covered in strands of white fur.

Bea continued. "He ever mention anything about generic drugs?

Or China? Or Brandon Doyle?"

Claire stroked the cat pensively. "Probably means nothing, but a few days before David was murdered, he came home all anxious. Insisted on knowing what generics I was taking and where I got them. When I told him all I take is an occasional OTC painkiller, he was relieved. When I asked why he was so upset, he just kind of blew me off. I didn't press it."

Bea finished her wine. "Did you mention this to anyone else? The police?"

"No, didn't seem important."

"Let's keep it between us for now, okay?"

Claire's brows furrowed; her eyes opened wide. "Can you tell me—"

"No. Nothing to tell. Just have faith that David trusted me for a reason. I'll fill you in when I have something besides idle speculation to report. Right now, we're just casting a wide net. It's what we do."

Bea refilled both their glasses. "Did David speak any foreign languages?" She plastered a crostini cracker with brie and popped it in her mouth.

"Actually, he was a linguist in Army Intelligence before he got his first job in journalism." Claire stared into her wineglass. "They sent him to the Defense Language Institute in Monterey. He ended up fluent in Russian and passable in Mandarin or Cantonese, can't recall which." She shooed Polar off the couch. He leaped toward the roses. "What's this about, Bea?" Claire's forehead furrowed with concern.

Before she could answer, Polar yowled. The vase of flowers shattered onto the floor. He sprinted away.

Both women leaped to the scene.

"Oh, my God, Bear, look what you've done!" Claire disappeared into the kitchen and returned with paper towels, a min-vac, and a garbage can.

Bea picked up the larger glass shards and placed them carefully on a side table. Then, something caught her eye in the puddle. Stuck to a dark-green leaf, she fished out a gray plastic disc the size of a nickel with a wire sticking out. Bea held up the item. "Cat toy?" she asked Claire.

"No, he only likes the feathery kind." Claire quickly sopped up the water and glass bits with the towels. She shooed Polar Bear away as he slinked close again. "Damn, would serve him right to get his paw cut." She sighed. "I didn't really mean that. We can salvage the roses. They're fine—I'll put 'em in a plastic vase."

Bea continued to hold out the object she'd found. Her pulse began to race. She recognized what it was but couldn't quite put her head around it. "You're sure this doesn't belong to your naughty kitty?"

Claire took a distracted glance. "Maybe something he randomly dragged in from the patio. Who knows with this dude. Just throw it in the trash." She continued to focus on getting all the little glass slivers rounded up.

Bea slipped the object into her pocket.

Claire stopped cleaning and gave her a hard look. "Why are you keeping that?"

Wiping her hands on her trousers, Bea stood and mouthed, *"I think it's a bug."*

"What?" Claire appeared to hyperventilate for a moment, then she shrieked. "A bug? An electronic bug? Like in spy movies?"

Bea winced. So much for keeping any listener out there thinking the device was still in play. The water had probably shorted it out anyway, but she pulled off the antenna wire to be sure. Either way, if there were spooks, they'd already gotten an earful.

Claire leered at the fallen bouquet. "Someone is listening to us? Well, listen hard, you motherfucker." She jumped up and began stomping the roses. Polar Bear fled in panic. "Come near me, and I'll kill you. *K-I-L-L-Y-O-U.* Just like you did David." Roses were flattened as she belted out each letter.

Bea patted the woman's shoulder to comfort and calm her—to no avail. That train had left the station.

The quietly grieving Claire was now righteously enraged. She grabbed a fistful of long stems and beat the flower heads against the wall. Petals flew in all directions. Bea was almost glad to see the fury let loose. The whole situation was outrageous.

Stepping away from the floral mayhem, Bea dialed Pete. No

answer, so she left a voicemail. "We need a team back at Claire Thompson's place. Send somebody ASAP who can scan for electronic surveillance. We found something—could be more."

Claire dropped what was left of the roses and collapsed onto the couch in tears.

13

Perched on the edge of his desk, Bea passed a bag of chips to Pete, who stared out the window of his West Hollywood office. Uncharacteristically, he waved the food away. Bea joined Lucy to huddle in the perp chairs across from him, hungrily sharing a turkey sub. Bea licked her lips and glanced up. He slicked his wavy dark hair back on the sides with both hands, like John Travolta preening in the classic film *Saturday Night Fever*.

Particles of chronic attraction hummed between Bea and Pete. The man was getting to her big-time. More and more she asked herself—what the hell was their relationship? He was traditional at heart—she, not so much. What did that mean for them? The ambiguousness of their seemingly casual commitment was unsettling. They both had kids, exes, jobs, all the baggage of life that often pulled them in opposing directions. When they were together, however, it was outrageously good, especially the sex.

Pete studied his smartphone and fingered the gold St. Christopher medal around his neck, the patron saint of travelers. Bea daydreamed about a steamy trip they'd made to Costa Rica just after the Covid travel bans had been lifted and they'd both had their vaccines. The beach was a spectacular bed. She came home with sand in crevasses she never even knew she had. That week, life was simple.

Abruptly, she hauled herself from distractions and kicked focus into professional mode. That's all they should be concerned with.

She asked Pete, "You think the bug in the roses was the only one?"

He seemed to be barely listening. She raised her voice. "Pete!"

His head snapped up. "You said something about the, uh, bug?" The detective sucked in a little breath.

Bea leaned his way. "No additional devices in either condo, is that correct?"

"Right, all clear. Lance Ludlow denied knowing about any kind of surveillance. And he also confirmed that the woman he and Thompson were with at the funeral was a Sandra Kellogg."

"Claire Thompson corroborated that ID," Bea said.

Pete nodded. "Supposedly, Kellogg has her own consulting firm, which seems legit, but we're still looking. Something's off with Ludlow, but I don't know what."

"What was the florist's story?" Lucy asked.

"She was clueless—an elderly Lebanese woman who only wanted to talk about her grandchildren and her nasty daughter-in-law. But the delivery driver..." Pete poked at his cellphone and held up a photo. "A Raul Aguirre, originally from Nicaragua, has been in LA for ten years. Said he was paid a hundred bucks to place the device in the flowers and was threatened extradition by a dude with authentic-looking ICE credentials if he didn't agree to do it. Evidently, my creds looked even more official, so he spilled the frijoles. I've got him in temporary custody."

Lucy tossed a wad of napkins at the trash can, hit it dead center. "Raul have a record?"

"Nada. Seems like a straight shooter. All his paperwork's in place for citizenship, flying colors on the exam. He's scheduled for the final swearing-in next month."

Bea frowned. "Probably scared shitless, like most immigrants right now, thinking that it'll somehow all fall apart at the last minute and he'll be tossed out of the country." She stood and shrugged into her gray silk blazer, straightened her trousers.

"You gonna let him go?" Lucy asked Pete.

"He's with a sketch artist trying to come up with a likeness of the ICE guy. We'll cut Raul loose as soon as they finish. Nothing to hold him on. His wife and three babies are downstairs crying their eyes out. I sent them a Domino's pizza and gave the crumb-snatchers those teddy bears we have for kid crime vics."

"That was thoughtful of you, Detective." Bea leaned over and kissed his cheek. "You're such a softie beneath that hard-ass exterior."

"Yeah, well, keep that to yourself. As soon as they're outahere, the better."

"Speaking of outahere, I have to get home." Lucy grabbed her camera case and headed for the door. She slipped her phone in a pocket of her khaki cargo pants. "Elsa's been with the baby all day. Her niece from Norway, my new mother's helper, is at some Pepperdine event. Elsa's in her eighties, probably exhausted. Working on a homicide investigation is a vacation compared to caring for a feral toddler."

Bea chuckled. "No kidding. So, where's your baby daddy? I thought he was in for parenting this week."

Lucy's face darkened. "He's in Santa Cruz with his adult children, both of whom he neglected for a decade."

"And his ex?" Bea frowned.

"Yup, with her, too. All part of the family healing process. His alcoholism fucked them up big-time. He's dead serious about making amends."

"He's up north a lot." Pete rubbed at his late-afternoon beard.

Bea could tell he did not like what he was hearing. She knew Pete could feel almost as protective of Lucy as he did with her.

Seeming to deflate, Lucy slumped against the doorjamb. "Just told me last night he might have a job offer in San Francisco."

"You're kidding." Bea's phone chirped. She took a quick look and silenced it.

"Nope." Lucy's voice was weary. She clutched her camera to her chest like a shield.

Bea cut a glance at Pete. "I thought Michael was going to stay based in SoCal and work as an indie producer. Last time I talked with him, he had a local gig with *Politico*."

"Yeah, it went well. But it's over, and he doesn't have much more lined up."

Pete grimaced. "You two won an Emmy for your Guerrero black tar heroin cartel documentary, and he can't find work?"

"His fourth Emmy, my first." Lucy shrugged. "It's a fickle business, and he's still living down a hard-drinking reputation—burned a few too many bridges over the years. In the meantime, the guy has two college-aged daughters he supports."

"Now that he's unemployed, do you think he feels like a *kept man* with you?" Bea asked. "I mean, in this day and age, he shouldn't give a damn about who has a bigger money bag but—"

Pete sneered, looking at Bea like she was crazy. "Of course, he feels like a kept man. Hell with wokeness and all that bullshit. We can't help that we're macho types." He slid off the edge of the desk.

Bea placed her hands on her hips and raised an eyebrow.

"Maybe we're not so far evolved." Lucy looked toward the empty hallway. "Unfortunately, I can see joblessness grinding away at his self-confidence. We are who we are. And damn, he's an international war correspondent, not a gentleman rancher, even though he tries to be one for me."

Bea crossed the room and gave her sad girlfriend a hug. "Forget the war of the sexes. I know he loves you and Henry to the moon and back. Is that getting to be a cliché?"

"Big-time."

"Okay, but you know what I'm saying." Bea released her.

Lucy shrugged and turned to leave. "Yeah, I know he loves us. But I also know that's not enough."

Bea wondered if that same thing was true for her and Pete.

—

Mary O'Hanlon felt like a beggar. Standing in front of the huge, custom cherrywood front doors to her ex-husband's Brentwood mansion, she realized she'd need a battering ram to breach his pricey fortress. She checked her watch, pounded again, and pressed the bell. If he didn't answer in the next sixty seconds, maybe launching the front bumper of her car through the portico would get his attention.

She wondered how he'd suddenly acquired the money to move from their respectable Agoura Hills ranch-style to this monstrosity. A recently deceased rich aunt? Hidden accounts in the Caymans? Probably the latter.

She rang the doorbell for the last time. No response. He knew she was coming. Why the hell was he stonewalling—other than to simply be a prick? That was usually reason enough.

A familiar voice came over the intercom. "She went out," Doyle said. "Not sure when she'll be back."

Mary felt heat rise from her collar. Her face flushed. "You remembered to tell my daughter I was coming and taking her to lunch, didn't you?"

"Hmmm, I might've forgotten."

After the altercation at his campaign rally, the judge had reminded him to allow Mary and Molly to meet whenever they wanted. "Fuck you, Brandon. How cold-blooded can you be, trying to keep me from my child?" She hoisted a five-gallon-sized container of prickly pear cacti and heaved it at the door. Dirt and pottery shards splattered.

"What the hell are you doing?"

"Open up, Brandon, 'cause I'm just getting started, you asshole." She picked up a second pot.

A shiny new Mini convertible steered into the drive, a pretty blonde at the wheel. Molly? A blonde? Her long, coppery curls weren't stunning enough? She'd always prided herself for those gorgeous locks. How like Brandon—every woman was better bleached and sculpted, even his child. And what doctor had signed off on her being behind the wheel again? It hadn't been six months since her last convulsion.

Mary dropped the flower pot with a clunk, and it shattered. She pushed her ginger curls away from her face. Taylor Swift, singing loudly on the radio about needing to calm down, went silent when Molly turned off the ignition.

"Mommy!" She hopped out of the car and ran toward her mother. The girl's limp was barely discernible.

They embraced like only death could separate them. Mary's pulse raced with joy and relief at seeing her daughter. And it flared with homicidal fury at her ex-husband who'd kept them apart.

"He didn't tell me he was taking you away," Mary gasped. "You just disappeared. I couldn't reach you. He'd cut off everything." Tears tightened in her throat. "I was losing my mind with worry!"

Molly pulled back, face confused. "You were too busy, and Daddy needed me to help with his campaign. Daddy said—"

Grabbing her daughter's shoulders, Mary lasered into her child's brain. "I don't care what your father said, I am never, ever too busy for you. *You* are all that matters to me. Understand?"

Molly nodded her head like a bobble doll. "Yes, I understand, Mom."

They hugged again. The door opened, and Brandon Doyle stood surveying his front porch. His black silk Hugh Hefner-type pajamas draped nicely on his buff frame. Mary wanted to stab him.

He smirked. "You've made quite a mess. I should report you for harassment."

"Go ahead." Mary took her daughter's hand. "The police'd have a field day with what they'd find inside this ridiculous place. More space for all your little *hobbies*, huh, Bran?"

A fleeting look of fear pinched his self-satisfied smile. The soulless sociopath knew he was vulnerable to discovery at some level. Whatever level that was, Mary swore she'd find it. Maybe the murdered journalist's thumb drive that Bea had held the key. She wanted to threaten but kept her mouth shut. With help from Bea, Lucy, and Detective Anthony—they'd meticulously collect the ammunition to take Doyle and his minions down. They'd hit him so hard he'd fly right out of his jammies.

Turning to her daughter, Mary asked, "You want to come back to Savannah, honey? You had classes at school you liked, good therapists, some new friends. You were doing really well there, weren't you?"

Molly opened her mouth to reply, but Doyle cut her off.

"She's got all that here, and more. Plus, a purpose—she's helping me with the Senate race. Doing a great job, too." He winked at his girl.

"Daddy needs me on his campaign." Molly smiled with obvious pride.

Mary winced and narrowed her eyes. So desperate for his attention, all he needed to do was throw his daughter a bone, and she was happy. "Is Molly your little *Ivanka*, Brandon?"

His jaw clenched and unclenched. "I can give her the best of everything she wants and needs, as well as a foothold into a promising career. Better here than in that backwater, bug-infested nowhere that's still fighting the Civil War."

"I like Savannah, Daddy. It's beautiful. The people are nice and more progressive than you think."

Mary felt herself holding on to the child for dear life. She took a shaky breath and forced herself to release her grip on Molly's arm. Molly was newly twenty-one, however she felt years younger. Mary could see the girl gaining ground, though. Independence flickered. The traumatic brain injury from the terrible accident that almost claimed her life was slowly healing.

Molly kissed her mother's cheek. "I have stuff to do with Daddy this afternoon. Can we have lunch tomorrow—you and me and Bea? And maybe Dexter?"

"Of course, honey." Mary struggled to keep her cool. The thought of having to leave her child with this vile man was excruciating. She could hear the blood raging through her veins and tried to slow her breathing.

"Dad finally gave me your new contact information," Mary said to her daughter. "You should double-check it and make sure it's correct. I'll touch base with Bea and Dexter and text you later about meeting with them." She turned to her ex. "And Brandon, I want the list of all Molly's healthcare providers—they should have access to her records from Emory."

In bare feet, Doyle started to step onto his porch, then quickly stumbled back from the uprooted cacti and nasty, sharp pottery shards.

Mary smiled.

Doyle scowled. "Yeah, sure. And about this Dexter kid, I don't want Molly seeing him. He's a radical, not the type a daughter of a senator consorts with."

"You're not a senator yet, Daddy, so I'll *consort* with whoever I want to." She gave him a sweet, naïve grin. "I like Dexter. We're friends."

Doyle unsuccessfully tried to hide an ugly sneer.

Mary chuckled, face devoid of humor. But she was encouraged by the sense of self beginning to glimmer in her daughter. Would living with Brandon destroy the progress? He was a dangerous predator who saw their child as a tool for his boundless avarice, but Mary could prove nothing. She wanted to weep. Instead, she smiled, blew a kiss to her daughter, and walked away. For now.

14

Sitting at the kitchen island peering into the pale blue screen of her laptop, Lucy watched a video for new parents on the topic of surviving sleep deprivation. The cup of chamomile tea and the melatonin-rich half-eaten banana that sat on a napkin weren't having the desired effect. Both Elsa and baby Henry had been snoozing by eight thirty in the evening. Elsa's niece, their mother's helper, was off to Catalina for a few days with a group from Pepperdine. Again.

Two-and-a-half hours later, Henry was up and hungry. Finally, at half past midnight he seemed to be, God willing, down for the count—like maybe for another three more hours.

Lucy was too agitated to fall asleep. Her email pinged. She tabbed to her mailbox—it was David Lee. Her groggy brain went on alert. What did he have?

Lulu—

I know you're asleep, but I just finished the translations. Once I got going, it was like crack for an international contracts geek like me. LOL. Looks like a deal with a Chinese conglomerate to start up a generic drugs manufacturing plant in the Coachella Valley, somewhere near Thermal. Actually, the documents are three years old, so probably all's up and running. Your man Doyle is one of the signatories. The whole thing skates on the legal edge. One red flag is that it has no provision forbidding the parties or its subcontractors from making "prohibited payments" under the Foreign Corrupt Practices Act or any other applicable US anti-corruption laws. The FDA might be interested in this stuff, but I'll leave that to you. How do you want me to hand off the info? I put the translations on a second zip drive. Just a reminder—I don't want anyone to know of my involvement.

Be careful. Xo

Lucy immediately typed back, offering effusive gratitude. She arranged to collect the material at the talent agency's front desk first thing in the morning. She had "Mommy and Me" yoga with Henry at the YMCA in Santa Monica at 10:00 a.m., so the early timeframe would work. She sent Bea a quick note about the pickup.

Looked like Bea was having an episode of insomnia as well—she responded in seconds. The two women agreed to meet for an early lunch at the beach. There could be new revelations to discuss.

—

Brandon Doyle lounged on his stunning, Tuscany-inspired back terrace overlooking a small vineyard with the Pacific in the distance. The old Moody Blues band played *Nights in White Satin* at the volume of a whisper. Su Jin Pang, MD, sipped sake at the expansive, alfresco teakwood dining table. Portly, with tortoise shell glasses, he wore an expensive European-made white linen suit. On a chaise behind him, perched on the edge of the seat, sat Marshall Chee, Pang's young, wispy-bearded assistant and nephew, poised to do his bidding. *Contracts? Supply chain? Blow job? Yes, sir.*

Doyle graced his guests with a warm smile. "So, the purchase of the additional facilities is complete? Any snags? My contacts should have paved the way, loosened up regulations." He massaged the skin-like silk collar of his shirt.

The nephew waved his hand for attention. Chee wore a bespoke suit of excellent but lesser quality than the boss, his uncle. He held up a packet of documents in a leather binder. "No problems—phase one of the lab and warehouse expansion finishes next week. With your help, sir, we were able to expedite the permits with Riverside County." He bowed toward Doyle.

Eyes flicking around like an aquarium fish looking for food, young Chee held up a second binder. "The licensing is complete for Riverside Pharmaceutical's three-prongs: *Good Health for Life*, which includes our cardiac drugs and blood thinners. Phase-Rx is the umbrella for high blood pressure, cholesterol, epilepsy, and antidepressant generics. Five-hundred-million pill output by this time next year. And then, prong three, we have the custom pain relievers that help with anxiety as well. That's Sanitas-Rx. We're ready to rock and roll."

The senior Pang's dense black brows drew together in confusion. "We ready to what?"

Marshall struggled not to roll his eyes and patiently explained. "Means we are completely ready to go forward. All is in order, Uncle."

Dr. Pang scowled. He took another pour of sake, then popped a rainbow sushi roll into his mouth.

Price Burgess stood watch at the room's main doorway. The group's German attorney, Edgar Neckar, sat at the table and shared sake with Doyle and Pang. Neckar, tall and slim with cheekbones that could slice granite, looked to Doyle like a Hollywood version of a Nazi general.

Pang continued. "Until now, almost eighty percent of our raw material has been sourced from China and India. This is changing as we open businesses based in economically depressed parts of the US. We'll be bringing our key ingredients directly to California via Shanghai. We're following the opioid use and distribution maps from your Federal Drug Administration website for our target markets."

On his laptop, Doyle pulled up a graphic of the map. "FDA did a brilliant job of pinpointing our most economically vulnerable populations. Makes our work that much easier." He chuckled.

Neckar nodded agreement. "With this new business model, generic prices will remain low for the consumer, and we'll be able to distribute medication with identical packaging everywhere from inside the US. We'll manufacture here and save billions in shipping and transportation costs. Moving product was always our biggest challenge."

Marshall Chee's eagerness made a squirmy puppy look lethargic. "Plus, customers will order everything online. Only digital pharmacies. Even though the active ingredients will come from anywhere we can get them most inexpensively, the meds will be marked *Made in the USA*. Quality assured."

"As you're all well aware," Pang said, "the media's stoking public concern about so many widely-used drugs being produced solely in Asia. The last plant in the US that produced antibiotics closed in 2004. Shortsighted move, as usual, for immediate-gratification Americans. Not a shred of long-term thinking. Just imagine the leverage we will have if they need penicillin, and outside of China, only we can provide it." He chuckled.

Neckar stretched; his long legs protruded like sticks from navy-blue Bermuda shorts. "Then, of course, the quality issue with your off-brand medications has been getting attention. And also that problem around contaminated active ingredients. Some of your products didn't contain any active ingredients at all." Neckar snarled. "You can never be that careless again if you want to maintain my involvement. We'll scale down active contents by 10-15%, which will ensure reasonable therapeutic value but save us millions at the same time."

Pang's nostrils flared. "Old news about active ingredients. All was upgraded, and the flawed products were sent to developing countries. Our North American and European customers were barely affected. Nobody misses 10%."

Doyle didn't give a shit about the crap they doled out to third world markets. Chump change in the big picture. "We'll capitalize on North America's growing fear of being dependent on China for critical meds. The pandemic really stoked that fire. Our timing is perfect for switching production to the States."

"We'll be flooding social media with rave reviews of the products as soon as they're available," Marshall Chee interjected. "In about six weeks from now, we'll be launching our campaign. Doctor Pang and my dear cousin Lance Ludlow will lead the media blitz."

"Glad we're gonna get something out of investing in that worthless rag of a newspaper," Doyle growled.

Dr. Pang's beady eyes gleamed. "Yes, indeed. And let's not forget what's new and significant with our business design. The popular drugs will all contain small amounts of our newly developed benzo-like compound as a filler. It's virtually undetectable using current FDA assessment tools. Just enough molecular change to be invisible and does much less damage. Patients not only take their prescriptions as ordered but will soon be happily hooked on our brands. Ultimately, it'll be a good thing for their health—they'll never miss a dose." He grinned and helped himself to more sushi.

"You mean"—Burgess stepped forward from his guard position at the doorway—"people are going to be craving Lipitor and penicillin? That doesn't make sense. There's no physical high to get them to wanna take their meds."

Doyle wasn't pleased about his bodyguard taking the initiative to ask a question, even if it was a good one. Shit, the guy had gotten his GED and thought he was a genius all of the sudden.

Pang swallowed a bite of sushi. "We'll focus on long-term prescriptions for chronic conditions—depression, anxiety, high cholesterol, and so on. As a result of this micro-addiction, patients will experience low-level but uncomfortable anxiety and will need our brilliantly promoted non-benzodiazepine sedative and pain reliever, recently developed in our Huzhow laboratory."

"We never quite got to final clinical trials," young Chee added, "but the FDA took Uncle's research at face value—they're too overworked abroad to do anything else."

Dr. Pang nodded. "The beauty of it is that the user doesn't need higher and higher doses to maintain dependency. Just ten milligrams daily. Forever." Pang smacked his lips. A small piece of seaweed from the sushi stuck between his front teeth. "Consumers won't be walking around like half-conscious meth zombies—they'll function normally, unless they don't get those little pink pills. I chose the color myself—they look so tender and innocent, *wugu*, as we say." His eyes lit up. "I call it wugoxydone."

"Brilliant product, market-altering," Marshall Chee gushed. "Ongoing, forever, cha-ching." He clapped his hands. "Perpetual pinkies." He raised his hands and wiggled his pinkie fingers.

His uncle snickered.

"With wugoxydone in the pipeline, we need to be open to moving beyond online pharmacies rather quickly," Doyle said. "With the *Made in the USA* label, we could contract with the big insurance companies, HMOs, big box retail, Amazon, and of course, the military." He could almost hear the clink of millions dropping into his little, pink *wugu* piggy banks.

Pang poured himself more sake. His eyes were beginning to glaze. "We will see. Must move carefully, gain user confidence, be sure our new products perform as expected. Old Chinese proverb says—'Be not afraid of growing slowly.'"

Slowly? Shit. Doyle struggled to curtail his natural impulse to jump ahead. The Chinese had such a frustratingly long-range approach to things. It wasn't practical in this day and age. With Pang in charge, they could all be toothless and drooling in their oatmeal before the big money started rolling in.

Neckar asked, "What is the status of the reporter who obtained the contracts? And how the hell did he procure them?"

Price Burgess stepped closer to the table. "He got the stuff because of Pang's inept brother-in-law, Ludlow." He glared hard at Pang. "But Pine's no longer a factor."

Pang turned to Doyle, ignoring Burgess. "I told my sister not to marry the dimwit."

Doyle grimaced. "Ludlow says he accidently left the documents in the general printer tray over at the newspaper. The printer on his desk was out of ink. Pine must've grabbed the papers and ran them through the copier, or took pictures or something, before your brother-in-law could retrieve them."

Neckar groaned and muttered something in German, heavy with throat-clearing sounds.

"High school stupid stuff," Burgess said.

"Yeah, like the melee at my kickoff event," Doyle spat. Burgess needed to be reminded of his place.

Burgess flinched.

Neckar glanced at the bodyguard, then at Doyle with a cynical twist of his reedy lips. "We are sure the information is no longer in play?"

"We are sure," Doyle said. "Burgess has a recently hired assistant, and the guy knows how to do wet work." He was looking forward to the new dude kicking Burgess's ass.

Pang nodded. "And Ludlow was properly admonished. No more mistakes."

Neckar rolled his eyes. "These kinds of petty screwups are inexcusable. I will not put myself and my reputation in jeopardy."

"It's taken care of, Neckar. Your spreadsheets are safe." Doyle didn't like the arrogant German but knew the man was considered the best moneyman in the international OTC and generic drug trade. They were lucky to have him. Pang sealed the partnership by giving Neckar a fat retainer that would impress even a Saudi prince. Doyle hoped the asshole was worth it.

15

Cleaning his glasses, Winfrey Chambers sat at his desk across from Bea. He had the sour look that comes with drinking milk gone bad or biting into a Limburger cheese dip you thought was Brie.

Anxiety dampened Bea's palms. Was her position on the line? It had only been a couple years since she'd been deep-sixed from local KLAK-TV NEWS7 when they changed ownership. Was the fight at Doyle's campaign kickoff raising its job anxiety head again?

"What is it, Win? Tell me."

He leaned forward and tugged at his bow tie. "I know you're going to be very disappointed with this decision."

Bea winced. Was she still employable? Too old? Too sassy? Too whatever?

He continued. "The network has decided to move production for statNEWS to New York the first of the year."

No mention of being fired. A wave of relief replaced abject fear. She paused a moment to let her heart rate slow. "I thought they wanted to launch it in California, see how it did in our market. Is this because of how my first meeting went with the newbies? Aja just kind of freaked out when she heard 'mass shooting.' I think she learned a lot that day—a reporter can't throw up her hands and run away in awful situations. She's also coping with a few, uh, personal issues."

Win shook his head. "Has nothing to do with that. All part of young journalists gaining maturity, right?" He smiled and directed his eyes toward a photo of his son on the wall. Big eyes, skinny, and unsure of himself—it was taken during the boy's first month as assistant Middle East correspondent for Vice News.

"Our company priorities have changed. With midterm elections coming up and candidates springing from under every rock, leadership decided to commit current funds to ramp up streaming political coverage."

Bea took it in. "Makes sense, but what about Aja and Tito? We promised them jobs. I think they each have the potential to be outstanding."

"We definitely want to keep them onboard. We'll do three statNEWS segments which we'll air in December, then they'll be reassigned, probably to New York, if they've stepped up and done solid work between now and then."

"I expect they'll be terrific." Bea's stomach tightened. "What about this summer, like right now—is Dexter out of a job?"

Chambers glanced out across the bullpen. Dexter stood at the copy machine diligently feeding in pages. "We promised him an internship, and he'll get a good one. Your young man will continue to assist Jamison Earl on all things related to candidate coverage and social media."

Bea pegged Earl as an arrogant *prima donna*, but he was a solid newsman. Hadn't given her too hard a time about the altercation with Doyle's people, either. Dexter would learn a great deal from Earl. "Thank you, Win. I know you could have canned the kid after the fiasco."

"The cops said Doyle's bodyguard threw the first punch. And the second. Got it on a bodycam. No charges were pressed, just some egos a mite roughed up. All is well. And, I have to admit, Dexter's relationship with Molly Doyle is interesting."

"Always an angle, right?"

Win smiled. "That's what we do—search for a unique take that sets us apart."

He nodded to Elliott Katz, the assignment editor, jogging past the door with Aja, Tito, and Dexter following behind like ducklings. They wore gray t-shirts and ball caps with the statNEWS logo emblazoned in red and black.

"Looking good, team!" Bea called.

All smiled and seemed thrilled with their gear, even if the plug would likely be pulled on the show. Might as well learn the realities of the business early on.

Win turned back to Bea. "Katz will continue to manage the group day-to-day, but I need you to meet with them at least weekly to make sure they stay on point."

"Of course. And they know my door is always open.

We got together yesterday—they're already at work on interesting topics. I've got Aja moving beyond her lifestyle influencer comfort zone. She's researching a piece on generic drugs and the problems with active ingredients manufactured abroad, like in her home country of India. Tito's doing something on sexuality and young people with disabilities."

"Sounds like timely stuff, Bea. I know all this is over and above your usual load, and your commitment's not going unnoticed."

"Yeah, well, to be honest, I'm relieved we're only responsible for the kickoff. Supervising a full-on program start-up with a group of youngsters should be somebody's full-time job."

"Agreed. But in the meantime, I'll let you get back to work on the Pine murder. I expect an update first thing tomorrow. I have a real concern that the statNEWS project will drain too much of your energy from important reporting."

"I'll make sure it doesn't. But a heads-up—the David Pine story is getting more complex by the minute."

Win steepled his fingers. "As Shakespeare said—*oh what a tangled web we weave.*"

"Truer words seldom spoken."

—

Bea returned to her office feeling lighter to know she had a short haul with the newbie journalists under her wing. The responsibility of guiding all that youthful aspiration and creativity without letting it run amok was daunting. How schoolteachers did it day in and day out at pittance wages without completely losing their minds was heroic. Her friends who had to homeschool their kids during the pandemic could testify to that.

Pete and Mary were waiting in Bea's office—Mary at her work table and Pete in a chair across from the desk. Both munched McDonald's egg sandwiches. A bag of the same sat next to Bea's computer.

"Thanks for McBreakfast, my friends." Bea unwrapped a bacon, egg, and cheese biscuit and stood at her desk, hesitating before biting in.

"You look like the cat who swallowed the canary. What gives?" Pete asked.

She put the sandwich down next to her keyboard. "Well, I feel kind of bad, maybe a little guilty, because my statNEWS project will be relocated to New York the first of the year. Tito and Aja'll be out of here in no time. Already I miss them."

Pete took a long swig of latte. "Just as well. Patience with inexperience is not your strong suit."

"Yeah, patience—you don't have it, sister," Mary agreed. "And just like me, you're not very good at distancing yourself from emotional situations with young people."

Bea crossed her arms. "Come on, folks, I'm patient and dispassionate."

Pete laughed out loud. "Fistfight at Doyle's event says otherwise."

"Asshole was pounding on my baby boy."

"All six-foot-six, two-hundred-pound little Dexter, the barely coordinated son of a Division I athlete momma and an NBA star daddy. Surprised the kid can walk and chew gum at the same time." Pete laughed even louder, choked on his coffee, and it came out his nose. "Dammit to Hell."

Soon, they were all laughing. The levity felt good to Bea, even if it was largely at her expense. They were irritatingly right. She had mother hen issues.

Lucy walked into the office and plopped a hard copy transcript from David Pine's flash drive in front of each of them. All sobered up fast. Bea shut the door.

"Take a good look, folks," Lucy said, "and tell me how in over our heads we are on this one."

16

Mary finished the pages first. "So, these documents your pal translated are about the supply chain for bulk pharmaceuticals—the manufacturer's big batches of active ingredients. Seems sketchy as hell. Looks like international drugmakers can say the chemical compound is a proprietary trade secret, and nobody can actually get in there to regulate it. And there's no global authority for oversight."

"It's the wild, wild West, or East." Lucy tap-tap-tapped on the manuscript with an orange highlighter. "And the FDA's at the mercy of these people."

Bea shook her head in dismay, then eyed Lucy who shrugged and stopped the irritating tapping. "The feds have to pretty much take the word of folks who mixed melamine plastic into dog food that killed four thousand pups in the US and sickened two hundred thousand more. Beyond crazy."

"I remember reading about that," Pete said. "Assholes."

"And get this," Lucy continued, "a company can buy all their active ingredients from anywhere in the world, places with zero quality control, and the seller only has to list the principal place of business as the source of origin."

Pete sneered and slapped down the transcript. "Now wait, you mean to say the active ingredients for our meds can come from a garage in Bangla-fuckin'-desh, be shipped to California or wherever—and the seller can put *Made in the USA* on the box if the actual pill is made here?"

"Precisely." Lucy nodded. "Scary shit, huh?"

"And the money to be made must be mind-numbing," Mary added. "Sounds so much like Brandon. And I have no doubt he'd do anything to protect this kind of scheme. If he wins the Senate seat, he can ensure the laws, or lack thereof, stay to his advantage."

Bea stood and began to pace. "You thinking maybe your ex-husband could've killed Pine?"

"Had him killed. Brandon would never get his own hands dirty." Mary lowered her head and groaned. "Sweet Jesus, I have to get Molly away from him."

"We need to find out more about that bodyguard, too." Pete entered a number on his iPhone and waited for a pickup. He walked to the window when he had the connection. Spoke to someone in his office and assigned them deep background on Price Burgess.

Bea looked around at the group. "So, what's our plan, people?"

"Mary has to stay focused on getting her daughter squared away and safe," Lucy said. "I'll continue research on the China connection. I also have a doctor friend from my UCLA days who worked for the Federal Drug Administration. I can see what he knows."

"Sounds good," Pete said. "In the meantime, we need to track down Doyle's connection to any potential manufacturing or warehouse properties in California." He turned away and dialed again, gave another assignment to one of his minions, then scrolled through his phone messages. "Some shit's coming up with Price Burgess. Looks like he might have an interesting paramilitary history."

"Let's regroup first thing tomorrow," Bea said. "Winfrey Chambers wants an update then, too."

"Copy that." Pete dashed out the door. Camera in tow, Lucy hustled in his wake.

—

Bea and Mary entered Middleton's Santa Monica bungalow to bloodcurdling shrieks and hoots coming from the backyard.

"What the hell?" Bea dropped her briefcase and purse onto a chair and dashed toward the open French doors. She stopped short. Twenty-somethings frolicked in the pool and hung out on the deck drinking beer, schmoozing, and playing yard games. Ariana Grande's voice sang out from speakers on a coffee table. Dexter's friends from high school, including BFF Shawn Hayes, plus Tito, Aja, Molly, and several others, all turned to call out greetings.

"Hey, Ma." Dex cannonballed into the water splashing his mom and Mary.

"Ah! I'll get you for that," Bea screeched, scurrying out of range seconds too late.

"You said I could have a few friends over this afternoon, remember?"

"I guess I did," she muttered, wiping her face with her sleeve.

Molly dropped her corn-hole bean bags and skipped in from the yard to hug her mom. Bea noticed many eyes follow the young woman's scarred, but otherwise perfect little body, tucked into a tiny yellow bikini.

"Dexter invited me—wasn't that sweet?"

"The sweetest." Mary's face clouded. "You're still not medically cleared to drive. You didn't, did you?"

"No, Mother." She rolled her eyes. "You know I'm only allowed to drive to Starbucks and back—a measly six blocks from home. I Ubered, *of course.*"

"Good girl." Mary smooched her daughter's forehead and whispered, "So glad you can have the opportunity to be with friends your age."

Tito came up to join them. The hitch in his step was noticeable. His dark, curly hair was loose. He wore tattered sweatpants and a black t-shirt with a vintage *La Bamba* graphic. "Hey, ladies. Thanks for opening your house to us, Ms. Middleton."

"My pleasure. Uh, great to have you guys. Next time, maybe my son will give me some notice. And I told y'all to call me, Bea."

"Yes, ma'am, Bea," Tito said.

"Excuse me—bathroom?" Molly bounced on her toes.

"Through the kitchen and around the corner to the right," Bea directed.

Tito couldn't take his eyes off the girl. He turned to Mary. "Molly's amazing. She has, like, no filters, says just what she's thinking in a really good, kind way. Asked about my injuries. Usually I get all defensive, but not with her."

"Maybe because she's had her share of wounds, too. She 'gets' it."

Tito nodded, smiled as Molly returned. "Aja and Hayes challenged us to a corn-hole match. You in, girl? Gotta take these suckers down."

"For sure, come on." Molly trailed after him, then stopped, looked back at Bea. Tito stopped, too. "Dexter made twenty-seven corn-holes in a row," Molly said. "And then we threw him out of the competition. He's unbelievable, he could be a world champion. But he said his father would have a heart attack if he gave up real sports for corn-hole."

Bea laughed. "That's an understatement. His dad would definitely have a coronary over that one. He freaked out enough when Dex switched from b-ball to lacrosse."

Molly nodded, but looked like she didn't quite grasp it. "You're a para-athlete, Tito, what's your sport?"

He laughed. "Basketball. I already challenged Dexter to a one-on-one." He grabbed Molly's hand and pulled her toward Aja and Hayes, busy tossing the bean bags, missing the holes by a yard.

Bea glanced at Mary. Mama's eyes still clung to her daughter. "I think those two got a little something-something brewing there," Bea said. "Two sparrows with broken wings finding each other."

Mary frowned at her friend. "Don't start."

At eleven o'clock, Bea finally threw everyone out. "Party's over, peeps. It's a weeknight, and I expect my employees to be bright and bushy-tailed, not hungover, first thing tomorrow morning."

They groaned in unison.

Molly walked into the kitchen wrapped in a wet beach towel,

working her phone. "Gotta text Uber. They take forever lately."

"I'll be happy to drive you home. You're in Brentwood, right?" Tito asked. He slipped a hand around her waist.

"That would be amazing, if it's not too much trouble."

"No problem."

Molly dropped the phone into her bag. Decision made. "See 'ya soon, Mom." She kissed her mother.

"Thanks, Ms. Middleton—Bea, it was really fun." Tito gave her a shy hug, then he and Molly walked out the front door, hand in hand.

Bea slid a glance at Mary, knowing her friend's life was about to get even more complicated.

17

In Brentwood a half hour later, Tito pulled his rusting Jeep Wrangler up to the front door of the Doyle house and turned off the ignition. "Wow. You, like, live in a mansion."

"Yeah, my dad got rich a few years ago. I miss our old house. This is too much."

"He's a lawyer?"

"Uh-huh. Used to be an LA County prosecutor. Now, he's running for Senate."

Tito's eyes widened. "I didn't realize you were *that* Doyle. I've been so focused on my own work lately."

"Yep, I'm *that* Doyle. Other than politics, I can't quite figure out what my dad does, and he won't tell me anything. He's working with some foreign guys I don't have good vibes about. I overheard them talk about buying, or maybe it was building, a warehouse in the desert. What for? Who knows? Anyhow, you want to come in? I'll give you the tour and then we can hang in my room for a while."

"Sure, if you think it's okay with your dad."

"He's probably asleep."

Molly leaned over the gear shift and kissed Tito full on the mouth. His brows raised, and he let out a little puff of surprise. She chuckled. "I've only had sex once—junior year in high school. It wasn't too great. Maybe I'd like to try again."

Tito smiled and rubbed the back of his neck. "Yeah, good to give things like that a second chance."

"With your injuries, does your, you know…"

He glanced down and then back up. "Yep, still works. But let's not rush it. You got your whole life to make love."

Molly nodded. "Okay, but come on, the view from my room is cool. The Santa Monica Bay shoreline looks like sparkly, white fairy lights at night. So pretty."

"Like you." Tito pushed a wayward lock of hair from her face.

The two climbed out of the Wrangler and headed for the front door. Molly tapped the entrance code onto a keypad, the door swung open, and they went inside.

The foyer was round with a white marble floor and a ceiling over two stories high. Molly twirled, arms out, as if revealing the shiny new remodel in a reality fixer-upper show. A wrought iron staircase wound along the wall, and a matching chandelier hung over a round table filled with a lavish flower arrangement.

"Whoa," Tito said, eyes wide.

"My thoughts, exactly. Let's go upstairs."

"Stairway to heaven, huh?" Tito chuckled.

Molly playfully punched his shoulder. "We'll see."

Tito stopped and pulled her close, ran his finger along her rosy lips. "We're gonna take our time, Molly, not just jump into this. We're both wounded warriors. Don't want to accidentally inflict any emotional damage on each other. Know what I mean?"

She paused, drinking in his shadowy, dark eyes. "Yes, I know exactly what you mean. And thank you." She paused. "Sometimes I try so hard to be normal, whatever that is, I force things. I'm all dead stop or a hundred miles an hour. Sorry."

"Nothing to be sorry about. Ever."

As they approached the steps, Brandon Doyle emerged from the darkened living room, wrapped in a butterscotch-colored silk robe. His jaw was clenched hard.

Molly gulped. "Hey, Dad."

"Molly, who is this?"

"My friend Tito Luna. We met at Dexter's house at the party this afternoon. Tito, this is my dad, Brandon Doyle."

"A pleasure to meet you, sir." Tito extended his hand.

Brandon ignored it. Molly winced at the insult.

"Why have you brought a stranger into my home?"

"I thought it was *our* home." She narrowed her eyes. "Tito's not a stranger. He's very nice, and I like him. He used to be a Marine, and now he works at CNN."

Doyle blanched. "CNN? Well, sorry to ruin your plans tonight, Tito, but my daughter isn't on booty call. And reporters are welcome in my house only upon invitation, *my* invitation. Are you using my very vulnerable daughter to get a story?"

"No, sir. I just like your daughter. Didn't even realize you were her father until about five minutes ago."

Doyle sneered. "That's hard to believe. Or you're a total shit reporter."

"Daddy, don't talk to him like that." She clutched Tito's hand in both of hers.

"My child suffers cognitive impairment from a TBI. In case you didn't know, that stands for traumatic brain injury, and I resent to hell that you're taking advantage."

"I know what a TBI is, sir, and I would never take advantage." Tito's eyes narrowed.

Molly felt her fear morph to anger. Her heartbeat accelerated. "I'm not stupid, Dad, I know what you're implying. Just because I've had some brain injuries doesn't mean no boy will like me."

"Enough of this." Doyle stomped to the front door, yanked it open. His robe swirled like golden bat wings. "You'll have to leave, Mr. Luna. Molly, time for you to go to bed. Alone."

Molly blinked back tears. "Sorry, Tito. Your place, next time. And thanks for the ride home." She pecked his cheek.

"There will be no next time." Doyle was livid, sweat filming his fake-tanned face.

"Daddy, you're being so rude. He's my friend. I'm nice to your friends."

Tito disengaged from Molly. "Sorry, Mr. Doyle, but you got the wrong idea. Your daughter's beautiful, yeah, and she's special and smart in ways that most of us aren't. I'd never disrespect her."

"Leave, immediately." Doyle's face was a mask of disdain.

"Good night, Molly." Tito stepped out onto the porch.

Doyle slammed the door behind him.

Molly stood at the foot of the stairs, shimmering with rage. "What is it, Daddy?" Her voice was low and throaty. "Are you jealous?"

Doyle sucked in a breath. "Don't be ridiculous."

"I know you watch me, ever since I was little. I never told anyone, like you asked. I love you, Daddy, but I am *not* yours."

o-o-o

Brandon Doyle sat in bed, leaning against a stack of black satin pillows. He poured himself another brandy from a crystal decanter and grabbed his cell phone. Glanced at the digital clock—it was just after midnight. He thumbed in a number and waited patiently for a response.

"Doctor Berman. Brandon Doyle, Pang's associate. Sorry to call so late, but I need you to stop by tomorrow. My daughter's TBI seems to be getting worse. Her impulse control is eroding drastically. I think we need to review her current medications and see if there's something we can do."

The appointment was made. Doyle drained his glass, then turned off the light.

—

The news department was quiet. Bea couldn't sleep and was in the office at her desk just after dawn. Several hours had passed, and the bureau would soon begin to bustle. She glanced up. Standing in the doorway was Tito Luna, looking like he hadn't changed clothes since he'd left the party.

Bea gave him her disapproving eye roll. "I think I said I wanted all my people bright-eyed and bushy-tailed this morning, not hungover."

"I'm not hungover. Been on my laptop all night. I took Molly home, and Doyle threw me out. I was upset, couldn't shut my brain down."

"The guy's always been an asshole," Bea said, wondering what had happened but knowing she should wait for Tito to offer the information.

"He said Molly and I couldn't see each other. I'm ex-military, decorated, with a good job, but I'll always be just a Mexican rapist invader to some people."

"Yeah, you will, to the idiots. Fuck 'em, Tito. Don't let people like Brandon Doyle be the measure of your worth. Negativity and belittling others are what people like him thrive on. Tune him out, or you're the dummy."

He nodded, standing a little straighter.

Bea continued. "I read that the genius Albert Einstein once said: 'There are two things that are infinite—the universe and human stupidity. And I'm not sure about the universe.'"

Tito laughed out loud.

"And if you're meant to be with Molly, it'll happen. Now go home and clean up. You look like shit."

He smiled. "Yes, ma'am."

"Anything else?" Bea asked.

"Actually, yes. When Molly and I were talking last night, she mentioned she'd overheard her dad and some associates talk about buying a warehouse in the desert. I know you're checking out Doyle, not sure for what, but I thought I'd pass that piece of information along. I feel kind of guilty—her dad accused me of hanging with her to get a story, but that's not why—"

Bea held up her hands. "You don't need to justify anything to me, Tito. Do solid work and tell the truth—that's all we can hope for. *Capiche?*"

He nodded. "Thanks, Ms. Middleton. Bea. If Doyle is a bad player, I'd like to help expose him." He laid a printout in front of her. "I searched the high desert—Coachella, Mojave, Riverside County, Imperial

County, and I think this might be it. Formerly a date-processing plant in Thermal." He pulled at his shirt. "Guess I'll go shower."

"Great initiative. I'll take the warehouse tip from here. Tito—good job."

18

At a coffee and brew shop unappetizingly called *Pick Your Poison,* just off San Vicente near the West LA Sheriff station, Bea sipped an iced tea and glanced at her watch. Pete was driving in from Monterey Park where the county homicide bureau headquartered. It had been a long day, and the traffic on the I-10 freeway was likely hideous as usual, perhaps accounting for his being forty-five minutes late but not for her unanswered calls. She checked local news. A Sig-alert, meaning a major traffic event on said highway, was in progress. A madman throwing bricks at motorists from an overpass had closed things down. Finally, her phone rang.

It was Pete. The psychic hammer that was Bea's worry reflex slowed to a faint tap.

"Sorry, babe," he said. "I got called out on a—"

"Brick thrower?"

"Well, aren't you all over what's happenin'. Guess that's how reporters roll, huh?"

"Yep. I always check the news when I can't get through to you."

"Yeah, me, too, when you disappear. Anyhoo—I'm fifteen out.

Order me a double of the strongest shit they got."

"Coffee or booze?"

"Got a lot of paperwork goin' on tonight, so hit me with the caffeine."

"Copy that, Detective."

Ten minutes later, Pete arrived looking disheveled with a tired slump to his shoulders. He took Bea into his arms and buried his head in her neck for a moment, breathing in her scent like taking a hit of oxygen, then let her go. "One sixteen-year-old girl dead, first week with her driver's license. Face crushed by a cinder block through the windshield."

"Oh, my God." The sharp pain in Bea's heart that stabbed when innocents were victims twisted hard.

"The SUV behind her, with a soccer dad and five eleven-year-old boys, plowed into her rear end. His son was in the passenger seat. Door crumpled like tin foil. Was bad. I dunno if the kid'll make it."

"How heartbreaking. Did you catch the thrower?"

Pete nodded. "The dude was a psychotic vet off his meds. Shot dead at the scene."

"Oh, my Lord."

"A fuckin' tragedy." Pete winced. "My Gianna goes for her permit in a month. I dread the crap out of that."

"Alyssa's two years out. I'm on the wait list to buy her a used Humvee."

"An all-terrain armed vehicle? Sounds like a great idea. Get me on that list, would 'ya?"

They sat down at a corner booth with an open window overlooking the busy avenue. Bea pushed a latte with a double shot Pete's way. He took a long gulp, closed his eyes, and let the warmth settle for a moment.

"So," he continued, "let's compartmentalize and go to Doyle's goon, Price Burgess. He's interesting."

Bea shoved the dead girl and crushed boy into a mental drawer and slammed it shut. Denizens of the gruesome contents pounded and wailed for release but soon stilled. "Fill me in."

"Okay, so, Burgess is a Kansas farm boy—both parents dead in a sketchy house fire when he was thirteen. Listed as a likely meth lab explosion. After that, he lived with his aunt who ran a small poultry farm. She OD'd when he was sixteen. She was only twenty-four."

"Shit. Lovely childhood."

"He quit high school right after his aunt died and joined the army. Had papers that said he was eighteen and legal to sign on. Doyle and Burgess met in the military."

"Doyle joined up as a kid, too?"

"No, he was ROTC at Berkeley," Pete said.

"Reserve Officer Training Corps, right?"

"You got it. He finished with a rank of Second Lieutenant, Army Infantry. Just months after college graduation, Doyle was off to the Persian Gulf and Desert Storm."

Bea rattled the ice in her glass of tea. "That's when Lucy's man, Michael Burleson, started his war correspondent career. CNN was the first to send reporters into live conflict. Michael's still a wounded warrior, like so many, including your brick thrower." Her eyes followed a gaggle of teenagers crossing San Vicente. Insane to send such babies into combat. To Bea's mind, there was a sickness baked into human DNA that was cruel, malign, and utterly incomprehensible.

Pete continued. "Turns out, Burgess was in Doyle's platoon. Saved Doyle's life during a major gun battle. The guy took out a nest of snipers practically single-handedly. Got decorated for it."

"So, they're brothers to the end. And clearly, he'd kill for Doyle. Did kill for Doyle in the military. Friend, fixer, and occasional hit man?"

Pete nodded and finished his coffee. "After a four-year stint, Doyle was honorably discharged and went to law school on the GI Bill. Burgess stayed in the military for another two tours. He trained as a ranger, deployed twice to Afghanistan. Then he disappeared into the ranks of private security forces, ending with Blackstream Consulting. When Doyle became a prosecutor, he hired Burgess as an investigator. They've been working together ever since."

"He married? Any children?"

"We searched county records—he just filed for a marriage license. Also owns a pricey truck and a small home in Sylmar. No kids or previous nuptials on record, but who knows?"

A barista walked through the room picking up empties. Bea nodded to him, then rested her elbows on the table, chin in hands. She looked up at Pete. "Doyle's living in a mansion, and Price Burgess is out in Sylmar about to be married. You think he's going to start wanting a bigger piece of whatever pie Doyle's cooking up?"

"I'd say that's a no-brainer." Pete pushed away his cup and checked his phone. "I'm gonna drop in and talk with Burgess tomorrow morning, early, before he heads out."

"I'm your wing woman, sweet pea."

He smiled and pressed her hand. "Guy's not gonna open up to the chick who took a swing at him a couple days ago. Not to mention you being a reporter and all."

Bea frowned. "Guess you're right."

"As usual. I'll fill you in afterward."

A group of middle-aged men in grass-stained baseball uniforms flooded into the shop, raising the sound level to an annoying pitch. A sponsorship logo from a local transmission shop was plastered across the backs of sweaty red jerseys. Bea finished her drink, grabbed her purse, and followed Pete through the throng out to the street. The scent of coffee faded into the gritty stench of exhaust and melting asphalt. Hot winds from the desert picked up debris and swirled it across the sidewalk in tiny cyclones.

Bea took his hand. "I forgot to tell you. One of my new reporters thinks he found a warehouse Doyle and friends purchased recently. They'd pulled permits for expansion. Lucy and I are headed out to Riverside County tomorrow to check it out."

Pete drew Bea close and gently kissed her. "Be careful, sweetheart."

The Glock in his shoulder holster pressed into her breast.

"I'd come over tonight," he said, "but got paperwork up the wazoo. Gotta get brick thrower squared away. And keep this Price Burgess information to yourself for now."

"Of course, but can I share it with Lucy?"

He smiled, nodding. "Is there anything you *don't* share with Lucy?"

Pete walked Bea to her car. She squeezed her key fob, the door clicked open. "Freaks me out to have sleazebag Doyle and a possible assassin anywhere near Molly."

"No shit."

"I hope she doesn't continue to live with the bastard much longer." Pete touched Bea's cheek, then stepped back and opened her car door.

"Mary's working hard on getting her out of there." Sliding into her silver Beemer, Pete closed the door with a thunk. Bea opened the windows and blasted the air. "Later, my Peety-pie."

"Peety-pie..." He groaned. "And you say it in public. Woman, you're killin' me."

In her rearview mirror, Pete stood on the sidewalk and watched her drive away.

o-o-o

Pete had pulled an all-nighter finishing reports, slept in his office, and just finished a bag of Cheddar Gold Fish that had been in his glove compartment since the millennium. The cop shop coffee was decent, but he was not in a good mood as he parked in front of Price Burgess's Sylmar ranch house—one of hundreds that sprouted up on the northern edge of the metro in the mid-eighties. Once home to pastoral olive groves and equestrian facilities, in past decades the area had struggled with economic hardships, changing demographics, drugs, and crime. Recently, the neighborhoods seemed to be making some positive progress.

The Price Burgess place appeared to be well-kept. Pots of bright red geraniums lined the small porch landing. The lawn was mowed, and the house's paint job looked fresh. If he hadn't been before, Burgess was definitely going domestic.

Pete stepped to the front door and rang the bell. A camera looked down from overhead, and another digital eyeball peeped from above the doorbell. Burgess was a believer in home security. He would definitely know how to plant a bug.

A voice sounded from a speaker. "Yeah?" The dude was not happy.

Pete held up his credentials. "Detective Sergeant Peter Anthony,

LA County Sheriff Homicide Bureau."

A woman's voice trilled in the background. "Who is it, honey?"

The voice muffled. "Just business. Get that coffee going, dollface."

She giggled.

There was a pause. Pete continued. "Price Burgess, I'd like a moment of your time, sir."

"What's this about?"

"David Pine."

"Who?"

Pete clenched his jaw. He was not in the mood for fun and games. "Reporter who had all kinds of shit on your boss."

"Don't know a David Pine."

"I'm tired and in a piss-poor mood, the kind that gets warrants and tears your house apart. So, open the fucking door."

After a pause, several locks disengaged, and the door slowly opened. In a black karategi with a Japanese logo over the heart, usually the sign of an instructor, Burgess eased out onto the porch. His smooth physical movements crackled with danger. His bare feet were wide as kayak paddles. Pushing a cigarette between his lips, the man pulled out a lighter and flicked it—the result looked like a mini flamethrower. Pete stepped back. Burgess smirked.

"What can I do for you, Detective? Like I said, I don't know no Davis Prine."

"Pine, David Pine, reporter for the Daily News. He walked away with some very interesting information on Brandon Doyle's plans to do some shit with generic drugs."

"Generic drugs? I dunno what you've been smokin', man, but—"

"Don't bullshit me, Burgess. Where were you on the afternoon of July nineteenth?"

The man took a long drag from his cigarette and fixed his narrowing gaze into middle distance. "Hmmm. That was, what? Last Thursday?"

Pete nodded.

"I was in Brentwood at a meeting with Mr. Doyle. Was there until early evening. We ate dinner at Sweeney's Bar and Grill. Nice place— you been there?"

"I'm not here for a fucking restaurant review, Burgess. Can anyone vouch for you?"

"Sure, Brandon Doyle, former LA prosecutor and US Senate candidate." His smirk was snake-like. He looked at Pete like the detective was a rodent who'd better run or die as a meal.

A smiling woman holding an aromatic plate of fresh muffins appeared in the doorway. She was pretty in a round, definitely-not-from-Hollywood way. Her bovine eyes shined with kindness. Pete saw Burgess's face soften. The guy had it bad.

She held out the plate. "Right from the oven. Have one, boys." Burgess obediently took a muffin, and Pete did the same.

"Thank you, honey. Girl's a helluva, I mean, heckuva cook."

She handed them each a dainty, blue paper napkin.

"Thank you, ma'am. Didn't get much breakfast this morning." Pete took a bite. Cranberry orange. "Mmmmm, fantastic."

Burgess held his muffin untouched in the napkin. The man looked like he'd be more comfortable holding a hand grenade.

"Glad you like it. I'm off to school with the rest of the batch. My first graders did such an awesome job with their library projects this week, I promised them a treat." She disappeared back into the house.

Pete took another bite, finished it off. "Looks like you got yourself a real sweet lady there, man. Don't blow it." He licked his lips. "They don't bake 'em like this at Lompoc."

"Fuck you, Anthony."

"I'm watching you, Burgess," Pete growled. "For the murder of David Pine." He crushed the empty napkin in his fist, shoved it into Burgess's baseball mitt-sized hand. "And hell, Romeo, we put you away for life, maybe she'll bake pastries for me."

If looks could kill.

19

At six the next morning, Bea was in the garage loading a small cooler into the back seat of her car when Lucy pulled up to the curb in her dusty Jeep SUV.

"Hey, girl," Lucy called. "We're not driving."

Bea raised her head. "What are you talking about?"

"Can't be away from Henry all day and can't face the drive to Thermal—too many hot, miserable hours on the road."

"Then, what—"

"Our old friend Ren Gelber. He's waiting for us at the Santa Monica Airport."

Bea grinned. "Well, ain't that fine! How'd you wrangle it, Miss Lucia?"

"I called him last night and begged. Offered him a mediocre deal money-wise, and good dude that he is, he agreed. He was heading in that direction anyway. Has to pick up a couple golfers at an Anza-Borrego resort and ferry them to San Diego. Then, he'll come back to Thermal for us around two this afternoon."

"Fan-frickin'-tastic. Best news I've heard all week."

Ren was a decorated Vietnam War vet who ran the private FBO terminal at Hawthorne Airport. Bea and Lucy had bonded with the chopper pilot big-time when he saved their butts during a dangerous foray into the mountains above the Coachella Valley the previous winter. He knew San Bernardino, Riverside, and Imperial counties like almost no one else.

"The chopper awaits," Lucy said. "I've had my meds, so I'm ready to lift off, so to speak."

Bea smiled, grabbing her day pack and the cooler. Lucy was flying phobic. She'd gotten better over the years, but a little too much turbulence could still push her over the edge into sheer panic.

The Santa Monica Airport was a small, municipal facility tucked into a residential and mixed-use commercial area just two miles from the ocean. Ren stood next to his twin-engine Bell 212, the civilian equivalent to the Huey he'd flown in Vietnam. He'd relentlessly saved every penny and bought the bird two decades ago, converting the bare-bones chopper into a cushy machine he used to transport celebrities, hotshot politicians, and other luminaries around the region. He named his pride and joy *Sister Rose* after his beloved sibling who died of breast cancer. She'd been a chopper pilot, too. A red rose across a heart of gold was stenciled on the passenger-side door.

Bea, Ren, and Lucy exchanged greetings and hugs, then clambered into the bird, donned their earphones, and secured their safety belts. The propellers began to whirl. A slow *whomp-whomp* quickly built to a high-pitched pounding roar. Then up they went.

Bea saw Lucy fix focus on the horizon to avoid looking down. She adjusted her Ray-Bans and grasped Bea's hand.

After a momentary hover, Sister Rose cruised low along the single runway, then cut east, climbing fast. In minutes, downtown LA was beneath them, and they were on their way to Coachella Valley, most famously known for the small city of Palm Springs.

Ren communicated with air traffic control and remained keyed in to radio chatter until they were farther away from the busy metro area. Soon, the San Gorgonio Pass through the San Bernardino mountain peaks offered a stunning view of the sprawling Sonoran Desert before them. Boasting miles of wind farms, they were entering the second windiest spot in the western United States. Point Reyes was the first. Bea readied for Lucy's death grip as the turbulence hit.

Bea knew Ren was well aware of Lucy's flying struggles. She was relieved when he attempted some diversion. "So, Lucy, what are you two wild women up to this time? You didn't tell me much last night. Not another battle with a drug cartel, I hope."

He chuckled and glanced into his rear view. The women sat behind him in two of the four comfy leather passenger seats. They weren't smiling.

"We want to check out a warehouse-type facility near Thermal," Lucy said. "Used to be a date-processing plant, but it's been purchased by a Chinese conglomerate with ties to a local political candidate."

"You're talking about the old Mecca Golden Date Company site."

"That's it," Lucy said. "May have been retrofitted to produce generic drugs, a US-based pill mill. So, yes. We may have another drug thing going on."

"Holy shit. A pill mill? Like in opioids?"

"We don't think opioids, but maybe generics with questionable ingredients," Lucy said.

Bea was relieved as Lucy's nervous handhold eased, allowing some blood flow back into Bea's fingers.

Ren's eyes followed an eastbound Southwest 737 jet a couple thousand feet overhead. "So, something's fishy about this warehouse deal?"

Bea watched Lucy's gaze switch from the wild blue yonder to the back of Ren's head. Any place but down.

"We're not sure what's going on," Lucy said. "A reporter friend of ours, who had a thumb drive full of information on the Chinese company, was murdered last week."

"Holy shit," Ren said.

"So," Bea continued, "you can bet Sister Rosie here that something's not on the up-and-up."

—

In less than forty-five minutes, the Salton Sea, which was about sixty miles southeast of Palm Springs, shimmered in the distance like a desert mirage.

"Winds are north-northeast at five knots, and the temperature is already ninety-five degrees with a high of one hundred nine," Ren reported. He went on to talk with the controller at the Jacqueline Corcoran Regional Airport, named for a local woman who was the first female pilot to break the sound barrier.

The chopper flew above emerald-green postage-stamp golf courses and residential neighborhoods, interspersed with tracts of barren desert. Finally, he cruised over the hangars and terminal building to land. Ren touched down about a hundred yards from the rental car kiosk. Lucy and Bea thanked him profusely for the transpo.

"You gals be careful now," he ordered. "See you after lunch, all safe and sound. Got it?"

"Roger that, sir," Lucy called out, clutching her baseball cap as they hunched beneath the rotors.

Ren and Sister Rose were quickly airborne again. Bea felt a pang of nausea from the smell of jet fuel swirling in hot air blasting from the downwash.

The two women scurried across the melting tarmac to pick up a bullet-gray Taurus that had seen better days. Perfect for their surveillance plans.

Despite the dusty, mud-spattered exterior, the rental car was clean inside and its air-conditioning prodigious. In no time, the interior became arctic. Twenty minutes later when Lucy and Bea arrived at the pill plant, they found a parking spot on the far edge of a lot near the entrance. There was no identifying signage on the utilitarian stucco building.

The entire area clearly had once been date groves. Only a few trees had been transplanted as part of a meager attempt at landscaping in front of the building. Most trees in the groves were dead. Hundreds of giant palms, at least seventy feet high, were topped with lifeless fronds hanging like dissolute broom heads. They provided a choir of scraping saws in the hot breeze.

Bea glanced at her watch. It was 8:33 a.m., and workers were beginning to congregate. Shift start was supposedly at 9:00. "Let's see if there's a coffee shop or a breakfast joint nearby where we can hang. Sitting in the car in these killer temps is not gonna happen."

Across a narrow, poorly maintained street at the side entrance to the old date factory sat a row of downscale commercial businesses. *Pepe's Cucina* was the only eatery. The women collected their belongings and ambled through the parking lot in that direction. As they approached, a small group of workers exited with to-go bags, chattering in Spanish among themselves.

Bea and Lucy went inside the small, neat restaurant. Its adobe-style walls were decorated with traditional Mexican crafts, woven rugs, and strings of dried chili peppers. A mariachi band crooned *Cielito Lindo* over a speaker. The menu, written on a chalkboard, featured a dozen dishes, mostly breakfast and lunch combo plates.

A middle-aged mom and pop team appeared to run the place. Behind the cash register, an array of family photos hung in cheap frames. A picture of twin girls in white quinceanera attire was prominent. Bea and Lucy slid into an empty table at the front window overlooking the loading dock. The rear half of the manufacturing building was surrounded by an eight-foot, chain-link enclosure topped with concertina wire. Spindly strands of strangleweed snaked up the fencing.

A small-boned woman, pretty in a crisp violet blouse and a black skirt, came to take their orders. She brought two ice waters and a pot of coffee. Her name badge read *Juana*. Likely, Senora Pepe.

Lucy ordered a breakfast burrito, and Bea went for huevos rancheros.

"You ladies here to visit vitamin plant?" Juana asked.

"Vitamin plant?" Lucy repeated.

"Uh, yeah," Bea cut in. "The vitamin plant. We have an appointment over there. Doing a story for the newspaper. Got here a little early—heard Pepe's has a *muy bueno desayuno*."

She blushed. "Gracias. *Mi esposo*, Pepe, he good cook. I hope you like." She hustled off to the kitchen.

"Vitamins, huh." Lucy pulled out her camera and snapped a telephoto of two semis backing into the loading bay. They carried forty-foot, two-and-a-half-ton when empty shipping containers, the kind that were off-loaded from massive cargo ships at big seaports like Long Beach and LA Harbor. These were painted gray with COSCO stenciled in dark blue. A half dozen workers materialized to begin unpacking the contents.

Bea googled the insignia. She'd seen it many times but didn't know its origin. "COSCO's out of China. Third largest container shipping company in the world. We see the logo all the time on the Savannah River back home."

Senora Pepe returned with breakfasts and *mas* coffee. "Lots of trucks, in and out, all the time," she said. "Day, night. We very happy."

She obviously loved to talk. "Since date factory close down, we almost go out of business. People like vitamins. They good for health." She raised her arm and made a muscle, chuckling. "The company grow. Dirt movers on other side of building make new addition."

"Yes, indeed, people like their vitamins." Bea reached into her purse and pulled out her own bottle of One-a-Days. Popped a pill and followed it with an ice water chaser.

Juana smiled and crossed herself. "Business stay good, maybe *mi dos niños* go UCLA someday. They very smart."

Bea felt her throat tighten. She wanted to press Juana's hand. If the factory was manufacturing crooked drugs, the woman's UCLA dreams would be ashes.

Lucy said, "I hear they make medicines over there, too. *Si?*"

She nodded. "I no sure. Mostly vitamins."

Juana returned to the kitchen. Bea and Lucy, famished, dug in. "*Mucho bueno.*" Lucy licked her lips.

Mouth full, Bea nodded agreement.

20

After they settled the bill, it was back outside into the bludgeoning heat. Lucy took off her ball cap and fanned herself with it. She wiped her forehead with the back of her hand. "Has to be upward toward a hundred twenty already. Thermal's aptly named, isn't it? Like sucking air straight out of a hair dryer."

Bea winced and adjusted her sunglasses, peering across the street. Another semitrailer truck with a COSCO stencil had pulled up beside those currently being unloaded. Pallets of gray bricks of product wrapped in plastic disappeared on forklifts into the dark warehouse.

Bea pulled a visor out of her purse and put it on. "With this kind of volume day and night, as Juana said, you can see why Doyle and his cronies want to expand."

"Yeah, for sure." Lucy shot several more images, then tucked her camera into a black, nylon fanny pack. "What's our next move, Beebs? Slip through that chain-link gate into the warehouse? Or try the front door and introduce ourselves nicely?"

Bea smiled. They hoofed it toward the loading dock trailing a group of women in aqua-colored scrubs who appeared to be cleaning staff or lab techs. Passing beneath a tangle of barbed wire over the gate, Bea spotted a card swipe mechanism for entry, but a curling Post-it said it was temporarily out of service.

She shook her head, frowning. "Fools should be more concerned with security. But sweet for us."

The employees took a hard right turn to enter through the front of the building, but Lucy and Bea made for the dock. The warehouse worker bees remained focused on their tasks, initially ignoring the two visitors who climbed the steps to the tepid, dim loading bay.

Lucy marched up to a young fellow who had the stony look of a hard-ass. She asked him, in the Spanish she'd been working hard to improve, what was being delivered. Then she glanced around like she owned the place and deserved an immediate answer.

He replied in English. "I don't speak Spanish."

Lucy frowned. "Why not? Thermal is almost entirely people of Mexican descent, and it looks like most of your co-workers are Hispanic."

Bea sidled up close to Lucy—ready to mitigate her friend's occasional "my-way-or-the-highway" approach. It had gotten them into trouble more than once.

"I'm Iranian." His eyes narrowed. "And I don't speak Farsi either."

Bea hit her friend with serious side-eye. Lucy'd recently been gripped by a Mexican pride obsession since bonding with an awesome great-aunt from Guerrero she hadn't known existed. Bea edged between Lucy and the warehouse guy. "We're fascinated with your up-and-coming enterprise here, sir. Perhaps you could tell us about it."

He looked at the women like picnic ants he wanted to crush. "Who are you? And what're you doing here? No visitors allowed on the loading dock. It's dangerous. Shit can happen."

"Is your supervisor around?" Lucy asked.

"You're talking to him, lady."

Lucy flinched just the smallest amount. "Ah, okay, sorry, Mister—"

"Tahan."

"Mr. Tahan." Lucy offered her hand, and he ignored it. "I'm Lucia Vega, and this is my colleague Beatrice Middleton."

Bea gave him a friendly little wave and stepped away to observe the workers and let Lucy dig herself out of the hole with Tahan. Nasty-bladed forklifts like steel praying mantises buzzed around a huge interior space.

Lucy continued. Her tone modulated from demanding to casual, maybe even a smidge contrite. "We're reporters doing a blog on new economic development in the Coachella Valley. We heard that you manufacture generic drugs. We wanted to learn more about forward-looking new businesses in the region."

His frown was menacing. His face was beginning to dampen. It was either his proximity to the outside heat or the topic of conversation. "Vitamins. We do vitamins. Maybe a couple generics. You need to go now. Make an appointment with the communications people. *Adios.* That Spanish enough for you, *senorita*?"

Lucy frowned.

Next to Bea, a small, ferret-like dude picked up gray plastic bags of product that had fallen loose from a broken pallet. "Guy's an asshole," he said to Bea in a low voice. His eyes were transfixed at boob-level. "They don't just do vitamins here. Manufacture all sorts of generic shit. Let me buy you a beer sometime, and I'll tell you all about it. Maybe even slip you some samples." He yucked at his double entendre.

The supervisor turned toward ferret guy. "Skunk, shut your fuckin' mouth and get moving. This is your last warning."

Skunk winked at Bea, then slinked away.

Bea dropped a tissue onto the floor in a dusting of power from a broken package and surreptitiously wiped up as much of the substance as she could. Stuffed it into in her pocket.

The super frowned at Lucy. "Ladies, you have exactly ten seconds to get the hell out of here before I call security." He glanced up at an overhead camera.

Bea followed his gaze to the silvery eye. *Hello, Doyle, you asshole.*

Grabbing the radio from his belt, the man in charge pressed a button and growled, "Security, we have gate-crashers who need to be ushered out."

"Copy that," a staticky voice responded.

"Okay, we're going." Bea took one last scan around the warehouse. It was chock-full of product, whatever it was.

—

Marshall Chee stood in the darkened security camera room surrounded by a dozen big screens. Ellen Crandall, a chemist who helped oversee production, was huddled at his side.

"What are we going to do?" Chee asked, voice high and shaky. "That's Bea Middleton from Network News."

Crandall adjusted her glasses. "I thought she was MSNBC or ABC."

"Whatever." Chee gritted his sparkling white teeth. "The point is, media is here! How did this happen? How should we handle this? Oh, my gawd." He was beginning to sweat.

"Transparency," Crandall said. "The illusion of transparency, at least. We have to let them in, give them a cursory look-see, then send them off placated."

"Placated? Oh, my gawddddddd!"

"Marshall, calm down." Her face was hard and business-like. "Be your charming best, sweet man, and leave the chemistry babble to me."

She turned, stepping from the room and into the hall. Chee, pulling at his tie, pranced toward the door to the warehouse.

—

As Bea and Lucy turned to leave, the double doors from the interior of the building flew open. A small-statured, young Asian man wearing a nicely cut suit jogged through. A woman of similar age, a harried-looking brunette in a white lab coat, was at his side.

"Hello, hello! Ms. Middleton, Ms. Vega." He grinned, arms wide in greeting. "Had we known the press was coming, we would have organized a grand tour of our facility. CNN, right? I'm a fan."

Bea nodded; she hadn't mentioned the name of the network to Tahan. The security footage, along with their identity, had made its way to the administrators in nanoseconds. Guess they decided to control the narrative by putting on a sudden, ingratiating play of hospitality. She'd join the dance, see where it was going.

Tahan smirked and turned back toward the half-empty truck.

"I'm Marshall Chee, and this is Doctor Ellen Crandall." Crandall nodded, her face as expressionless as a sidewalk. They all shook hands. "Doctor Crandall is the assistant to Doctor Sandra Kellogg, head of our Research & Development Division." Chee enunciated the word *doctor* as if the visitors were expected to genuflect and kiss a ring.

Lucy and Bea stole a quick look at each other. Pete had thought a Sandra Kellogg ran an HR firm. It was likely the same person. *Surprise, surprise.*

Marshall Chee soldiered on. "We'd hate to have you leave without seeing the manufacturing division of our enterprise. We turn out a quarter million pills a week. Vitamins mostly, but also popular generics for over-the-counter drugs like Advil and Tylenol. Everyday stuff."

Chee was an overly enthusiastic camp leader orienting new campers. The two newswomen hung back for a moment.

Lucy and Bea followed the duo from the dim belly of the warehouse into the irritatingly bright, purplish fluorescents of a long white hallway. The temperature dropped about twenty degrees, and the place smelled of antibacterial wipes. A hefty security guard trailed in their wake.

"Thank you, Mr. Chee, Doctor Crandall," Bea said. "Great to see your operation in action. And sorry for just showing up. It was totally serendipitous. We're doing a story on economic development in the desert communities since Covid-19, and we landed at Pepe's for breakfast."

Lucy continued. "Figured while we were in the neighborhood, we'd just take a little walk over and see what was happening."

"So glad you did, yes, so glad, uh-huh." Chee seemed to make an effort to still his flighty, bird-like hands. Bea guessed he must be really nervous. It was her understanding that making broad hand motions while speaking and calling attention to oneself was considered rude in Chinese culture. But this thirtyish fellow could be generations from the traditional ways.

Bea and Lucy followed him down the hallway. Lined with windows, it provided a viewing balcony over the manufacturing floor. Pills were vomited onto conveyors that flew across the space and were counted and dumped into brown plastic bottles. Caps and labels were slapped on. The percussion of machinery was audible through the glass, which vibrated ever so slightly from the beat.

Blue-clad workers with bouffant caps to cover their hair, latex gloves, and Covid-familiar surgical masks checked the meds, bottles, and labels for imperfections. Bea visualized Lucy and Ethel in the old *I Love Lucy* TV show doing a hilariously poor job of wrapping chocolates as they sped by.

Lucy raised her camera to take a photo, but Chee's hand popped over the lens, practically knocking the camera from her grasp. "Oh, sorry, so sorry but we can't have pictures taken inside here. Security reasons, you know. So sorry. I'm sure you understand."

"Of course." The camera's audio mode kept recording as Lucy tucked it back into her pack. At least they'd have the conversation.

The group moved along the hall to where vats of pinkish slush simmered below them, reminding Bea of the pharma version of a microbrewery. Dr. Crandall looked down onto the kettles and began to speak in a nasally and tour guide-ish voice. "Fillers are needed in pill manufacturing because the tablet must be comfortable for human fingers to readily manipulate. That's why pills are, of course, quite a bit larger than the active ingredients they contain."

Lucy piped up. "We've all heard about the fillers—plastic fragments used by Chinese drug companies that killed people and pets. And I heard about glass in a generic for high cholesterol. Do you import from China? Or India?"

Crandall's face turned the color of skim milk on Cheerios. "Like most companies, we bring in active ingredients from Asia, but all are FDA approved, of course. Never an issue."

Lucy pressed on. "I hear the FDA barely checks pharmaceutical products manufactured overseas."

Crandall's lips puckered like she'd just sucked on a lemon. "Our products are manufactured in the United States, and I assure you we abide by all rules and regulations." She raised her chin with more than a hint of defiance. "And regarding fillers, we employ lactose, microcrystalline cellulose, cornstarch, sugars, whey, and yeast. All harmless and easily digested."

Lucy nodded. "Good to know, Doctor Crandall. I'm sure your supervisor, Ms. Kellogg, is on the same page."

The woman huffed. "*Doctor* Kellogg. PhD in Biochemistry, Stanford."

"*Doctor* Kellogg, sorry," Lucy said. "So, you and Doctor Kellogg lead R&D. Y'all have any new patents in development here?" Her eyes went to the pink slushie.

Chee did a quick but intimate touch of Crandall's arm, then jumped in with a fawning smile. Bea wondered—was she his girlfriend? Whatever their relationship, Lucy's questions were getting under their skin.

"We mostly leave true research and development to the universities and big companies with deep pockets. Doctor Kellogg and Doctor Crandall are with us to make sure our manufacturing processes remain top-notch, all in accordance with government regulations." Chee danced around like a game show host primed to open door number three. "Doctor Crandall, why don't you tell these fine people about the binders, disintegrants, and coatings?" He ushered them further along the sterile hallway.

Crandall was immediately back in her comfort zone. She droned on for more than a quarter hour about how tablets are dissolved and how polymers, cross-linked polyvinylpyrrolidone, and cross-linked sodium carboxymethyl cellulose—all help to break things up so the active ingredients can be released. Bea figured if the doc was trying to bore them into a coma, she was making solid progress.

Glancing at her watch, Bea noted it was past noon already. They had to get back to the airport. Time for the last question—the elephant in the room. "So, Mr. Chee, Doctor Crandall—who owns this organization?"

Chee cleared his throat. "We're a private company, Ms. Middleton." He held his soft, narrow hand to his lips and intoned the statement as if sharing a secret between close friends. "We don't, you know, discuss our internal details."

Bea pushed on. "Brandon Doyle in the mix? I heard he's head of B. D. Keeter Enterprises LLC, affiliated with a Chinese pharmaceutical conglomerate."

Chee's Adams's apple bobbed up and down, and he tried to pretend he hadn't swallowed hard. "Ah, soon-to-be Senator Doyle. He's been a very valuable advisor. Promotes Asian-American partnerships, a very forward-thinking man. Incredible insight, way ahead of the curve. He's helping bring thousands of jobs to marginal economies, like here in Thermal." He turned toward the end of the hallway and the exit sign. Bea knew she was going to get nothing more from the antsy, young spinmeister. The young dude's phone rang. He yanked it from his pocket and scrutinized the screen as if he was looking for an answer to a million-dollar question—like, is there a God? Or how do I get rid of nosy reporters?

"Ladies, I'm sorry to say, Doctor Crandall and I are late for a meeting. It was so nice to meet you, very fun. Thank you for taking the time. Our new website should be up in about four weeks. Be sure to, you know, *friend* us and subscribe to the blog. Do come again. Call me anytime."

In minutes, Lucy and Bea were maneuvered down the steps and out the front door. They traipsed back through the parking lot. Bea pulled out her electronic tablet.

"That was interesting as hell," Lucy said. "Now we know how Doyle got that big, new mansion. Vitamins." She chuckled and opened the car door. A gasp of brimstone emanated from the black, heat-retaining interior.

Bea worked her tablet, then eyed Lucy. "There's a Sandra Kellogg from Arcadia, California who runs an HR firm, but she's African-American."

"Not our girl," Lucy said. "Pete's people missed the mark on that one. The woman with Lance Ludlow and Thompson at the funeral was a tall, older version of Crandall—kind of washed out and lab rattish."

Bea continued to tap on her tablet. "I'm looking at a Doctor Sandra Kellogg's American Chemical Association profile. Doctorate from Stanford in Biochemistry, postdoc in biogenetics at Genentech, and formerly Assistant Director of Research and Development at a big pharma subsidiary in Shanghai. Major experience." She turned the screen toward Lucy and displayed the photo.

"Bingo. That's her," Lucy said. "I guess the vitamins are a great beard." She slid into the driver's seat and winced as the plastic burned her skin. Turning on the ignition, she blasted the air. "But with that pedigree, you can bet they have something big slopping around in those vats."

Bea crawled into the passenger seat, sat for a moment, then shut the door. Aimed the driver's-side cooling vent directly at her face. "Whatever it is, if Doyle gets that Senate seat, he'll do everything he can to make sure we never find out what it is."

21

Molly rested in her room's pillow-filled window seat playing with the yellow-eyed, black kitten her father had just given her. She named the sweet girl Savannah. She loved having a pet, but if her dad thought a kitten was going to replace budding true love at this stage in her life, he was sorely mistaken. She was not eight years old.

The morning following Tito's upsetting visit, a new doctor arrived and conducted a full physical. He adjusted Molly's medications and talked about how head injuries could affect one's impulsive behaviors. She wiped away a tear, kissed the kitten on her moist black nose, then put the furball onto the floor where the little one entertained herself attacking a sock. If only life were that easy.

There was a quick knock on Molly's bedroom door. Before she could say, "Come in," a grandmotherly Hispanic woman tiptoed into the room with a glass of water and a paper cup of pills in hand. Molly tensed. Taking certain meds to continue getting better was important, but she no longer knew what they were giving her. She was tired of everything being out of her control, including her medical treatment.

Reluctantly, Molly accepted the water and pills. She peered at the contents of the paper cup and sighed. "I'm young. I shouldn't be on all this stuff. I should be getting less medicine, not more."

"Medicine make you all better," the woman sing-songed.

"What are these?" Molly asked. There'd been a pink one added. And a yellow one.

"Doctor say take. All good for you."

She felt too tired to fight. This time. The woman stood over her, breath smelling of garlic. Molly leaned away.

"I don't know the doctor who prescribed these."

"Nice Doctor Berman. He do your checkup."

"Berman? Does my mother know about him?"

"Oh, yes. She know." The woman nodded vigorously. Her head was big and her neck stalklike. "And your father say he the best."

That was not reassuring. Molly had discovered her father often lied. That's how he'd gotten her here in the first place. She sighed and downed the pills.

An hour later, she felt more relaxed but uncomfortably dizzy. Stretching out on her bed, Molly picked up the phone and dialed Tito. She needed to talk to a friend, but his number had been blocked. Definitely her father's handiwork. Anger knotted her chest. Why did he keep trying to cut her off from the world?

Molly called Network News directly and, after dropping Bea Middleton's name to the receptionist, got through to Tito's voice mail. Disappointed that he didn't pick up, Molly left a message. So very tired again, she rolled over and snuggled with Savannah.

It was dark outside when the woman came again with more pills.

—

After spending most of the morning at the courthouse, it was early afternoon when Pete returned to the county sheriff headquarters in Monterey Park. Famished, he picked up spicy wonton soup from Yunkun Gardens on Garfield. With a majority Asian population, this part of the San Gabriel Valley, about seven miles from downtown LA, boasted some of the best grub in the metro at affordable, non-hipster prices. He breathed in the tantalizing aroma while he unwrapped his plastic utensils.

The homicide bureau bullpen was quiet. Pete checked his phone. Bea had left a message about needing some analysis of a powdery substance she'd mopped from the floor of Doyle's druggie warehouse in Thermal. He was relieved when she mentioned they were safely back in town.

Grabbing his desk phone, he direct-dialed the crime lab in nearby Westlake and gave them a heads-up on the incoming mystery dust. They'd add it to the pill analysis Bea'd twisted his arm to put through just a couple days earlier. County had one of the premier labs in the nation, but if Bea was wanting results fast, it wasn't gonna happen.

A uniformed officer, a short-haired blonde in her mid-twenties named Courtney, tapped on his door frame. "Sarge?"   "W h a t ' s shakin', Court?" She was a nice kid. Smart, but anxious and apologetic.

"Austin Dombrowski's parents are here to see you, sir. They don't have an appointment. Should I ask them to come back another time?"

Pete scratched his head. "Who's Austin Dombrowski?"

"The brick thrower."

"Ah, shit."

"They say they got information you need to know." She shrugged. Stepped up and handed him a manila folder. "Here are the basics."

Pete took the folder, gazed longingly at the bowl of wonton soup, took a fast slurp, then pushed it aside. "Okay, put them in the small conference room. I'll be right there."

This was a part of his job he hated. Grieving families who think their loved one is a misunderstood innocent. He took a long swig of Diet Coke for a caffeine boost, then went to deliver condolences to Audrey and Sid Dombrowski.

While walking down the hall, Pete made a quick perusal of the folder's contents. Sid, the father, was military—a flight engineer tasked with midair refueling of fighter jets at thirty thousand feet. That kind of dude had certifiable balls of steel. Audrey was a middle school teacher—steel balls there, too.

They looked up expectantly as Pete entered the room. Despite comfortable leather chairs and a sunny view of the mountains, their faces spoke earthquakes, storm fronts, and death. The couple held hands and took a quick look at each other. Sid, in his early sixties with buzz-cut silver hair, appeared ten years younger than the file indicated. Audrey had a plump, matronly build with sporty brown hair in a ponytail and a face that was still a head-turner.

"I'm so sorry about your son, folks." Pete flashed on how he'd feel if his own kid ended up throwing bricks from an overpass onto the freeway and was shot dead by faceless SWAT gunners. Unfathomable as a parent. His neck muscles tightened. "I understand Austin was a vet. PTSD involved. Is that correct?"

Sid answered, "Yes, sir. But the reason we came in is because he was doing really well, going to therapy, taking his medication, better than he'd been since he got back from Sudan. Special Forces. Then, over a period of a couple weeks, he stopped communicating, stopped taking care of himself, and locked himself in the basement playing video games. We didn't know what the hell was going on."

Audrey dropped her husband's hand and went to work twisting a Kleenex. Turning to Pete, her watery blue eyes were rimmed in red. "It was like the slow-motion flipping of a switch."

"What do you think happened?" Pete asked.

Sid answered, "We think there's something wrong with his medicine."

"The wrong prescription?"

"He was shifted to a generic antidepressant just over a month ago," Sid said. "That's when he began to go downhill. Supposedly, the medicine takes a while to wear off, but this seemed to happen fast, like he wasn't on any medication at all."

Audrey pulled a plastic freezer bag from her purse and placed it in the middle of the table. "We know it sounds crazy, but please, Sergeant Anthony, could you have these analyzed?"

Pete was taken aback. Three requests for drug analyses within a couple days was highly unusual. "Did he get those meds through the VA?"

"The scrip was from the VA, but he said he found it cheaper online." Audrey's lower lip trembled. "They were delivered through the mail."

Pete stared at the plastic pill bottle in the bag. Austin, thirty years old, had been shot dead when he turned away from the freeway and threw a cement block at a deputy. Were the drugs to blame? Was this generic thing legit? Or was it the desperate grasping of distraught parents who didn't want to accept the reality around their boy's death?

Pete rubbed again at his cramping neck muscles. The kid was a vet, had given his sanity to protect this country. "All right, folks. Tell me everything. I'll see what we can do."

—

The group of principal investors in the pharmaceutical start-up, just christened with the benign moniker "Riverside Pharma: Good Health for Life," met together again in Doyle's expansive family room. Dr. Pang claimed most of the custom-made couch with his hefty girth, along with a tray of pastries, a teapot, papers, and files. Doyle was cramped at the edge of the sofa, growing more resentful by the minute. Neckar and Marshall Chee lounged, comfortably sipping coffee, in matching leather club chairs. They were all waiting to hear young Chee's report on Vega and Middleton's gate-crashing at the plant.

"I think they were just fishing." Chee stretched his neck, appearing strangled by his shirt collar. His usually perfect spiky hair stuck out at odd angles, as if he'd slept on it wrong. He'd shaved off his wispy, inadequate beard. "Doctor Crandall and I gave them a nice, bland tour. I figured a sense of transparency would be a good thing to communicate. We were friendly, tried to look relaxed, but we were freaking out. Free-king-out!"

His words accelerated until they spewed out fast as a jackhammer. "I mean, we were, like, face-to-face with a major network—CNN. I mean, Christiane Amanpour and that smokin' hot Don Lemon. I'm not a liberal, but Don Lemon. Oh. My. God." He fanned himself with his hand. "Anyhow, Crandall started to get bitchy, and I did my best to keep the happy face, but really, I could only do so much. Those newswomen were, like, scary intense."

Dr. Pang continued to expand, pulled out a handkerchief, and dabbed his brow. "You did fine, nephew. Slow down, take a breath."

Chee continued, unable to stop himself. "And the tall black one, Middleton, looked like she could take you out with a snap of her fingers. And the shorter one had these freaky blue eyes, chilled you to the bone. And when they asked if I knew Lance Ludlow, I about fainted."

"Enough, Chee. We get it. And I trust Lance to keep his mouth shut, or we'll sell that goddamn hack paper out from under him." Doyle gritted his teeth and impatiently nudged a couple files back toward Pang. "Vega and Middleton are pit bulls after a bloody bone. We gotta keep an eye on those bitches. They're both friends of my ex-wife—a shit-show of ballbusters. Wish we could wipe them all out in a single plane crash or something. Any ideas?" Doyle glanced over at Burgess who stood at his usual post by the door. He shrugged and stepped away into the hall.

Stick-up-his-ass Neckar, the German attorney, gazed down his nose at the gathering. "At this point, naught has come of their visit, except the knowledge that we have a functioning warehouse and small manufacturing center providing jobs for an economically depressed community in the desert. All very benevolent. I fail to understand the concern."

Doyle fought his frustration. "The concern, Mr. Neckar, is that these females are potential spoilers. Two journalists with a detective sidekick who is my insane ex, all with histories of digging up dirt that should've stayed buried." Doyle swiped away beads of perspiration dampening the back of his neck. He extricated himself from the couch and moved to perch on a leather footstool. This was his home, his deal, and he was on the goddamned footstool.

"Doyle, settle down." Pang raised his hands as if staving off an onslaught. "Everybody's getting too excited. We will monitor the women closely and consider applying leverage—if necessary."

Doyle heard the doorbell ring. He hated unscheduled visitors. Before Burgess could even leave his post to get the door, loud knocking turned to outright pounding.

Moments later, Burgess exchanged low words with someone, and then the yelling began. A woman's voice shrieked. "You motherfuckers deserve to die!"

Pang looked at Doyle. "What the…"

Claire Thompson burst into the room, shrugging off Burgess with a furious slap to the side of his face. "Don't you touch me." Burgess almost went down.

She stomped over to the sofa and pointed at Doyle. "You damn murderer. You're a murderer!"

Doyle could feel himself sweat more profusely. Damn. "What the hell are you talking about, Claire?"

"David Pine is what I'm talking about."

"If you think I killed Pine—"

"You piece of shit. Just because you didn't pull the trigger, doesn't mean you aren't responsible. You ordered the hit! You're gonna pay, all of you!" Her eyes assaulted each guilty face.

"You need to calm down, Claire," Doyle said in a faux soothing tone of voice.

"You told me to watch him, find out what he knows. Never, never did you suggest he would die! I cared about him!"

Her hair was wild, and spittle flew from her mouth. If she'd had a gun, she would have used it then and there. Doyle took a quick glance around the room. All were stunned. Pang came out of it first.

"Claire, dear, you knew what you were getting into when you accepted this job. Big money, stimulating science, but high risk. And sadly, David Pine was on the verge of ruining everything we'd worked so hard for."

She gritted her teeth. "I am not your goddamned *dear*, you chauvinist pig. And if you'd given me a chance, I could have guided him in another direction. I'll never forgive you people. You disgust me."

Doyle stood and cleared his throat. "Claire, you're the brilliant scientist who developed the opioid alternative which is about to make our fortunes. I don't think you really want to walk away from that."

"I do, and I will." She grabbed a blue-and-white porcelain vase from a tabletop.

Doyle gasped. "No! It's Ming Dynasty!"

She hurled it across the room and smirked as it smashed against the fireplace.

"Get her out of here!" Doyle shouted. The vase was worth a fortune.

Burgess grabbed Claire's arm and wrestled her, kicking and screaming, back to the front door. He slammed it shut on her amid much cursing.

The sound of pottery breaking on the front stoop was grating. "Fuck," Doyle cursed. "She's finishing what my ex-wife started a few days ago. What is it with angry bitches breaking my things?"

Burgess, scowling, returned to his post. A red hand mark swelled on his cheek. He licked a bloody lip.

"Pass the sake," Pang said. "We need sake. I think we're going to have to reassign Ms. Thompson to our Wuhan office."

"We don't have a Wuhan office," young Chee said.

Pang nodded. "Precisely."

22

After the Claire Thompson episode, the meeting was over, and all left quickly. Pang was the only remaining partner. "You must concentrate on your candidacy, Brandon," he said, draining a final cup of the hot rice-based liquor. "We have a big rally in Sacramento tomorrow——you need to prepare."

Doyle glanced at his watch and tried to get the trashed $20,000 vase out of his mind. Let go of minor things. Focus on the prize. He was supposed to meet with his speechwriter in half an hour.

As Pang collected his folders, Burgess, cheek swollen, scurried into the room with Molly's elderly nurse in tow. "Boss, your daughter isn't doing well." He nodded to the old woman. "Go ahead, tell him."

The nurse clutched her hands prayerfully. "Mr. Doyle, Doctor Pang, you check Miss Molly. She no good, much shaking."

"A seizure?" Doyle jumped to his feet and hustled to the stairs. Dr. Pang turned from slug to gazelle and moved quickly behind him.

Doyle rushed into Molly's room. Almost stepping on the mewling kitten, he grabbed the edge of the desk to keep from falling. His daughter was unconscious on the floor, lying on her side. Saliva dribbled from the corner of her mouth. Her face was ashen.

"Move over, Doyle. Let me in." Pang pushed him aside and crouched down to take her vitals.

Doyle hovered. "Is she okay? Is she going to die? What's going on?"

Pang held up a finger asking for silence, then said, "We need an ambulance. Her pulse is thready, breathing shallow."

Molly convulsed again—her body went rigid and spasmed for about fifteen seconds. Doyle skittered back onto the bed. Panic burned in his belly. "No ambulance. I can't risk this leaking to the press, especially the night before a major rally. Assholes'll suspect a drug overdose. They'll plaster it all over social media and say I'm a shit parent. Not what I need to deal with right now."

He pressed his temples, breathed deeply, and tried to slow his hammering heartbeat. A thought materialized. "What about your clinic? Can't you take her?" Doyle slid down onto his hands and knees next to Pang.

"Yes, of course. I should have suggested that immediately. We don't want your, uh, issues in the public eye." Dr. Pang tapped numbers into his phone. Seconds later, he connected. "This is Pang. Please send medical transport to this address stat, and have the staff ready to receive a young woman. She's seizing, post-traumatic brain injury, TBI."

Doyle looked on the verge of convulsion himself. "Sweet Jesus, I can't believe this is happening to me."

Suddenly aware that his blathering sounded less than fatherly, Doyle asked, "Will she get the care she needs? Is your clinic as good as an ER?"

"My facility's better, unless major surgery is needed. For this type of attack, we just want to keep her safe and stabilized. She should see her regular neurologist as soon as possible."

Reassured that Molly would likely survive, Doyle assigned Chee to accompany her to the clinic. Just before transport arrived, she regained consciousness but was clearly disoriented and limp as a fresh corpse.

Ten minutes later, they were off to Pang's clinic in Calabasas where his staff ministered to high-profile luminaries with enough money to procure full-service secrecy for their medical and addiction issues.

Doyle felt a wave of relief. The problem was under control.

—

Late that afternoon, Bea watched Pete lean against the credenza in her office, coffee cup in hand. Three sets of eager female eyes—brown, green, and blue—belonging to her, Lucy, and Mary, were aimed in his direction. Tito sat on the windowsill wearing aviators. The Hollywood Hills skyline rose behind him like a movie set.

"You said you found something?" Bea slid back from her computer. "Anything interesting?"

"Nothing on the pill from your cub reporter yet—what's her name, Aja. But I got results on the stuff you wiped off the floor in Thermal."

Bea sat up straight. He had her attention. "Lay it on us, Sarge."

Pete sat down on a chair across from her desk. "It's vitamin C."

Bea deflated. Her bottom lip stuck out in disappointment. "Damn. I was hoping it was some kind of contraband and we could call in the DEA."

"Sorry, folks." He sipped his brew and stepped across the room.

"Ninety percent of our vitamin C comes from China," Lucy said, having recently become quite knowledgeable on drug and supplement imports from Asia. "Maybe they really are making vitamin pills out there."

Pete finished his coffee and tossed the cup in the trash can. "Despite what might be going on in Thermal, we have nothing that'll legally grant us entry to the plant or the warehouse. We're screwed on a warrant, at least for now."

Tito slipped off the windowsill, removing his shades. "Here's an idea." His eyes glistened with intensity. "I could get a job there at the plant, work undercover. From how you described the place, I'd fit the demographic."

The office went dead quiet, intensifying the white noise of the bullpen outside her door. Bea's gaze flitted from Pete to Lucy and

Mary, avoiding Tito.

"Let me do it." He hustled into Bea's line of vision; his face lit up like a Hollywood Klieg light. "Come on, there's no other way."

Bea responded immediately. "I don't think it's a good idea. We can't put you at risk. We've already had one journalist murdered. Plus, what are you qualified to do at a pill mill? Probably *nada*."

"They have openings for forklift operators," Molly read from her laptop. "You know how to do that, Tito?"

"Hell, yes. Did it in the Marines for a couple months." Tito paused, wary eyes to the hills beyond, as if waiting for an enemy to breach the crest line. Then he shifted focus to Bea again, arms across his chest, chin raised. "A veteran newswoman once told me that risk is part of being a great reporter." He tilted his head in thought. "Wait, I think it was *you* who said that."

Bea rolled her eyes. "Forget anything I told you, kid. Was all bullshit."

"In small print, it says they're military friendly," Molly noted.

"Even better." Tito scuttled next to Pete, *mano y mano*. "Sergeant Anthony, you can see that this is a great idea, right?"

"You're not law enforcement, man. We can't provide backup."

Tito gritted his teeth. His jaw locked and unlocked. Bea worried that the double amputee would sacrifice his own safety and risk too much to prove his worth.

Pete continued, "But it's not a bad idea. Probably have to clear it with your boss. That could be the toughest part."

Bea scowled at Pete. Lucy chuckled.

Mary's cellphone beeped. She checked the screen.

Tito turned to Bea. "Give me a week in there," he pleaded, both hands now splayed atop Bea's desk. "I'll apply online. Tonight."

"Oh, my God." Mary jumped up; her laptop clattered to the floor. "Molly's been taken to the hospital, a clinic. She had a convulsion. I've gotta go." Hands trembling, she retrieved her laptop, stowed it in her backpack, and bolted unsteadily for the door.

Bea's face darkened. "Mary, you shouldn't go by yourself. You're too upset."

"I'll take her." Tito darted after Mary. "Wait up, Detective O'Hanlon." With a quick glance over his shoulder at Bea, he called, "We'll go over my new resume later."

Mary and Tito disappeared out the door.

23

The exclusive clinic was in a generically bland, two-story stucco office building just off Agoura Road in the high-end western suburb of Westlake Village. Tucked between Westlake Driving School and a real estate magazine publisher, there was no identifying signage.

Mary pushed a speaker button set into the wall next to the door.

"May I help you?" a warm female voice asked.

Mary's throat felt dry as sand. "I'm Mary O'Hanlon, here to see Molly O'Hanlon Doyle. I'm her mother."

"Thank you, Mrs. Doyle."

"It's O'Hanlon." Mary's hands gripped into fists. "I divorced the bastard four years ago."

Tito pressed her arm.

Mary pulled herself together. "Sorry, ma'am. I'm so worried about my kid." She was glad to have Tito along.

The voice replied, "No problem, Ms. O'Hanlon. I understand your concern. I'm checking the access list but don't see your name on it."

Mary felt ready to start shrieking and breaking car windows. She paced and muttered, "How dare anyone try to keep me from my daughter. This has Brandon's stain all over it."

Tito spoke into the intercom. "Could you check directly with the patient, ma'am? There must be some mistake. Ms. O'Hanlon is her mother, and she's worried sick."

"And you are?" the disembodied voice asked.

"Tito Luna. A family friend. Please, go check with Molly."

"All right. One moment, please." The voice's obsequious façade cracked with a tinge of huffiness.

Why was this taking so long? Mary checked her watch. Her disgusting ex had purposely kept her name off the visitor's list just to twist the knife. Again.

After pacing for eight minutes and twenty-seven seconds, the door buzzed open. She stomped through with Tito at her side.

The clinic's interior foyer was a stark contrast to the building's plain brown-wrapper exterior. The clean architectural lines of a modern Malibu beach mansion was plush with pricey oriental rugs and cushy, leather-and-chrome Euro-design furniture. It screamed money.

"I can see the Kardashians dropping in for their lip fillers and boob lifts," Mary whispered to Tito.

He rolled his eyes, not inspired by the image.

A platinum-haired Barbie named Ashley, dressed in black leggings and Dansko clogs beneath a swishy gray silk tunic, greeted them.

"Welcome, Ms. O'Hanlon, Mr. Luna. Please leave your drivers' licenses in that container on my desk." She pointed a flawlessly manicured finger at a small, hand-carved box that looked worthy of a museum.

"Why do you need to keep our licenses? Can't you just look at them?" Mary asked.

"Part of our security protocol, ma'am. We go the extra mile to keep our patients safe."

Mary wanted to argue, but seeing Molly as soon as possible was more important. With sweaty fingers, she struggled through various grocery and credit cards until she found the license. Tears of frustration welled in her eyes.

The platinum-haired receptionist, her name badge read Siobahn, but probably was really Sandi from Sacramento. The woman motioned for them to follow her down a hallway of cast concrete beneath skylights. The artwork on the walls was ultramodern and original.

"Sheee-it, I think that's a Basquiat," Tito murmured, obviously a fan of the brilliant graffiti artist.

Farther along, they passed an atrium with chirping white parrots on faux birch branches. Soothing nature sounds were piped in through speakers, and monitors featuring calming ocean waves were mounted overhead. A hip-looking twentysomething guy, with a man-bun and lots of bracelets, carried a tray of culinary magazine-worthy salads through the hall.

"I feel healthier just looking at that stuff," Tito whispered.

Then, they turned into Molly's room. Mary gulped when she saw her baby girl looking so frail in a pair of pastel yellow scrubs, amidst a large arrangement of white roses next to a pottery vase exploding with an assortment of colorful blooms.

In seconds, mother and daughter were crying in each other's arms. Tito waited quietly while the women reunited.

Molly spotted him and reached her hand out. Tito came to the bedside where she pulled them all in for a group hug.

Molly laughed out loud, then choked down a sob. "Oh my God— what a relief. Two of my favorite people! I hope you're here to bust me out of this place. Don't know what happened. I haven't had a seizure for, what, almost nine months?"

"Nine months and thirteen days," Mary said. She kissed Molly's cool forehead.

"I was afraid Daddy wasn't going to call you. He says he's so busy with the Senate race, he forgets stuff."

Mary hugged her daughter again. "He texted. Knows I'd scream bloody murder in front of *The Hollywood Reporter* offices if he didn't keep me informed." Mary smiled and conjured an evil twist to her lips.

Molly chuckled. "And that's a bigger deal than Network News here in LA. I couldn't call you myself—they took my phone. I'm like a prisoner. I mean, they're nice and everything, but I have to ask someone to just take me to the bathroom. I'm not totally disabled, for God's sake."

Tito pulled a burner phone from his pocket and pressed it into Molly's hand. "Thought they might have hijacked your comms. They want you to, you know, relax and shit."

"You are just amazing." She kissed him on the cheek. "Isn't he amazing, Mom?" She immediately stashed the contraband under her pillow.

"Yeah, totally." Mary shook her head. "Not sure if he's an always-prepared boy scout type or a budding criminal."

An athletic-looking man, fiftyish with curly salt-and-pepper hair and a stethoscope draped across the shoulders, stood at the door in a white lab coat. "Hello, Molly. I'm here for the afternoon check-in. Is this your family?"

"Hello, Doctor Berman." She turned to her mom. "He's the medical director. Doctor, this is my mother, Mary—*Detective* Mary—O'Hanlon and our friend Tito Luna from Network News. They're here to take me home."

His eyes widened, but he made a prodigious effort to look nonplussed at the revelation that a cop and a reporter were nosing around his clinic.

"Detective O'Hanlon, Mr. Luna, nice to meet you. But let's take a good look at Molly here before we send her off." He turned to the visitors. "Could you kindly step outside while I do the exam? Let's give the patient some privacy. There's a nice waiting area just down to your left. Coffee, snacks."

"No!" Molly grabbed her mother's arm. "I want them to stay. I mean, it's not like you're gonna do a pelvic exam or anything, right?"

Berman hesitated for an instant, then forced a smile. "Not the area we're concerned about today. Okay, make yourselves comfortable over there, please, folks."

Mary and Tito sat on cushy visitor chairs across from the bed.

"With my daughter's permission, I'd like you to go over her treatment plan with me, Doctor Berman." Mary moved to the edge of her chair. "I need to be updated on what medications she's taking and the therapy she's receiving. I want to take a look at her blood work, too."

Molly swung her legs over the side of the bed and perched on the edge. Her eyes were glassy. Mary had seen the look after a seizure and sometimes before. Her daughter had not fully recovered despite the good energy she projected.

"Give her everything in my file," Molly said to the doctor.

Berman sniffed. Readied his stethoscope to listen to his patient's heart. "Our policy is…"

Mary cut him off. "My daughter is of age and has full legal rights, unless my former spouse is up to some shenanigans. He's quite the manipulator."

Berman blanched and licked his full lips. "I'm sure we can honor your daughter's wishes."

He listened carefully to Molly's heart and lungs, then hung the stethoscope back across his shoulders. Next, he clicked on a penlight and peered into the patient's pupils, then asked her a series of questions about dizziness, nausea, and confusion. There was just enough hesitation in her daughter's answers that Mary knew all was not perfect.

"I want my mother to have all my medical records," Molly said again, face strained. "She's the one who's been taking care of me every minute since my car accident. And way before that. Knows my whole history, even better than I do." She drew herself up tall, asserting whatever power she could muster.

Berman stuck the penlight in his breast pocket next to assorted prods and writing instruments. "Certainly, no problem. I'll notify Doctor Pang."

Molly's brows scrunched together. "I don't want to wait for Doctor Pang. Please ask the nurse to bring my files in, now."

"Who's Doctor Pang?" Mary's antennae began to buzz.

"He's our CEO, ma'am," Berman said, face pale.

"And Daddy's good friend," Molly added. "Pang owns this place. I heard them talking."

Mary frowned. Tito caught her eye, then stood and went over to admire the flowers.

"Everything looks good," Berman announced, switching focus away from Pang and back to the patient. "She's stable. I'd suggest Molly stay with us for tonight, however, just to be sure she's properly monitored. Now, let me go check on those records." He scuttled out of the room.

"I'm not staying, Mom. I'm fine."

"I googled this clinic on our way up, honey. Has a very good reputation. I think you should be here one more night, like the doctor suggested. Just to be sure..."

Molly started pulling at her hair. "I want to come home with you. I don't want to be with Daddy anymore. He's never around, and when he is, he never lets me do anything. I'm suffocating. I can't stand it."

"Okay, sweetheart, we'll talk about it tomorrow, first thing. I promise."

The earlier animation seeped from Molly's face, leaving her wan and deflated. "Okay, one more night." She gazed out the window across a shaded rock garden. "Then you have to get me out of here. Promise?"

Mary nodded. "Promise." Maybe it was time to talk about bringing Molly back to Savannah again.

A nurse, a gray-haired and matronly woman wearing yellow scrubs like Molly's, entered the room as Berman exited. She pushed a cart carrying one of those wonder salads, a glass of something that was likely iced tea, and a chaser of pills in a paper cup.

"You folks want anything to eat or drink?" The woman was rose-cheeked and pleasant.

Mary thanked her but refused. Tito did the same. She noticed Tito straining to see what was in Molly's pill cup.

"I'll be back soon to see if you or our dear patient here needs anything else."

The woman patted Molly's hand, waited until she downed the meds, then left the group to go about her rounds.

"Pretty flowers," Tito said. He pulled out one of the white roses and handed it to Mary.

She looked at the rose, then side-eyed Tito.

He continued. "Who's your special fan, Molly?"

She looked at the arrangements and sighed. "One bunch is from Daddy, and the other is from the News Network staff. Mom, I figured you and Tito were in on that."

"We just found out what happened a couple hours ago, honey. All I could think about was getting here to make sure you were okay. Bea probably ordered them. She's very thoughtful."

Molly picked at her salad, then laid back on her pillows. She yawned. Her eyes flickered and closed.

Tito continued to inspect the white roses.

It suddenly occurred to Mary—wasn't that what Bea said had been in David Pine's girlfriend's place? White roses?

And then, there it was.

"Fuck," Tito whispered. He pulled out the bug tucked inside the rose petals.

Mary's eyes widened. "What the…"

He held up a finger to his lips asking for quiet. She nodded. Tito dropped the tiny device onto the floor and crushed it with the heel of his boot. He bent down and pocketed the remains.

His attention turned to his phone for a few minutes, then back to Mary. "I've been in and out of hospitals for long enough to recognize all those pills, except the pink one. I'm checking the pharmacy handbook online, and there's nothing shaped quite like that. I think you should ask Berman about it."

"It's just a mild sedative and painkiller," Berman said as he stepped into the room again. This time, he had a file in hand which he gave to Mary. "The color and shape of medications change depending on what company is currently manufacturing them. Happens all the time with generics. It's basically a stronger version of Advil. No worries."

Mary thought he blinked his eyes several times too many. The dude was nervous. But why?

"I must get back to my patients," he continued. "You may take this copy of Molly's file with you, Ms. O'Hanlon. Give me a call if you have any questions. My contact information is on the inside flap. In the meantime, if all goes well, which I fully expect, she can check out tomorrow morning after breakfast."

Mary looked over at her daughter—she was asleep.

"Okay, Doctor Berman. I'll be back at 9:00 a.m. tomorrow. Is that a good time?"

"Perfect. I'll make sure she's had her final check-up. So nice meeting you both." He tried for an enthusiastic smile and missed.

Mary stepped over to Molly's bed and kissed her forehead. "Thank you for taking good care of her, doctor."

"That's what we do here." Berman ushered them out.

Siobahn waited just down the hall and speed-walked them to her desk where she returned their IDs. The front doors buzzed, and Mary and Tito were off to their car.

"Three things," Tito said as they climbed in.

"Number one, the listening device was probably similar to the one Bea found planted in Pine's girlfriend's condo. Number two," Tito continued, "that pink pill isn't pictured anywhere in the current pharmacy pill book. If it's a generic super-Advil, the Pope's a Muslim."

"And three?" Mary wasn't sure she could take another hit.

"Berman's rated online as a really good doc. I think somebody has something on him, or he wouldn't be passing out the pinkies."

"I shouldn't have left her there." Mary slammed on the brakes.

Tito reached over and touched her arm. "She'll be safe. He's a competent doc, and if anything happens to a Senate candidate's daughter while she's in this clinic, there'll be hell to pay."

24

Baby Henry, now eight months old, was recovering like a trooper from his premature birth on a mountainside next to a burning SUV. Lucy shook her head. Seemed like all her loved ones either entered or exited this world with a car wreck involved.

She buried her face in Henry's sweet, silky brown curls. A beautiful boy indeed. She lifted him from her shoulder and placed him onto his cot next to her desk. He stretched and gurgled in his sleep. For a moment, his arms swung around like he was leading a band. Bugle the beagle immediately snuggled in next to him. The dog had claimed ownership of the tot from the minute the two met.

Lucy's phone buzzed. She checked caller ID. It was Michael. He was supposed to be coming home tonight. She had a niggling sense that he wasn't going to make it. Something felt off in their relationship lately. He'd been restless, at loose ends without a job such as a documentary in production or some kind of journalistic project to work on. He'd been sober for a year, which was a blessing. As his sobriety gained strength, so did his need to get back into the work fray. An award-winning war correspondent couldn't enjoy long-term ranch life unless the spread was located in a temporary green zone between conflicted nations with oil fields blazing in the distance.

"Lucy, hi, honey. I'm just south of San Luis Obispo." His voice was normal and reassuring. "Should be at the ranch around dinnertime." She noted that he always called it *the ranch*, seldom called it home. "Want me to swing by Zuma and pick up a pizza?"

"That would be nice. Elsa and her niece went to Solvang for the weekend. So, it's only us." Lucy looked forward to having just their little family together.

"We need to talk," Michael added.

Lucy's stomach tensed. So much for normalcy and reassurance. "Oh yeah? About what?"

"I'll fill you in when I get there. A job opportunity, not brain cancer."

"Oh, okay, good to know. Sounds interesting."

"Talk soon. Love you." He clicked off before she could say *I love you, too.*

Lucy gazed down at her son. *What does your daddy have in the works, little man?* She had a feeling it was going to be complicated, like everything always was.

Shifting thoughts away from pointless speculation about Michael's "we have to talk," she returned to her research. Dr. Max Berman, Molly's doctor at the clinic, was complicated, too. She texted Bea to call her. Lucy was ready to share the full summary on the guy. The phone buzzed five minutes later.

"Hey, Luce. So, what's the skinny on Berman? Mary told me he seems decent, but Tito's really concerned about some drug he's dispensing. I know zero about it, but looks like a red flag."

"Yeah, this medication thing is tough to get a handle on, but the Berman info is definitely enlightening."

"Okay, lay it out." The network news feed chattering in the background was muted.

"His full name is Max Marans Berman. Originally from San Francisco, his dad was an orthopedic doc, mom a watercolor painter. Both deceased. No sibs. Degrees from Berkeley and then UCLA Med.

All his subsequent postgrad training is based in LA. After ten years in a Westwood internal medicine practice, he opened the Calabasas facility." Lucy took a drink of water and cleared her throat.

"Launching a high-end clinic must've cost him a bundle," Bea said.

"That's where family money comes in. His parents left him about twelve mil. That was probably enough for a solid down payment. The clinic's officially called Westlake Valley Wellness Center, LLC. Rave reviews from former patients, and no dings for malpractice. He used to be the sole owner."

"Used to be?" Bea asked.

Lucy rose from her desk, phone on speaker, and wandered into the living room so as not to wake the baby. She sat down on a comfy leather sofa with views across the chaparral. "He did well financially for quite a while, then got divorced. Very pricey settlement, plus he has twin boys at USC and a daughter who's a sophomore at a very expensive private high school. The girl's big into the equestrian scene, an Olympic hopeful, or so it seems from her social media. Barns, horses, vets, competitions, transportation for the equines—totally a money pit. He had to declare bankruptcy."

"Oh, wow. Is that when Pang came into the picture?"

"Bingo. They formed a limited partnership. Appears that Berman runs the medical stuff and Pang's the moneyman. I couldn't find any particulars beyond what's in public records. Oh, and I forgot to mention, Berman owned a huge oceanfront estate off PCH that he couldn't sell. Was on the market for several years, and it finally went into foreclosure."

"Sounds like he may have had to make a deal with the devil to hang onto the clinic," Bea said. "Keeping those kids in schools and horses would cost a fortune all by itself."

"No kidding. Berman started the clinic and is very proud of it. From news clippings, seems like his whole identity, at least professionally, is wrapped up in it. Anyhow, that's all I got for 'ya, sistah. I found out a bit more about Doc Pang, though."

"Excellent. What's his deal?"

"Had a nice, long research session last night with an old friend of mine from the FDA. Turns out Pang's a former Chinese national who did a postdoc at Berkeley and an MD in internal medicine at UCLA in the early 1980s."

"About same time Berman was there," Bea said.

Lucy could feel puzzle pieces easing together.

Bea continued. "Sounds like Pine, Berman, Pang, and Doyle were all at Berkeley and UCLA around the same time. We need to check that out."

"This is getting crazier by the minute," Lucy said. "But there's more." She cleared her throat. "After Pang got his medical degree, he returned to China and worked for more than a decade at a now-defunct drug laboratory that was a subsidiary of a company from Hong Kong. Pang oversaw benzodiazepine and opioid research and manufacturing until a major contamination issue shut them down. But it seems they weren't really shut down. The names were changed, and the location shifted from Hong Kong to the mainland."

"International corporations get away with that shit all the time," Bea said. "Pharma whack-a-mole. When did they start developing the US angle?"

"In the last couple years," Lucy said, "they opened plants in Alabama, Arkansas, West Virginia, and the latest one in Thermal. No issues during their FDA inspections, but that doesn't mean they don't have shadow accounting, manufacturing, and other parallel systems. Sneaky bastards."

"When did Doyle join the party? Dude clearly thrives on riding on the edge of what he can get away with."

"Came onboard about three years ago after a trip to China sponsored by some entity called the Sino-Southern California Economic Development Committee," Lucy said. "Functioned for a year, then disbanded. Could be where Doyle and Pang hooked up again." Lucy took another swig of water. She could hear the baby begin to stir. "You think Pang's involved in Doyle's run for Senate? Or rather, stupid me, how deep is Pang's involvement in Doyle's run for Senate?" She stood and went to the doorway to the porch. Henry was awake but peacefully playing with his toes.

"I'd be shocked if Pang's not the bankroll behind the campaign," Bea said. "The pill people need a hook into the government, and Doyle's the perfect stooge. No moral compass, addicted to making a buck, and has that slimy charisma that makes people think he's all the things he's not."

"You know he's going to get elected." Lucy slumped into a chair next to the baby.

Bea's laugh was dark. "Not if we have anything to say about it, Lucia. We're gonna bust this sucker wide open."

—

Later that evening, Molly slipped the burner phone into her toiletries bag and locked herself in the bathroom. She was still a little dizzy, but they'd okayed her to make the ten-foot trip from her bed into the loo unaccompanied, finally. God, she wanted out of this place. Despite the staff's cheeriness and kind service, she had a generalized sense of being spied on. Probably just a post-seizure effect.

She sat down on the toilet seat and called Tito. She needed to hear his reassuring voice.

He picked up immediately. "Hey, beautiful. How's the patient?"

"Better now that I can call out. Was feeling really anxious, trapped. I can't thank you enough for sneaking in the phone."

"A phoneless young hottie sounded pretty grim to me. How're you feeling? Ready to be home tomorrow?"

"I'm not going back to my dad's. And he's gonna have a coronary." She tugged at her baggy yellow scrubs. "He's a control freak. Doesn't want me to have a life, especially one with my mother involved."

"Why not? She's cool."

Molly felt her throat tighten. "Someday I'll tell you the whole story. But when I was damaged, he barely communicated with me. Now that I'm recovering, he wants me again. He's a user. Likes to watch me, show me off to his friends."

"That's pretty fucked-up."

"It's all I knew as a kid. But now I'm understanding more. My dad and I kept bad stuff from Mom. When she found out, she divorced him and moved away with me. I was a mess. Tried to kill myself with a car." Molly picked at a ragged cuticle until it started to bleed.

"I'm so sorry. I didn't know. Does he still…"

"He leaves me alone." She felt her gaze disappear into a middle fuzzy distance. "Were you a confused mess when you lost your legs?"

Tito's chuckle had no humor in it. "Big-time. I thought about a gun to my head. Click. Boom. *Finito.*"

"Glad you didn't do it and that we met."

"Me, too. There's a reason we survived."

"I believe that. Mom made me talk to a therapist when I was in Savannah, helped me begin to see the bigger picture of my life. I miss my sessions with him. I may go back for a while. My mom can't be away much longer without losing her job."

Molly's phone read 6:00 p.m. "My dinner and medicine'll be delivered any sec. Gotta bounce."

"Molly, wait. Do me a favor?"

"Anything."

"See if you can nab one of those pink pills the nurse gives you. I want to see what it is."

"You think it's like poison or something?"

"No, not poison. Settle down. I'll explain when I see you. Can you do it? Get the pill?"

"For sure. I hear the meal cart. It's squeaky. Bye now. You're the best, Tito."

Molly clicked off. Stepped out of the bathroom and over to her bedside table just as the kind older woman named Kathleen wheeled in dinner and meds. Sweet, brain-injured Molly Doyle would obediently consume everything except the pink pill. How was she going to make that happen? She had about two seconds to decide.

Kathleen held out the paper cup of medication and a glass of water.

Molly stumbled backward onto her bed and knocked the cup. Meds scattered.

Kathleen gasped. "Oh, heavens."

"Clumsy me. I'm so sorry." Molly scrambled onto the floor under the bed. She popped the scattered pills into her mouth. "Don't worry,

I'll get them. No problem."

"No, dear, we'll dispense fresh ones for you. Heavens, please don't eat them off the floor!"

"Five-second rule. No stress. This place is so clean—not even dust bunnies under the bed."

Should she put the pink pill in her mouth and spit it out later? Simplest would be best. Still on the floor, she surreptitiously stuffed the pink pill into the pocket of her scrubs.

Molly stood, took the water from the woman, and drank it down.

"Oh, my goodness, child!" Kathleen looked pallid as a fish belly.

Molly smiled. "A little dirt never hurt anybody."

25

The next morning, fifteen minutes after the clinic opened, Mary gazed with relief at her daughter who now sat next to her in the rental car. Molly looked smaller and wan, but her eyes didn't have the glazed look of the previous day. She squeezed her child's hand, then turned on the ignition.

Tepid air blasted from the vents, and NPR played over the speaker with the weather report. Mary turned off the radio. It was summer in Southern California—every day had the same beautiful face. Unless there was an earthquake or a brush fire. Then, everything cracked and burned and went to hell.

Molly reached into the pocket of her sweatpants. She retrieved a crumpled tissue and handed it to her mother. "It's the pink pill Tito was worried about. He wants you to get it to Detective Anthony so he can send it to the lab and find out what it is. Actually, I think it's a lighter color and a different size than the ones I'd been taking. Wasn't exactly studying the meds, just took them. Was too blotto to do anything else, at first."

Yet another pill for the county crime lab. What the hell was going on? Mary accelerated hard out of the parking lot. "Tito asked you to nab it? That's dangerous. I don't like that at all."

"Was easy. I had to do it. I mean, if they're giving people bad medicine, don't you want to know?"

Mary looked over at her child—no longer a child. "Of course. Was brave of you. I'm thankful you didn't get caught."

"I've learned a few skills from being a cop's daughter." She smiled at her mother. "And anyway, what would they do if they caught me? Kill me? I mean, get real."

Mary shuddered. They had killed, at least once.

"The flowers were gone when I woke up this morning." Molly picked at her fraying cuticles. "I wished I could have kept the ones from Bea and you guys, but I was glad to have the white roses out of there. Felt like I was in a funeral home. Mom, if I die before you do, swear there won't be white roses on my coffin."

Mary's heart almost stopped. "That's such a morbid thought, honey. You're doing so much better. This seizure was probably just a passing setback. May never happen again."

Molly nodded. "I know, but promise me about the flowers."

"I promise. Now, no more death talk, okay?"

"Okay, but what are we going to do, Mom? I'm done living with Dad."

Mary let out a heart-wrenching sigh of relief and glanced over at Molly, a bright purple overnight bag sitting on her daughter's lap. Somehow purple seemed too young a color for her now. Mary'd get her some new luggage soon, something for a more mature traveler. She was moving so quickly along the road to grown-up womanhood.

Molly tugged at her seat belt. "Mom?"

"Yes, yes, we'll go to your dad's place right now and get your belongings, including the kitty. Sound okay? Lucy lent me a pet carrier to put her in. It's in the trunk. I was hoping, no, praying, you'd come to Bea's with me."

Molly reached over and squeezed her mother's hand. "I sure hope the housekeeper was feeding her."

Mary pulled onto Las Virgenes Road heading east toward the

Ventura Freeway. The scar on the hillside where Kobe Bryant's helicopter had crashed, taking nine lives, was still a tragic, dark gash.

Molly gazed up into the dusty hills. Two skinny horses munched on scrub across the fence from an exclusive green-grassed subdivision. She turned to her phone screen and frowned. "I texted Daddy that I was gonna pack up my stuff and go with you to Bea's. He pretty much said, 'no way in hell.' Needs me for the campaign. Doesn't want to be up on stage without family members around—meaning me. It'll look bad. And I think he hates Bea."

Mary let out a laugh that ended in a snarl of anger. "He should have thought about losing his family before he made all those really bad life choices."

"Did you know he has a big safe room?"

"No, I didn't." Mary felt something crawly under her skin. Doyle had that effect on her.

"He says it is in case bad guys breach security, with him being famous and all. But I saw inside once, accidently. Burgess ushed me out, but I saw stuff."

"What do you mean, Molly? What kind of stuff?"

"It's a safe room, but it's something else, too. So many monitors. There's a button behind a bookcase that swings out. And I saw bad stuff, porn, and Burgess was talking about some kind of business they're in. I think Bea should know about it."

"Porn is not illegal." *What the hell was Brandon into?*

"I know, but there are just really bad vibes in that room. But it will catch up with him one of these days, right?"

"I sure hope so." A driver laid on the horn behind Mary. She'd let her focus slip. Remembering how handsome and charming Brandon Doyle had been—reeling her into his self-absorbed life like a trout on a string. But Mary wasn't a trout anymore. She was something dangerous, with fangs. She gave the dude a bad hand as he roared by in his shiny gold Porsche. "Let's go get your belongings. Kitty, too."

Molly laughed out loud. She hooted out the open window. The wind tousled her long, sun-streaked hair with wild fingers.

—

The next day, Tito gazed out the meeting room window in the West Hollywood Sheriff Station overlooking San Vicente Boulevard's lush green median. It was late morning, and the sky was uncharacteristically overcast. Pedestrians dribbled from breakfast eateries along the street. Sitting across from Pete Anthony, sipping a diet cola, Tito's legs ached like hell today. Was a bitch to have something that wasn't even there cause so much grinding misery. Why the hell did he still get the phantom pain? How long would his brain take to finally rewire? Maybe never. But the new fake job assignment was gonna be one helluva sweet distraction.

"They called me an hour after they got my online application," he said. "This was meant to happen."

"When's your first day of work?" the sergeant asked.

"Tomorrow. It's a temp job. Guy got hurt, so I'm running a forklift until he comes back."

"Perfect. I cajoled my captain into giving up some support for this action. Got you an impounded car—a piece of shit Camry with almost two hundred thou on it. Will be more convincing than that shiny, little Jeep of yours, and it'll get you to Thermal and back, no prob." He tossed over a key fob with a Red Bull logo on it.

"Thanks, Sarge. You won't regret this."

Pete leaned back in his chair, eyes narrowed. "Sure as hell hope not, dude, or my girlfriend's gonna have my ass."

"Copy that, sir."

"Once you hit town, check in with Sergeant Tonia Delgado. Her number's programmed into your burner phone. You'll meet her at the coffee shop Yucca Joe near the Riverside County-Thermal Sheriff Station on Airport Boulevard and Grapefruit Avenue. She's your liaison. They have a downscale condo used for a safe house that'll be yours 'til you're done out there. Got it?"

Tito nodded. A shot of adrenaline roiled into his bloodstream. This was the kind of work he craved. This was what he wanted to experience and write about.

Pete passed him an envelope. "This has your new fake ID and a prepaid cash card with five hundred bucks on it. Should cover gas and food for a week. Keep your receipts. And use the burner for all communication with me and Delgado. We're the only ones you talk to. *Capiche?*"

"Yes, sir." Tito felt himself grin. "Thank you, sir. I'm on it."

Pete chuckled. "I remember my first undercover. Was a rush taking on a secret identity." His face hardened. "But never forget these people are assholes who've already murdered one reporter. That we know of. Don't let your guard down for even a second, Señor Carlos Hernandez."

"I won't. Thanks for taking a chance on me, Sargent. I'll do you proud."

"I hope so. Be safe, kid."

The two men stood and bumped fists. Then, Tito was on his way to pick up his shitty new ride. He'd never been more excited about a car in his life.

26

The sound of his vehicle rolling up the long gravel road was elating to Lucy. The dogs barked an excited welcome, the truck door slammed. She left Henry in his playpen, dashed through the house and out across the patio. The screen door slammed behind her.

He had only been away two weeks but seemed like months. Michael Burleson was home.

Several years and one baby since their first meeting, Lucy still felt the flutter of butterflies loose in her body every time he returned from a trip and stepped back into their life at *Rancho de la Vega*. When he'd leave, there was always a nagging shard of dread in her heart. Would she ever see him again? But here he was. Those indigo eyes, disheveled blond hair, and that schoolboy grin still did it for her. She rushed across the drive and into his arms.

He hooted, lifted her off her feet, and hugged her hard. Howard the cat yowled, the goats bleated, and Henry cried out from his digs inside the house.

"Where's my boy?" Michael demanded.

He set Lucy down and dashed for the ranch house. She jogged

behind him as he sped through the living room and the kitchen, dodging toys and baby equipment like a wide receiver rushing for a touchdown. He scooped up his son, who immediately calmed and began to coo.

"How's my little man?" Michael kissed the child's warm, peach pie cheeks.

Henry squirmed and kicked his feet with delight. Then he babbled, "*Dada.*"

"Oh, my God." Michael's eyes shone like polished glass marbles. "Did you hear that?"

Lucy's heart swelled with pleasure.

"Did you hear that?" he demanded again, incredulous.

"I heard it!" Lucy grinned. Now Henry said three words. Dada, Ma, and bah for bottle.

"Brilliant child!" Michael smooched the baby's belly.

This father-son reunion was one of those moments that gave existence meaning. But Michael had mentioned a job opportunity. That was great, right? Lucy hated that she was such a cynic when good things came her way. Not every hopeful occurrence had a devastating price. With Michael back at a job doing what he loved to do professionally, life would be even better. He and Henry would continue to bond more deeply every day. She threw her arms round both of her men and hugged tight.

After a solid hour of admiring their fabulous offspring and consuming neglected, cold pizza, newly crawling Henry settled back into his playpen. Stackable rings and an array of wooden creatures would serve for entertainment until he was hungry again.

Lucy cuddled up next to Michael on the couch. "So, my love, what's this job news you've been so cagey about?"

Michael cleared his throat. Lucy could feel his body tense. Her pulse rate quickened.

"Might as well jump right in," he said. "I got an offer from MSNBC."

"Oh my God!" She raised her hands into the air, thanking the universe, then did a fist pump. "That's fantastic!"

He grinned. "I met with their people at the San Francisco office."

"Why didn't you tell me?"

"Didn't want to get your hopes up. Felt like a long shot. I still can't believe it. Anyhow, the money's good. I'll produce one major spot per quarter. I'll have lots of flexibility on what gets covered."

"Congratulations—that is beyond cool! I'm so proud of you." She kissed him soundly.

His smile was humble, and he bowed his head. "Never thought I'd get this chance again, Luce. I thought I'd completely burned my bridges. I let the booze take over my life. You helped me dig out of that dark, shitty hole. I couldn't have done it without you, sweetheart."

Lucy sniffed. Her eyes filled with moisture. If only she could trust his resolve. He meant it with all his heart, but addiction was a ruthless savant who knew every chink of human vulnerability.

He took her face in his hands, wiped away tears with his thumbs. "I promise you I'm not going to blow it."

Months ago, she'd taken the leap of faith with this man. For better or worse, she was there for him but would not be destroyed or let their son be damaged if he succumbed to addiction again. Michael understood and accepted this hard fact. Lucy kissed him deeply and prayed for strength. "You'll be amazing. They're so damn lucky to have you."

He smiled and gazed out toward the ocean. The sky had purpled like a fresh bruise against the pale chaparral scrub. Yucca plants outside the window were shadowy, dagger-like bouquets. He twisted a tendril of Lucy's dark curls in his fingers, then pushed it behind her ear. "But you knew there'd be a downside."

Her excitement tempered. She pulled away and hugged a throw pillow tight to her chest. "Okay, what's the catch?"

He took her hand. "It's based in New York."

Lucy groaned. "You'll have to live there?" She could barely keep track of friends and acquaintances in the news and entertainment industries whose relationships were destroyed by time and distance.

He nodded. "Afraid so. I'll be bicoastal, home every weekend that I can. Unless you want to come with me to New York. For part of the year? Give it a try? That would be amazing."

Henry, now hanging from the edge of his playpen, whined like a trooper and held his pudgy arms out to his father. Michael rose and picked him up, cuddled him close. Henry was already a daddy's boy. She couldn't bear to see that relationship threatened.

The two loves of her life. Why did she always surround herself with men who either died early or otherwise abandoned her? And leaving the ranch—her spiritual home, her center—would be like peeling off her skin.

But she would go to New York. It was their only chance to survive as a family. Cool ocean breezes, the smell of dry creek willows, and red-tailed hawks floating on the thermals would be replaced by gritty heat bouncing off hot concrete, diesel fumes, and pigeons.

"When do you start?" she asked.

"Two weeks."

Her heart hammered with ambivalence. "We have a lot to pack."

—

The next morning, Bea set a box of goodies from Stan's Donuts in the middle of her desk along with a carafe of hot coffee. Pete, Lucy, and Mary gathered round. Winfrey Chambers slouched at the windowsill. No one seemed to feel much like eating—more like they should be passing around a bottle of Jack Daniel's. This David Pine drug manufacturing story was going in lots of directions, and they weren't getting a firm grip on any of it.

Pete stood with his feet planted, fists at his side. He looked ready to throw a punch. "Bad news, lovelies. The antidepressant that the brick-tossing army vet got online had nothing in it but fucking baking soda, caffeine, crushed insect parts, and some gummy stuff that held it together in tablet form. The parents were right. Their son was murdered, along with the teenage girl who happened to be driving under that bridge when the brick smashed through her windshield."

"Holy shit." Bea's face was ashen.

"And get this—it's the same garbage that your newbie reporter, Aja, was given. We've notified the DEA, the FDA, and the Center for Disease Control. This is far-reaching. And somebody's gonna pay."

Lucy winced. "What a nightmare. Must be tons of other innocent folks ruining themselves with these fake meds."

"Press releases are going out locally and across the country as we speak," Winfrey Chambers said. "The national evening news will feature it tonight. Healthcare providers have been given the lot numbers, and they're trying to get patients notified. About one in ten take them."

Mary looked like she was about to vomit. "I have a really sick feeling that my ex and his cronies are involved in this thing, or something equally rotten."

Bea poured herself a cup of joe and dumped in the stevia.

"Bijan, our dark web-meister extraordinaire, is on it," she said. "The pharmacy site where the brick thrower bought this contraband from appears to be AWOL. Was probably just renamed with a new IP address. Will be a bitch to track down, but if anyone can do it, it's Bijan. Won't be cheap, though." Bea looked over at her boss. "Sir?"

Winfrey sighed and nodded. "Send the invoice to Lorraine in accounting."

"Thank you, sir."

Pete took a chocolate crème twist from the box and continued. "Also got results back on the so-called 'pink pill' Molly snitched from the celebrity clinic. It's Inderal—used legitimately for circulation problems, migraines, and sometimes anxiety."

Mary shook her head. "My daughter says it's not the same pill she'd taken previously. Maybe they switched it after Tito and I visited."

Pete paced, holding the pastry in his hand and waving it around like a pointer. Little chocolate sprinkles went flying. "Nothing in the pharmacy manual fits the description Molly and Tito gave us of a bright pink pill. But you probably figured that. There was no inscription, and it was an eight-sided shape, an octagon, not a disc like the one she brought in. Could be some kind of custom mix. Pharmacies do that. Berman, of course, says he knows nada. But he's now hip to the fact that we're on his ass."

"I want to talk with the orderly, Kathleen," Mary said. "She seemed like a decent person, and she gave out the medications every day. Maybe I can hit her up in the clinic parking lot at change of shift."

"Good idea," Lucy said. "I'll be your wing woman. None of us should deal with these people alone."

"I'll second that," Winfrey said. "Good work, and keep me posted, folks."

Bea gave him a thumbs-up. "Copy that, chief."

He grabbed a maple-frosted cruller and returned to his office.

27

After signing in with Human Resources, filling out an hour's worth of forms, and getting his picture snapped, Tito was handed an ID affixed to a black lanyard. Finally, he was escorted to the warehouse by a pale, colorless woman in her twenties devoid of interpersonal skills. The place smelled of sweat and fuel. She introduced him to his supervisor, Rick Tahan, a wiry, middle-aged dude with ferret-like eyes and a pissed-off attitude. She turned and scurried back into the air-conditioned manufacturing building without a "good luck" or "have a good day."

"So, where'd you get your forklift training?" Tahan asked in way of a greeting. No handshake was offered. His shoulders appeared permanently hunched, like a man ready for something to drop on him. He reeked of cigarettes with a hint of weed.

"Marines, sir. I've driven a Clark and a JCB. I see you got Hyster-Yale's."

"Yup, here's the key. Use the helmet hanging on the rig. It's that one over there." Tahan pointed to an older model.

"Familiarize yourself, then report to Rios—the dude with the full sleeve tats over yonder. He's *semper fi*, too. We got a big load comin' any minute, so get moving."

"Yes, sir." Tito took the key, nodded at Tahan. "Thank you, sir." The new employee proceeded to his machine, checking out the warehouse as he walked.

The place seemed half the size of a football field with industrial storage racks packed almost to the ceiling, like in big-box home stores, only taller. The racks were automated and moved carousel-like for product access. Lighting was dim from fluorescents high above that gave the illusion of coolness despite the moisture-sucking heat blowing in through the exterior ramp doors. Tito took a long gulp from his water bottle.

At the other end of the facility, two Hispanic men, in their late twenties, operating forklifts moved pallets from a stack of around fifty units through huge roll-up doors opening into a bright white arena. Stainless steel manufacturing machinery whirred. Faceless workers in protective gear loaded cardboard boxes onto conveyors.

The former marine, Rios, was easily fifty. His face was leathery and sun-damaged, maybe had multiple tours in some Middle Eastern desert, or maybe it was just the result of a lifetime in Thermal. He glanced over at Tito, offered a quick nod, then turned his attention back to an electronic pad where he scanned inventory barcodes.

Just as Tito donned the helmet and climbed into the cab of his machine, an eighteen-wheeler hauling a shipping container began backing up to the loading dock. A loud buzz sounded a warning. Tahan waved to the driver. Rios jogged over to assist.

Tito fired up his forklift and adjusted the seat belt. Working his way through the gears, he raised the prongs, shifted into forward, and drove the rig toward the open dock. It had been years since he'd maneuvered a lift, but it was like riding a bike—easy to jump on and go. But this time, he depended on his prosthetics to press the accelerator and brakes. He was going to ache by the end of the day. Fortunately, most of the maneuvering and lifting was accomplished via hand-operated levers.

Tahan motioned him over to the semi. Tito lined up next to the two other lift drivers.

"Hey, bro." Tito reached over and offered his hand to a hefty dude with a shaved head and soul patch. They slapped palms. "I'm, uh, Carlos." Tito coughed; he'd almost introduced himself with his real name. He couldn't afford to make that kind of stupid mistake. "'Sup, man?"

Talk shifted from English to Spanish. "I'm Diego, and that's Skunk."

Skunk nodded. Short and compact with black hair intersected by a white stripe, the guy had the jittery body language of a meth-head.

Diego continued. "Glad to have some help, dude. We've been pulling way too much overtime. The money's good, but shit, man, I'm exhausted. I got a new baby on the way, too. I'm never home, and the wife's about ready to kill me. We need the bucks and all, but she's kinda overwhelmed. This heat is killing her. She's on maternity leave starting this week, *gracias a Dios*. Her mom always wants to come over to help, but she drives my woman crazy. Know what I mean?"

Tito nodded. Diego was a talker—that could be good.

"You married, man?"

Before Tito could reply, Tahan called out, "Diego, Skunk, new guy. Let's go."

"Wonder what we're unloading," Tito said, almost to himself.

"Shit's from China. Always China. Once in a while, India. They say it's all vitamin C or something like that. But I don't buy it, man. The Skunkster forked open a pack by accident a couple weeks ago. It's like pink talcum powder. We call it China Pink, you know, like China White, only pink." He laughed hard.

"Diego, move it. Now." Tahan was perturbed.

Diego winked at Tito, then put his machine in gear. Tito and Skunk followed him to the rear of the shipping container. At the same time, a slim Asian guy, late twenties, jogged across the warehouse. Primped up with an expensive haircut and a navy pinstripe suit, the dude was way too stylin' for this shithole in the desert. He grabbed Rios's inventory pad, looked it over, and handed it back.

"Appears to be in order. Twenty pallets directly to manufacturing.

Store the rest in sections 2B and C."

"Yes, sir, Mr. Chee." Rios turned to the forklift operators. "You heard the man. Get this stuff unloaded. First off, twenty to the cookhouse."

"Thank you, Rios." The skinny guy turned on the heel of his pricey oxblood Euro-styled ankle boots and returned to the administrative wing.

Was this young dude in cahoots with Dr. Pang, the supposed moneyman behind the Calabasas clinic? Tito'd expected someone older.

Pulling up to a pallet and inserting the prongs, Tito snugged the load against the back of the carriage, lifted the plastic-wrapped bricks of product, and followed Diego to the innards of the warehouse where his new work buddies had been busy earlier.

China Pink. Could it have anything to do with the unmarked pink pills Molly'd been prescribed? He was well aware that China White was street for primo heroin or fentanyl. If that crap was too concentrated, even skin contact could kill you. Maybe he should carry Narcan, the antidote for a toxic opioid reaction, just in case things went bad. Tito hoped he was not in over his head with this undercover gig.

Suddenly, he was bearing down on the rig in front of him. He slammed on the brakes, stopping inches from the rear counterbalance. Pain spiked from his shin to his hip and took his breath away.

He'd almost rear-ended Skunk's rig.

Tito wiped sweat from his face and glanced around. No one seemed to have noticed the near collision. The last thing he needed was to get fired before he had enough evidence to put these assholes away.

—

Lucy pulled her SUV into the clinic parking lot behind Mary's silver rental car. She cracked the windows for ventilation but remained belted in her seat. Her home, *Rancho de la Vega,* was only twenty minutes away through the Santa Monica mountains from Westlake Village. Michael reveled in his special day alone with Henry but would be off to New York on Monday to scout temporary housing in

Manhattan. Brooklyn sounded more family-friendly to Lucy. She still hadn't told Bea they were moving to the other coast in less than two weeks. She rested her forehead on the steering wheel.

Lucy's bones ached at the thought of leaving her beloved ranch. They'd just finished the arduous process of rebuilding after it burned to the ground during a wildfire. And now she was going away when she most wanted to stay tucked into her secure nest.

Maybe she was being a drama queen. Probably. People in the business of news and media moved around all the time. But *Rancho de la Vega* would always be her touchstone, her spiritual center. Elsa, Lucy's quasi-grandma, and Cheyney Hitchcock, retired stuntman and their neighbor across the road, would do a great job of managing the place in her absence. Cheyney had boarded his horses at the ranch for years, maintained the barn, and was already their go-to handyman. He and Elsa were the best support system anyone could have.

Why was she so anxious about sharing the Big Apple news with Bea? Maybe because it was the first thing in forever they hadn't discussed and dissected together. More likely, it was because Lucy was still in denial.

Mary knocked on the window. "Let's go, girl. Shift changes at 4:00—that's in five minutes."

"Sorry. Coming." Lucy unbuckled, jumped out of the car, and slammed the door behind her.

The two hurried to a grassy median at the edge of the lot. Mary carried a small gift basket with a Starbucks mug, coffee, and chocolates.

"It's for Kathleen. A small token of appreciation for taking care of Molly. Might warm her up a bit, too."

"Nice idea." Lucy scanned for surveillance. "Would be smart to talk with her out of camera range. Their devices look like the panorama type—wide-angle, night vision, very sophisticated. I see one at the main patient entrance and another above that side door—probably access for employees and deliveries."

Kathleen emerged from said side door.

"There she is." Mary began a beeline in the woman's direction.

"Wait, hold back until she clears the front of the building." Lucy stumbled over a sprinkler head.

Mary grabbed Lucy's arm and slowed. They followed parallel to their subject, then began to move in.

Dressed in her yellow scrubs, Kathleen toted a shopping bag and a big purse. A white sweater was tied around her waist. She skirted the clinic and strode toward tree-lined Westlake Boulevard.

Lucy spotted a bus stop kiosk a half block away at the far corner of the clinic building. "Looks like she takes public transpo."

Mary nodded and picked up her pace. "Miss Kathleen," she called.

The older woman looked their way. A moment of hesitation, then a broad smile of recognition. "Molly's mother! Mary, isn't it? Hello, dear."

"Good to see you again, Kathleen."

The older woman offered her hand in greeting, but Mary drew her into a quick hug.

"Kathleen, this is my friend, Lucy."

"Nice to meet you, Lucy."

"You, too, ma'am. Molly and Mary sing your praises."

"Thank you so much, dear. It's my job, and I really enjoy it. How's your daughter doing? Such a sweet girl."

"She's great, thanks to you and your colleagues." Mary handed the basket to Kathleen. "Just a little token for taking such good care of my kiddo."

The woman's eyes popped wide, as if the modest gift was a big check. She rested her heavy shopping bag on the ground. "Oh my, so kind, and so unnecessary. But *thank you*." Kathleen's eyeglasses hung on a beaded chain around her neck. She put them on and appreciatively inspected the gift. "Two of my favorites—coffee and chocolate."

"Mine, too. Enjoy."

Lucy edged closer. "We've got a quick question for you, Kathleen, if you have a sec."

"No problem. What can I help you with?"

"It's a quick medical question." Lucy tried to appear nonchalant. "About Molly's medicine."

Kathleen's eyes narrowed. "I'm probably not the right person to advise you. I'm just a nursing assistant, but go ahead."

Lucy nodded. "We're pretty sure Molly was given a bright pink pill without any inscription during her first two days in the clinic. Then, she said it was replaced with the common light pink Inderal tablet. You must keep careful track of all that, as the person actually administering the medications."

"Yes, of course. We're meticulous. But I dispense pills for lots of patients every day." She shifted from foot to foot and glanced at her watch. "Can't miss the bus—not another one to Newbury Park for an hour."

"We won't keep you. But the thing is," Mary said, "there's no mention of that first medication anywhere in her file. What was it? Was it a generic with the same active ingredients as Inderal?"

"Oh, goodness, I can't talk about medical protocols without written consent from the patient." Kathleen looked toward the street as if hoping the bus would fly down from the sky and rescue her from the conversation. "Confidentiality, HIPPA, I'm sure you understand."

Mary frowned. "You heard my daughter tell Doctor Berman to give me access to all of her records. So, anything you could share on this one little issue would be much appreciated. I want to keep my daughter's medical information updated, of course. I'm an organized detail person, just like you."

Kathleen nervously twisted the ribbon on the gift basket.

"I'm sorry, ladies. All I can say is that we often use generics. That's standard protocol everywhere these days. Size and shape of the pills vary, depending on where they were manufactured. But the active ingredients are identical. No worries."

"Not identical," Lucy interjected, "but bioequivalent, supposedly. Would you have access to a sample?"

Kathleen stepped back. "Goodness. Absolutely not. I love my job, and I won't risk losing it."

The bus rounded the corner, only a block away. Kathleen moved toward it.

"I must run. Send my best to your daughter," she called over her shoulder. "And thank you for the gift." The woman practically leaped into the bus.

Lucy and Mary sighed in unison and turned toward the parking lot. A security guard now stood outside the building's entrance.

"We've been made," Lucy said. "So much for getting anything out of the clinic. Place's tighter than Spanx under a sheath dress."

Mary's chuckle was devoid of humor. "Yeah, they're good. Really good." She glanced over at the guard—now there were two of them. "Doctors Berman and Pang sure as hell know how to keep a secret."

28

After getting Henry off to sleep, Michael and Lucy sat on the back porch, sipping iced tea and working on their laptops. Lucy was digging further into Dr. Sandra Kellogg's background, the head of Research & Development at the Thermal manufacturing facility, and that of her prickly assistant, Ellen Crandall.

Michael interrupted her off and on, insisting she take a look at one cool NYC loft or another. So much money for so little square footage. How would she breathe amid the sunlight-obliterating high rises? She quashed that thought fast.

Lucy was ready to turn in for the night when she came across an article in an obscure biopharmaceutical industry newsletter from several years back. It said that Sandra Kellogg's American Chemical Association membership was briefly suspended because of supposed irregularities in a research project she oversaw. Topic: *Opioid Derivatives and Molecular Manipulation.* The project had been funded by a grant from a Chinese pharmaceutical firm.

"Holy shit." Lucy grabbed her phone and hit speed dial.

"What?" Michael looked up from the real estate website.

Lucy waved him quiet. He crossed the room to grab a pile of real estate ads he'd printed out.

When Bea picked up, Lucy reported what she'd just discovered. "Kellogg is definitely a Stanford Chem PhD. That's legit. But get this. Ellen Crandall and—hold on to your socks—Claire Thompson, Pine's fiancée, were her graduate assistants."

"The girlfriend? Claire? Whoa!"

"I think it's time to talk to Ms. Thompson again," Lucy said. "She may not have murdered her honey, but her relationship with Kellogg and Crandall is one helluva coincidence. And we don't believe in coincidences."

"This is a major kick in the head," Bea said. "I totally believed her. Other than my first husband, nobody's ever lied to me so convincingly."

"And Bea, one other thing…"

Bea groaned. "Not sure I can take anymore and still sleep tonight."

"Michael got a job!"

"Whoa! Awesome!" Bea let out a wild whoop.

Lucy winced and pulled the phone from her ear. Michael smiled. He obviously heard Bea's shout-out.

Lucy continued. "One minor detail I should mention."

"Yeah?"

"It's in New York, and we're moving in less than two weeks."

—

Dawn had barely begun to brighten the eastern sky when Lucy and Bea unwrapped their breakfast burritos while merging onto the I-5 freeway toward Claire Thompson's place in Valencia. Bea had called the woman several times with no response. "I didn't leave a message that we were coming. We'll be on her doorstep well before she leaves for work. Surprise, you lying bitch." She took a long swig of coffee from her USC women's basketball commuter cup.

"So, you think she murdered David?" Lucy asked.

"The woman didn't seem like the killer type, but she sure had me convinced she was the grieving lover. My heart went out to her. Was an Oscar-worthy performance, I kid you not."

"Even if she didn't pull the trigger, she must have a pretty good idea who did."

Bea nodded. "Making her a possible accessory, at the least. I've got the Santa Clarita PD on speed dial in case we run into trouble. And I'm carrying."

The two were quiet for the next ten miles until they exited the freeway onto McBean Parkway. Traffic began to build.

"Thank you for not bringing up New York," Lucy finally said.

"Why would I? I have two exes that're history, kids who have moved on, and now my best friend is abandoning me. Why would I bring up New frickin' York?"

This was the reaction Lucy had been dreading. "I'm not leaving you. I'll be back every month or so."

Bea took an angry last chomp of the burrito, wadded up the wrapper, and stuffed it in the trash bag. "Things'll be different."

Lucy's breakfast was still unopened. Stomach acid roiled. "Maybe they'll be different in a good way."

"Never happens. But I don't want to talk about it right now. Let's keep focused on the case."

"Okay, agreed." Lucy was relieved to cut the conversation short. At least the topic was in the queue. "So, to review—we go to her place, she opens the door, realizes it's us—and slams it in our faces."

"She'll see us as friendlies. Has no clue we're aware of her tie-in to the two pharmaceutical chicks, Kellogg and Crandall."

"She may not be clueless." Lucy chewed at a fingernail. "If we found out about her online, she's gotta know the info's out there and that she's vulnerable."

"You're right. We can only hope we beat her to the punch," Bea said. "Okay, Plan A—when we get there, if she lets us in, we sit down on her Crate and Barrel couch and question her straight out, ask about a connection to Crandall and Kellogg. See how she reacts."

"Direct, no beating around the bush. Good. I'll be recording everything." Lucy patted the cell phone in the pocket of her denim shirt. "By the way, is your boyfriend aware we're doing this?"

Bea smiled and shrugged. "His people should be at Claire's place in..." she glanced at the console clock, "...in about an hour and a half." She pulled up to a stop sign but didn't fully halt the Beemer, instead doing a California roll through the traffic signal. "We'll have what we need and be gone by then. You know how the police marginalize us when they're on scene—barely let us question the perps."

"He's not gonna be happy, Beazy."

"Won't be the first time. You and I have a job to do, and it doesn't include calling the county sheriff for permission every time we make a move." She frowned.

The parkway narrowed, and they were now on the edge of a residential neighborhood. "Here's our turnoff." Lucy pointed to a driveway marked "Visitors."

Bea slowed the vehicle and took a hard right into the eighties-era stucco outcropping of boxy condos. She nailed a parking spot next to a landscaping truck. The sound of a lawnmower whirred in the distance.

As Lucy and Bea made their way toward Claire Thompson's second-floor condo, the sky turned from blue black to the pale gray of early morning cloud cover. Night-blooming jasmine was still fragrant in the air, and hummingbirds collected around a bird feeder.

The two women climbed the stairs and walked past David Pine's door. A shred of crime scene tape Bea hadn't snatched away in the first visit still hung despondently from the jamb.

"Here's her place," Bea said, "number 221." She banged on the door. "Claire, it's Bea Middleton. We need to talk."

A grizzled older man emerged from the next unit down the breezeway with a similarly grizzled black lab in tow. Both of their dark muzzles looked dipped in powdered sugar.

"You gals looking for Miss Thompson?"

"Yes, we're friends." Bea offered a benign smile.

"Moved out last weekend, she did."

"Damn," Bea whispered.

"A big truck came and took everything but the herbs and spices. I rescued 'em. They were gonna toss those pretty plants in the trash." His eyes narrowed, and he shook his head in disgust. "Can you imagine?" He limped past them toward the stairs.

"Yeah, very sad, leaving things to die," Bea said. If Claire was involved in Pine's murder, then killing a few plants would be a piece of cake. "She mention where she was going?"

"Nope. Didn't say a word. Must've been pretty freaked out by her fiancé's murder. Poor lady."

"The Oscar-worthy performance by Claire Thompson," Lucy muttered.

"Maybe the property manager can tell you more. He's in Building B, first floor."

"Thank you, sir. We'll go right over," Lucy said.

The dog began to whine.

"Gotta get Buddy out to do his business. Can't hold it like he used to. Me, neither. We're just a couple old dogs doin' the best we can." He chuckled and was on his way.

Lucy and Bea trailed the arthritic duo down the steps, then moved in the direction of Building B. A sign indicating the property manager's office pointed the way.

Although it was early, lights were on in the unit. The sound of a local TV news station leaked into the outside hallway.

Lucy knocked.

A toilet flushed. The TV was turned down, and soon, a spry gentleman opened the door. He had a head of silver hair bushed back from a severe widow's peak and wore a crisp white shirt and khakis with a knife-sharp crease.

"Hello, ladies. Are you the ones here about the condo for lease? They don't come up in this complex very often. Didn't expect you until ten, but we can go and see it now. No problem."

"Hello, sir. We're not here about the condo," Bea said.

He looked perplexed.

Lucy continued. "I'm Lucy Vega, and this is Beatrice Middleton. We're friends of Claire Thompson." They shook hands with the manager.

"Edgar McTavish, at your service. Been taking care of this place for twenty years, since I retired from my bookkeeping business in Van Nuys. How time flies."

"A pleasure, Mr. McTavish," Lucy continued. "We drove out to meet her this morning, and we found she's moved! Never told us a thing."

"We're quite concerned." Bea made a somber face. "She's in a very vulnerable space. Seems to have gone off the deep end since David Pine's murder. We were wondering if you know where she went?"

A little dog appeared at the door and began to yap. "Breakfast in a minute, Fifi." The manager stepped out into the hallway and shut the door behind him. The barking continued.

"All I can tell you is she broke her contract, wanted out of here, which I can totally understand. This is a nice neighborhood, good people. We're all horrified by what happened. Cost her a bundle in penalties to leave early, but she didn't care. I gave her a little discount."

"I'm sure she appreciated that, sir. Did she move out by herself?" Bea asked.

"Her brother showed up with a truck and a couple workers from a furniture rental company, can't remember the name. Truck was dark blue. But anyway, took them only about two hours, and they were on their way. Claire paid her bill and barely said goodbye."

Lucy was working her cell phone. Held a photo up for the man to see. "This her brother?"

Bea saw it was a picture of Molly's handler, the guy who started the fight at Doyle's campaign kickoff—a Mr. Price Burgess.

The manager pulled glasses from his shirt pocket, squinted, and looked intently. "Yeah, that's the guy."

Lucy side-eyed Bea.

"She briefly introduced me to him," the manager continued. "He's not the friendly type like Claire was."

"Okay, thank you," Lucy said. "Anything else you can tell us? We want to be there for her. Know what I mean? And we love Polar Bear."

He nodded. "Of course. I cat-sat for him a few times. Such a spirited feline. Got along with Fifi pretty well." He winked at the two women. "You're obviously kind people."

Bea smiled. Talk about an Oscar-worthy performance.

McTavish gazed out toward a sprinkler that had just come on.

The smell of wet grass became pungent and earthy as the fizzy flow of water jets crossed the lawn.

"This is probably nothing," he said. "But I heard them talking about which was the best route out to the desert from here. Death Valley, Pear Blossom, Palm Springs? Who knows which desert? That's all I can tell you. Sorry, ladies."

The yapping intensified.

"Got to feed my baby. Better run. Let me know if you're ever looking for a condo in Valencia. You both seem like you'd be lovely neighbors."

"Thank you, Mr. McTavish," Lucy said.

The manager retreated into his condo, and the yapping died down.

Lucy and Bea double-timed it to the parking lot. Lucy could feel electrons buzzing in her brain. "Better call Pete with this info ASAP. Price Burgess and Claire Thompson are connected. Yes!"

29

Three days into his forklift job with little intel to show for it, Tito pulled the piece-of-crap Camry into his condo's assigned parking spot and opened the car door. It was like putting your head into a hot clothes dryer and trying to breathe. Drought-stricken LA was a humid tropical paradise in comparison to this arid hell.

Tito yearned for a long, cold shower, but his stomach roiled. The PB&J he'd packed for lunch hadn't cut it. He recalled passing a food truck just down the block at a local sports field complex. A fresh plate of tacos, rice, and beans sounded good, and he needed a walk, despite his aching, gimpy limbs. Sitting all day and working the lift was getting to his back big-time. He was more than ready for the chiropractor.

From the center console, he plucked a baggie with the sample of pink powder he'd nabbed from a broken brick of ingredients at the warehouse and stuffed it into his pocket. He'd send the pink fairy dust by courier to Anthony in the morning. He slid from the seat and locked the car door.

Limping down the block toward dinner, the chile red food truck ahead was buoyed on a lake of shimmering heat waves rising from the surrounding blacktop. Tito spotted a small gaggle of customers treading water at the order window. Cheers from a Little League baseball game sounded in the distance. A breeze, hot as his grandpa's salsa, rustled spindly palm fronds high above the sidewalk. They sounded like dry, clacking bones.

In Tito's peripheral vision, he became aware of a police cruiser approaching from behind real slow, creepy slow, like the driver was looking for something, not just making a "serve and protect" presence known in the local 'hood.

The hackles rose on Tito's neck. Maybe it was Sergeant Tonia Delgado coming by to let him know everything was chill. He glanced over, hoping to see her reassuring face. A county cop's Ford Interceptor pulled just ahead and stopped. It was not Tonia Delgado.

Tito kept walking, surreptitiously pulled out his phone, and pressed Tonia's speed dial. Went to voicemail. "Call me," he whispered, then stuffed it back into his pocket.

"Sir!" A white guy, pumped and thirtyish with acne scars on his forehead and a disconcerting smirk on his face, hoisted himself out of the vehicle. His hand rested on his service revolver as he stepped onto the sidewalk. No bodycam was visible.

Shit. Perspiration began to dampen Tito's armpits.

"Hello, mister…" the cop said with forced friendliness.

"Hernandez." Tito almost forgot his undercover name again.

"I'm Officer Flynn. Where are you coming from, sir?"

Tito stopped and faced the cop. "Just got off work. Gonna get one of those taco plates to take home. I'm starved."

"You visit La Marimba liquor store on your way?"

"Liquor store? No. I came straight home from work, parked at my condo, and here I am. No liquor store, huh uh, not even the 7-Eleven."

The dude's face was expressive as concrete. "Let me see some ID."

Tito reached for his wallet, and the officer pulled his gun. Adrenaline gushed through Tito's veins and resounded in his brain like a noisy toilet flushing.

"Sweet Jesus, officer. I'm unarmed. Name's Carlos, Carlos Hernandez. Was just getting my driver's license for you."

Flynn re-holstered his weapon but kept his hand on it, trigger finger tapping. Finally, he took Tito's wallet and wrote down the driver's license information in a shabby notepad he pulled from his back pocket. That done, the cop rifled through the other meager contents. Twenty bucks, the prepaid credit card, and a free car wash coupon that fell out and floated to the ground. "Where's the money? In your car?"

Bad thoughts rioted in Tito's brain. He was being set up. "I don't have any more money, sir, in the car or anywhere else."

A second county sheriff's vehicle pulled up behind the Interceptor, lights flashing. A woman came to the window in a townhouse across the street, looked down on the scene, then disappeared. A teenaged boy with a skateboard situated himself on a nearby picnic table and pulled out his phone. Tito was full-on sweating. At least there were people around to see him die.

A tall, lanky officer in his forties with a dark complexion slid out of the backup cruiser to join Flynn. "Have to say, you fit the description of a man who just robbed the liquor store and pistol-whipped the proprietor about twenty minutes ago. Limped just like you do." Officer Flynn bounced on his feet like a pugilist ready to take a swing.

"I'm a paraplegic—Marines." Tito prayed that might buy him some points.

"We got a lot of vets out this way." Flynn stepped toward Tito. "All think they're fuckin' special." The man's affect was flat—obviously couldn't give a shit about Tito being a veteran.

The tall, dark guy fired up his taser. "Hands on the roof of the squad car, sir."

Tito complied. He had nightmares about being tased. His sphincter tightened reflexively. The dark-skinned officer, whose badge gave his name as Acevedo, frisked him. Pulled out the burner phone and the baggie with the pink substance.

"What the hell is this?"

Tito gulped. The moisture in his mouth dried to sand. What the hell was he supposed to say? He had no idea what the contents were. Was he gonna go down on illegal drug charges?

"I dunno, the pink stuff must be leftover from a donut I had earlier. And I can't afford a real phone." He knew both excuses were utterly unbelievable. And they'd find it pretty weird that the only two contacts on the burner were sheriff's deputies. Flynn grabbed the baggie and phone and tossed them onto the driver's seat of his cruiser.

"A fuckin' donut? Haven't heard that one before." Acevedo snorted, then snapped on the cuffs. "In the car, sir. You're under arrest for suspicion of robbery and drug possession."

Tito knew he had to stop freaking out and start talking. Once he got dragged into the system, things could go sideways fast. "Listen, check with Tonia Delgado, Sergeant Delgado," he pleaded. "She'll vouch for me. We, uh, have worked together."

"Worked together? In the service?" Flynn asked.

"Yeah, the service." Tito didn't want to reveal anything else. Who knew, maybe these cops colluded with the drugmakers. Paranoid? Maybe, but anything was possible. "Call her, please. Just call her."

Flynn yanked open the rear door to the cruiser. Acevedo grabbed Tito and pushed him hard into the back seat. Tito banged his head on the doorframe. The patrol car smelled of puke and hand sanitizer.

"Please, call her. Now. She'll stand up for me." Tito's heart pounded so loud in his ears he could barely hear his own voice. "I didn't rob that store; I swear to God. I've never even been past it."

A third black-and-white turned hard from around the corner and swerved to a stop in front of Flynn's ride. The woman from the window across the street sidled out onto the pavement with a chihuahua tucked under her arm. Skateboard kid seemed to be recording the whole thing, maybe hoping to get a homicide that would go viral.

Delgado hopped out of her car. Face twisted with anger, she stomped toward the officers. "What the hell is going on here, Flynn?"

Flynn's nostrils flared. "Suspect in the liquor store robbery, Sarge. Thirties, Hispanic, a limp."

Her eyes narrowed. "Did you actually look at the security cam images at all? Guy had a beard and a clearly visible scar indicating cleft palate surgery. Jesus, Flynn, Acevedo. Let this guy go before he sues our ass for harassment or something. I expect you to be better than this, officers." She planted her feet and folded her arms across her chest.

The two men hesitated.

Flynn spoke first. "He had a baggie in his pocket with a suspicious substance. And a burner." He grabbed both from his car seat and held them up for Delgado to see.

She snatched both from his hand. "I'll get this baggie to the lab, and we'll look at the phone, but until we find something incriminating, this man is free to go. Release him."

Flynn shuffled his feet, seeming unsure. Acevedo retreated to his ride.

"Now, Flynn!" she ordered.

He stiffened, yanked Tito out of the rear seat, and uncuffed him, cursing Delgado under his breath.

In less than a minute, Flynn and Acevedo were on their way, obviously pissed at their bitch boss.

"Those two are real assholes," she said. "Flynn's only been with us a month, and already he thinks he's the desert Rambo. Sorry 'bout all that. You okay, Carlos?"

Tito nodded and licked his parched lips.

Skateboard kid, disappointed not to see mayhem, jumped on his ride and zoomed down the sidewalk toward the ballgames. The old woman and her dog moved quickly to Tonia's side. Both women watched the retreating cruisers.

"How did you know I needed a rescue, Sarge?" Tito asked.

"Got your message. Something in your voice sounded off." She turned to the older woman standing next to her. "And thank you for calling me, *Tia.*"

"When I heard this young man shout your name and ask to talk with you, I phoned you immediately," the old woman said to Tonia.

"You did the right thing, as usual." Delgado turned toward Tito. "Carlos, this is my aunt, Mirabel Delgado. She was a 911 dispatcher for years in Riverside County. Now she's head of your Neighborhood Watch. Little gets by her."

"Gracias, Señora Delgado." Tito was ready to drop to his prosthetic knees in gratitude. "Such a pleasure to meet you," he said in Spanish, shaking the old woman's hand with both of his, then giving her a grateful peck on the cheek. Tia Mirabel blushed with pleasure.

"Can I buy you two dinner at the truck? Not fancy, but you saved me a whole lot of trouble, to say the least. *Gracias a Dios.*"

"Such a sweet boy," Tia Mirabel said. "And I heard you say marines. Lots of marines in the family. *Semper fi*, right, Tonia? Chachita and I'd love to have dinner with you both." She smooched her pup. "The truck over there *es muy bueno.*"

Tito and Tia Mirabel ambled down the sidewalk together with Chachita following in her pink leash. Tonia pulled ahead to park her car and stash the baggie.

Several blocks in the distance, what looked to Tito like Flynn's black-and-white crossed from a side alley and pulled east onto Church Street toward Airport Boulevard. Was the cop somehow onto Tito's cover with the drug company? Was the unwarranted stop a warning, or a messed-up attempt to apprehend a real criminal? He had to find the answer.

30

At her Santa Monica condo, Lucy scooped clothes out of her dresser drawers, including T-shirts, shorts, old swimsuits—the stuff of her life at the beach. Her throat tightened, but she refused to cry. Leaving this behind was tough. Substituting the Pacific for the Atlantic—they didn't even smell the same. This sweet little place had been Lucy's first home of her own—purchased with savings from photo gigs and a meager inheritance from her parents that she received at age eighteen when she was a first-year college student at UCLA. Since then, she'd used this casa as her hideaway, second home and *pied-à-terre* whenever long hours working in the city made the trek up the coast to Malibu impractical.

The walls of her bedroom and high-ceilinged living room were lined, gallery-style, with her best black-and-white photos of Los Angeles beach life. Bea'd always said she should have a show of her photographs—maybe she'd do that someday. But for now, getting ready for New York was on her mind. New adventures were coming like heavy surf. Ready or not, they'd either drag her under or give her a helluva thrill ride. Whichever the case, she'd come out dripping and on her hands and knees.

The cool smell of salty air wafted in from the open screen window while she finished her task. The filmy white curtains billowed like sails. After assessing her belongings, Lucy chose only her favorite pairs of jeans and a decade-old Venice, CA hoodie to pack for the Big Apple. Everything else was stuffed into plastic bins and jammed in the closet next to her wet suit and a couple old sundresses that were worn soft as baby blankets. Most of her things—clothes, books, and cameras—were already packed and waiting to be shipped out. Was she really doing this? She prayed it wasn't a monumental mistake.

Molly and Mary were in the process of moving in. The condo would be their temporary home away. Plopped in the middle of a sand-colored papasan chair, Molly pressed her lips into a tense line as she examined her cellphone screen and petted her dozing kitten. She punched out a message with the focus of a seagull homed in on an open bag of Doritos.

"Looking pretty intense over there, Moll." Lucy caught Mary's eye. There was only one person Lucy figured the girl would be that into communicating with.

Mary dropped the toiletries she'd just pulled from her suitcase onto Lucy's guestroom bed. "You're not texting Tito, are you?"

Molly looked up from her cushy perch, face unable to hide the guilt. "He's been gone for four days." Arms and legs drawing inward, shoulders hunched—she was like a turtle trying to avoid a predator. "I only wanted to check on him and make sure he's okay."

Mary shook her head, dismayed. "Molly, that's what Pete Anthony and the LA county sheriffs are doing—making sure Tito's okay. It's their job. They take it seriously."

"But..."

Mary began to pace. The kitten yowled and skittered under the coffee table. "What if the bad guys get his phone and track calls from you—the daughter of a big-time lawyer, a Senate candidate? You could blow Tito's cover and put him in danger. Come on, Molly, I told you— no calls to him while he's undercover. You said you understood."

"And how did you even get his number anyway?" Lucy asked.

Molly was not the sole culprit here.

The girl began to seriously yank at a strand of her coppery hair. "He called me yesterday, really upset because he'd been hassled by the police." She sat back down.

"Oh, man." Lucy pulled her phone from the pocket of her cargo pants. "Pete needs a heads-up on this."

Tears welled in Molly's big green eyes. Their usual clarity misted like overcast skies moving across early summer beaches. She rocked back and forth, hands pressing her temples, the phone abandoned on her lap.

Mary sighed, then squeezed in next to Molly and pulled her close, like she'd probably done so many times before. Lucy left the room to let mother and daughter talk while she dialed Pete.

Lucy walked out onto the terrace overlooking the beach. Strains of Ferris wheel honky-tonk on the Santa Monica pier sounded in the distance. The phone rang a dozen times, then he picked up.

"Lucita. Sorry, just got out of a meeting. What's up, good-looking?"

"Molly and Tito." She sighed. "Our little *Romeo and Juliet* have been talking on the burner."

"Shee-it," Pete said. "Shoulda figured that would happen."

"Mary's with Molly now, trying to get her to understand. No easy thing. Mother and daughter are staying at my condo in Santa Monica until they decide what they're going to do next with their lives."

"Nice of you. And, yeah, I know the girl doesn't have the best emotional control mechanisms in place. And Tito probably hasn't gotten laid since he lost his pegs. So anyhow, lemme get him ASAP and have him ditch the compromised phone with my contact in Thermal. She'll arrange for another burner, and we'll both give him hell for breaking the undercover code of honor. He'll understand that approach, ex-military and all."

"I hope he steps up, for everyone's safety." Lucy heard Molly crying from the bedroom. "He's much more likely to be able to put on the brakes than Molly. She's still very fragile after that seizure."

"She okay?"

"Actually, she's doing pretty well, all things considered."

Pete continued, "By the way, I just got the labs back on the sample Tonia grabbed from that asshole cop who gave Tito a hard time."

"And?" Lucy held her breath.

"Once again, we got us a benign vitamin. B12 this time."

She felt the balloon of anticipation in her chest deflate. "Maybe it really is a vitamin plant."

"Yeah, well, I'm not ready to go there yet. I'll give Tito a couple more days. Then, if nothing more turns up, I'll bring him in."

"Should I call Bea and get her up to speed on this, or do you want to?"

"I'm meeting her in a couple hours for dinner and a little romp in the hot tub, so I'll fill her in."

"Okay, Pete. Frolic on. More soon."

—

The desert morning dawned even hotter than usual in the Coachella Valley. At 8:00 a.m. the temperature nudged the sizzling underbelly of the century mark. Even the usual chirping birds were baked into shadowy stupor high in the dead fronds of palm trees ringing the pill plant. The air was still as death. This was the kind of heat that could kill.

Tito gulped from his water bottle, which had been in the freezer all night but already felt tepid to the taste. He stretched his stiff neck and slowly walked through the chain-link fence entry to the warehouse. Pete Anthony had reamed his butt the previous evening, and it still hurt. Tito knew he'd been careless. A good reporter, especially working undercover, could not afford stupid mistakes. He put thoughts of Molly—long legs, ginger hair, lips shiny with strawberry gloss—into a mental cabinet and muscled the door shut. He sweated at the effort.

"Hernandez," his boss shouted from across the floor. "Over here. Now."

Slapped back into the present, Tito trotted over to Rios, the big ex-marine. "Hey, man, what's up?"

"We got an early shipment over at the new place, and we gotta get it loaded in ASAP."

What was the dude talking about? "The new place?" Tito thought this was their only facility.

"Yeah, a couple miles from here. Just completing a big addition over there, so this shit wasn't supposed to arrive until next week, but here it is. Gotta get it taken care of right now, so I need an extra operator. The big bosses are coming today to inspect everything."

"Bosses?" Maybe he'd get a glimpse of the kingpins. His heart rate accelerated. He fingered the burner phone in his pocket.

"Yeah, the big guys from LA and Hong Kong."

Tito nodded. "Sounds intense. So, where am I off to?"

"South of here, like five minutes. Turn left onto highway 86, then left onto Rio Seco. The warehouse is behind the hill in a grove of date palms. You'll see a small reservoir with a herd of scrawny cows that like to stand in the water. Park in the underground lot, and meet Joe Estrada at the loading dock." He glanced at his watch.

Tito turned to acknowledge Skunk and Diego who were approaching to check in.

"*Ve rápido, Hernandez!*" Even Rios's "inside voice" was pure drill sergeant.

"*Si, si*, on my way."

Tito adjusted the backpack on his shoulder and rushed out to his Camry, anxious to get a look at this previously unknown facility. Maybe that's where they stored the bad medicine. Maybe this was going to be his one and only opportunity to find out what was happening beyond the vitamins. Maybe this was his shot at a career-defining story.

His car was already an oven as he turned down the Riverside County highway toward Rio Seco.

—

Joe Estrada, a sixty-something Native American with long gray hair tied into a ponytail, wore a fresh, white polo shirt with a casino logo tucked into pressed jeans. His leather belt appeared hand-tooled. Sitting at a workstation in the corner of the warehouse, he raised his hand as Tito approached. This warehouse was twice the size of the one at the old date-processing plant where Tito unloaded vitamin powder.

It was modern and light, actually air-conditioned. This was definitely the A game.

"Mr. Estrada? I'm Carlos Hernandez."

"It's Joe." The man stood and they shook hands. His grip was firm and dry. "Thanks for coming over. We need the help with a surprise early load-in. Our other guy called in sick."

Fifty yards in the distance, an African-American woman appeared on a shiny new forklift with two pallets of product just seared from the back of a semi.

"Go on down to Stella, and she'll fill you in."

Estrada's phone rang. "Sorry, gotta take this." He turned away.

Tito nodded and headed toward his new co-worker. The woman, mid-thirties and stocky, lowered her mask, revealing a great smile. Tito walked up to her rig.

"So glad they could send you over. I can't handle this all by myself. It's a whole flippin' double shipping container's worth."

They shook hands. "I'm Carlos. Glad to help."

"Stella Jones. The staff break room is over there." She pointed to an unmarked white door. "Lockers, showers, first aid and safety station, refreshments. It's pretty good. The locking mechanism on the lockers hasn't been activated, but it's only you, me, and Joe, so if anybody steals your stash, you know where to come." She chuckled. "And no phones on the warehouse floor. There are masks leftover from Covid in there, too. I usually use one when I'm unloading anything from a foreign country. I'm kinda paranoid—waiting for a rabid bat or something to fly out." She laughed again. Tito joined her.

"Okay, I'll get rid of my backpack and be right there."

"Your rig is parked over by Joe."

Tito turned and eyed a shiny new Toyota forklift. Definitely the A game.

31

Rubbing gritty eyes, Bea stepped unhappily from the elevator into the news bureau din. She circled the cube farm where the minions worked their digital devices with the ease of those who never had to deal with paper. Studying her cellphone through dark glasses, she took a healthy swig from the commuter cup. As she passed Dexter and Aja schmoozing at the copy machine, she muttered, "My office. In five. And bring your research."

"And good morning to you, too, Ms. Middleton," her son called in an annoyingly cheerful tone.

Bea was in no mood for pleasantries. She and Pete had downed way too much Chianti with the chicken parm and had kept the hot tub sizzling into the wee hours like they were idiot college kids. What were they thinking? They weren't.

She fired up her laptop and the Keurig, then dragged out the pain relievers. Her neck was killing her. She had to get back to yoga. And where was the damn Visine?

Dexter and Aja darkened the doorway. Dex knocked on the doorframe hesitantly. Aja pressed against his side, laptop clutched in her hands. Bea had the feeling that a little action was going on between her kid and the new reporter. A clear violation of company policy—one she'd broken a few times herself over the years, like when she'd married her news director. And then there was Molly and Tito making calls on a secured phone that could blow his cover. Young lust, middle-aged lust—she couldn't take any more drama. She downed a couple capsules of pain reliever.

"Okay, come in. Show me what you've got on the drug situation." She knew Aja had ditched the bad generics and had her meds under control with the help of her shrink. The girl looked cute in blue jeans and a classic gray blazer. Bea was hopeful Aja was back on a steady course.

"You okay, Mom?" Dexter's lips curled into a sly smile as he and Aja stepped into the office. "Party a little too hearty, *mamacita*? And on a weeknight?" He added a parent-worthy *tsk-tsk*.

"Don't be ridiculous. Just have a bit of a migraine." Was that a twang of defensiveness in her voice? Oh, yeah. She pressed her fingers to her temples while the kids pulled the two chairs across from her desk closer together.

"Okay..." Bea fumbled around the desktop for her reading glasses. Dexter handed them to her. She grabbed the specs, huffed, and quickly perched them on her nose. "Okay, so, Aja, tell me what you got."

"Right. The research." Aja sat up very straight and adjusted her laptop on a corner of Bea's desk. "First off, we know that, in the United States, the foreign entity where the generics' active ingredients are manufactured does not need to be noted anywhere on the bottle or packaging. Point of origin has to be disclosed somewhere online, but too often it's almost impossible to find. The dirty little secret is that, although the bottle will say *Made in the USA*, the stuff that counts is usually from China, India, or Thailand."

Dexter nodded. "When US pharmacies couldn't get enough ibuprofen during the pandemic, China, the source of most of the active ingredients, blamed a supply chain interruption. Our people started hoarding it."

"So, if we don't manufacture it in the US," Aja said, "we're subject to the whims of other nations' standards and regulations. Or lack thereof. You can see the danger."

Bea felt her Asian-sourced painkillers start to kick in. "I already know this. What else?"

Aja took a quick look at Dexter, and he nodded encouragement. She continued. "The law says the drugmaker can claim as the country of origin wherever the drug's various components were 'substantially transformed' into the final product. They can get ingredients from around the world, often from loosely regulated sites, and if they put it together in pill form here, they can legally stamp it *Made in the USA*."

Aja scrutinized her computer screen. "In a recent *Times* article, it said: 'The final pill assembly might be done in the United States, but the ingredients are more like an episode of Dora the Explorer.'"

"We're at the mercy of global supply chains and politics," Dexter said. "Covid-19 showed us some of that with PPE and Covid testing."

Bea pressed her thumbs against her eyes. "I think we're aware of most of this. Y'all have enough for a strong article on the subject, or is your info mostly derivative?"

"We're just giving you background first." Aja moved to the edge of her chair. "The really interesting finding is the role of a man named Su Jin Pang."

"I know about him. He's the moneyman behind the clinic Molly was sent to last week." Bea had hoped for something new from Aja and Dexter.

"Yes," Aja said, "and he also may be behind the pharmaceutical company in Thermal where you sent Tito."

"Pang funds the pill mill?" Bea's head began to pound again. "And you know about Tito?"

"Molly texted us," Dexter said. "Don't worry, we're keeping his situation on the down-low, of course."

"Oh, man," Bea groaned. "Who else did she tell this bloody *secret* to?"

"Just Aja and me." Dexter lowered his voice. "And Lucy and Mary, and Pete, of course."

"I hope to God, for Tito's sake, that's true. And how do you know

Pang is the money behind the pill mill? And let me remind you, all we have so far is proof of vitamin production out there."

Dexter smiled. "Ready for the big reveal?"

"The reveal? We're not hosting a home improvement show here, son."

Two sets of brown eyes sparkled at her.

Aja blurted, "Dexter hacked into a government database…"

"What!" *No*, Bea thought. No, she couldn't believe it. "My boy is not a hacker. Right, Dexter?" She was afraid to hear the answer.

He popped up from his chair. "I didn't, you know, like, personally hack in. But—"

"But, what?"

"But I sort of…facilitated it."

Bea could feel her burning eyes narrow to slits. "Facilitated? What does that mean?"

Dexter rubbed his chin the way he always did under stress.

"As you've shown me in the past, when you need digital expertise on a tough problem, you go to Bijan."

Bea choked on her coffee. "You talked to Bijan? And Bijan knows everything, too?"

Aja's face flushed with excitement. "Bijan is so nice. He checked out Doctor Su Jin Pang for us."

"Bijan Rachmaji provided this information? As a freebie for you two rookies?" Bea's irritation meter zoomed upward. Bijan didn't live in a Marina del Rey penthouse by giving his services away.

Dexter gulped. Aja touched his knee reflexively. "I kinda, well, I told him to put it on the statNEWS tab."

"This just keeps getting better and better." Bea pulled out the Baileys Irish Cream from her lower drawer and slammed the heavy bottle onto the desktop. She had only a few young reporters to supervise, and they were locking themselves in bathroom stalls, making illicit phone calls, charging unapproved sums to the company account, falling in love with each other— Bea splashed the liqueur into her cup.

"But wait," Dexter said, "it was totally worth it." His eyes were wide, hands gesticulating as he got up to pace the room. "Pang is a Chinese national who has dual citizenship because he married an American—Sandra Kellogg, PhD."

"He's married to Kellogg?" *Now we're getting somewhere.* "And sit down, Dexter. Your pacing is making me nervous."

He complied but twitched like bacon on a skillet.

Aja punched a few buttons on her keyboard. "Pang was head of one of China's largest synthetic opioid production labs until a scandal involving doctored research data forced him to leave the job. That was in 1983—the year before he turned up in the States as a postdoc in molecular medicine."

Bea felt a visceral jolt of electricity. "Don't tell me he was at Berkeley with Doyle and company."

"Yes," Dexter said, "at Berkeley."

Bea's pulse quickened. "I knew he'd done graduate studies at Berkeley. Lucy already turned up some of this information. But holy shit, this puts all of them together for sure—David Pine, Brandon Doyle, Pang, Berman, Thompson, and Kellogg. Add Burgess, too, because he was in the military under Doyle who was a Berkeley ROTC grad." The pieces were beginning to make sense.

"But there's another interesting thing, Mom." Dexter was still wound tight as a Tesla coil. "Lucy's friend." His voice lowered again. "David Lee?"

Bea put the Baileys back in the drawer and dumped the lukewarm contents of her commuter cup into the wastebasket. "Yeah, okay. He's helped us with this case. Did translations. What about him?"

Aja leaned in. "One of Lee's uncles completed his MBA at Berkeley in '84 and worked at the same lab as Doctor Pang before coming to the US. And, drumroll, Mark J. Lee manages his uncle's international business contracts. And there are accounts in sketchy places."

"Like the Caymans and Lagos." Dexter shut his laptop. "We don't know what all this means, but we got us some serious red flags."

Bea sat back in her leather chair. "We sure as hell do. Let me get with the rest of our team this afternoon and figure out how to proceed. Nice work, young journalists. I'm proud of you both."

The two hustled from her office, all smiles. She saw her son grab Aja's hand the second they'd cleared her office door. She ripped off her damn reading glasses and grabbed the Visine.

32

Tito gazed around the modern staff locker room. Light and bright, it looked like it belonged in a high-end fitness club. Where were the damn terrycloth robes and body lotions? He chuckled to himself. A bunch of hardcore warehouse mucks were not going to be anywhere near feeling comfortable in this hipster spa environment.

He opened the door to a gleaming white locker and stashed his shabby backpack. They'd said nada to phones on the job, but there was no way he was going to part with his now-compromised burner. He stuffed it in the back pocket of his jeans and pulled his shirt over it. Taking one last glance around the big room, he spotted a 360-degree camera mounted in a corner high above. Tito hoped his phone wasn't spotted. And there was nothing to steal but minimal first aid supplies, day-old donuts which were suspiciously near an OSHA Heimlich poster, and the coffee maker. Grabbing a blue Covid-era face mask, Tito stuck it in his pocket over the burner. He clanged his locker shut and thought of Stella's warning. She was being a little paranoid about bats flying out of shipping containers—the pharmaceutical shit didn't come from a Wuhan wet market. Did it? He pressed his pocket again, donned his hard hat and safety glasses, then returned uneasily to the warehouse.

Tito took an assessing walk around the forklift—all appeared copacetic. After securing his seat belt, he took a few minutes to work through the operation, familiarizing himself with the new rig. It was sweet, no doubt about it.

Two forty-foot containers sat at the dock. This would likely be a daylong project or more, but since he couldn't talk to Molly, he welcomed the overtime. He'd planned to meet Tonia at 6:00 p.m. to hand off the burner. He might have to push it back.

Stella's voice crackled over the radio that sat on his machine's front console. "Carlos, start with the K-line container. We'll block stack those pallets in section 3-A down to your far left."

"Roger that," he replied, glancing over at Joe who was still at his desk working the phones. There was definitely a sense of tense anticipation in the air. The bosses must be on their way.

An hour into unloading, the double security doors to another part of the building, probably the manufacturing section, swung open. In the lead, strutting and gesticulating, was a skinny Asian dude about Tito's age. He'd seen him in the other building. Obviously, he was the tour leader. Behind him came an overweight Asian man in a white linen suit and a tall middle-aged blond guy with creepy Aryan features right off a Nazi recruiting poster. Following the men were two women in their thirties or forties, both with a brown-haired wallflower look.

Tito's heart rate jumped, and he almost lost the forklift load. Brandon Doyle, along with his bodyguard, Burgess, stepped through the doors. The dickwad cop who'd hassled Tito the previous night was with them. Asswipe obviously worked a second gig as a security guard.

He pulled himself together and continued toward the block stacking area but not before he pulled out his phone and surreptitiously took a couple shots of the group. Brandon Doyle might be able to ID Tito. The cop certainly could. But out of context here on the job—if he stayed far enough away from them—he'd probably be okay. He stuck the phone back in his pocket, then remembered his face mask.

After adjusting his light-blue surgical mask for maximum

coverage, he eased the pallets into place and expertly released his cargo. Warning lights flashed and the backup alert dinged until he turned the lift truck toward the loading dock. In the rearview mirror, he saw the bigwigs heading his way. Tito's hands went watery with sweat.

The executives collected in the center of the warehouse. Joe signaled for his newest employee to bring over his forklift. Tito adjusted his mask again and powered up to the group, stopping several yards away. All wore green hard hats with a Riverside Pharma company logo on the side. He could also make out something about "good health," an afterthought in small print.

Heart hammering, was the cop checking him out? Yep. Seemed like the jerk had a habit of being on the prowl for somebody to aggravate.

Joe stepped next to the rig like Vanna White on Wheel of Fortune. "And we have three more Toyotas just like this one, plus a couple of stackers ready to be delivered later this week. In a way it's lucky the product came in early so you could see the beginning of the warehouse in action." He smiled and tapped on the cab, ran his hand down the mast, and actually kicked a tire.

Doyle moved up close and circled the machine like a kid examining a new Tonka toy. Tito held his breath. At least nobody asked him to remove his mask. Plenty of people still wore them.

Then, the worst happened.

Doyle stepped up close. "Mind stepping out of the forklift for a few minutes, *amigo*? I'd like to sit in and see how it feels."

He was not Doyle's damn *amigo*. Racist asshole. Tito was paralyzed for an instant, then engaged his stiff muscles and slid off the seat, stepping onto the warehouse floor with all the grace and control he could muster. If they saw his limp, it might cue recognition. Doyle knew he was a double amputee; Molly had told him the night he practically threw Tito out of their house in Brentwood. Flynn, the cop who had hassled him over near the park in Thermal, knew, too.

At that moment, Stella drove up, mask down with a friendly smile on her face. She was, thankfully, nicely distracting. After a mini-demo of the lift truck and some chitchat, the bosses began to straggle their way toward the exit.

All except for the cop.

Tito climbed back onto his seat, and in the process, his phone popped out of his pocket and clattered to the floor. He moved to grab it, but the cop beat him to it.

The son of a bitch scowled. "Didn't anyone tell you, no phones in the warehouse?"

"I told him," Joe said. Worry lines etched his forehead.

"Me, too." Stella gave Tito the stink eye.

Near panic, Tito's brain raced with excuses. Which one would sound the dumbest and therefore most plausible? Always choose a lie with a sliver of truth to it. "I'm sorry. No harm meant. I'm waiting for a call from my girlfriend. We kinda, well, we had a fight last night and—"

The cop doubled down. "This is a top secret facility. I don't give a shit about your chick problems. We can't have people sneaking around taking photos."

Tito flashed to their encounter on the sidewalk near the food truck. The guy was a dog after a bone. He had something to prove, big-time. "I haven't taken any pictures. Why would I take pictures? There's nothing here that's interesting. I'm just waiting for a phone call." Tito gulped. If they saw the photos he'd just taken, he'd be up shit creek.

The skinny Asian guy came back into the warehouse and joined the cop. "What seems to be the problem here, Officer Flynn?"

"This schmuck had a phone."

Tito opened his arms in supplication. "Only to talk to my girlfriend. I'll stick it in my locker immediately. I'm really sorry, I had no idea this was such a big deal. I thought it was like the other warehouse, kind of, you know, informal."

Flynn dropped the phone into his pocket. Tito was on the verge of freaking. Sweat pooled under his hard hat, threatening to run down his face in guilty rivulets. "I'm sorry, sir, but I need my phone, or I'm going to have to leave. This job is not the most important thing in my life, my girlfriend is. I was going to propose to her this weekend." He looked away.

Joe's eyes flitted to the packed shipping containers and back to Tito, then to Flynn and the skinny executive. "Carlos is a terrific worker, and we have to get those babies unloaded tonight. So, could you give him his phone back, Officer Flynn?"

The skinny exec chimed in. "Can't ruin a man's love life, now, can we? Lighten up, Flynn, give him the damn phone, and let's get going. The others are waiting, and they don't have a lot of time."

Flynn grimaced and extricated the phone from his pocket. Tito snatched it out of his hand.

As Flynn and skinny dude retreated toward the exit, Joe pointed to the locker room, eyes angry.

Tito saluted and sped away. He'd barely dodged the bullet on this one. Holding the phone close to his body, he texted the images to Pete, then deleted them. Although more than ready to bail, Tito still had to somehow walk out with a sample of what was in those containers. He mopped sweat from his forehead with the back of his hand. The whole scene was getting too hot to handle.

—

Chee pranced along the hallway inset with big windows overlooking the manufacturing floor, much like in the other building. He clucked at his gaggle of execs and motioned for them to follow. "I'm glad you enjoyed the warehouse. Here's the final stop on our tour of Riverside Pharma's impressive facility: the security center."

He opened the door into a large, dim room with black walls. "Come on in and we'll give you a quick demonstration."

The temperature dropped at least twenty degrees. The air smelled of new computers. A plump, middle-aged man, who looked like a Geek Squad clone in a white shirt and skinny black tie, dominated the expansive console. His hands moved across various switches and buttons as if he was the Phantom of the Opera playing an organ. Twenty video monitors popped to life—electronic eyes surveilling every work area and the staff locker rooms. Several workers were adjusting a conveyor on the manufacturing floor. On another screen, the forklift operator, Stella, loaded a pallet into a storage area as Joe looked on, electronic notebook in hand. Someone was in the warehouse staff locker room. Flynn moved in close to the screen.

Chee continued. "Our state-of-the-art security center will be staffed twenty-four seven to assure the integrity of our products and our workers. Officer Flynn, whom you've all met, will be leading the security team, coming onboard full-time as soon as we officially open."

Flynn's eyes were riveted to the warehouse staff locker room screen. Tito had removed his mask and was rummaging in his backpack.

"Fuck. That's the asshole I hassled the other night over by the sports complex. Was a possible suspect in a liquor store robbery."

Back by the door, Chee rose up on his toes to try and see the monitor over the heads of those blocking the screen. "You saying he's a criminal?"

Flynn snarled. "My boss showed up and rescued the asshole. Said he was a vet, a paraplegic. Dude walked kinda wonky. Turned out not to be the perp we were after, but there was something about him I didn't like."

Burgess joined Flynn at the screen with Doyle at his side.

Chee piped up with his usual high-pitched enthusiasm. "See how easy it is to keep track of absolutely everything with this security setup? Very nice. All happening in real time. Impressive. Does anyone have any questions before the luncheon? Sea bass and pineapple glaze. Fresh date shakes for fun."

Flynn, Doyle, and Burgess ignored him.

Doyle pushed the others aside and drew up closest to the screen. "Shit. A paraplegic vet; he looks really familiar." His eyes narrowed. "Fuckin' ay. I think this is a kid my daughter brought home. I threw him out."

Flynn looked completely confused. "This warehouse asshole? And your daughter?"

Doyle's teeth clenched. "He may be a crack forklift operator, but that's not who he is."

Burgess joined Flynn with a slack-mouthed WTF look on his face. "Molly and that dude? What are you talking about?"

Doyle turned and looked at the group, then at Burgess. "I think he's a reporter with Network News."

There was total silence, then a collective groan.

"You're sure?" Sandra Kellogg asked.

The console operator brought the image up onto the center big screen.

Doyle took another look as Tito pulled his mask back on, shut his backpack in the locker, and left the room. On another screen, he emerged into the warehouse, heading toward his forklift. "Yeah, I'm sure." Doyle stepped away, loosened his tie, raked his fingers through his lovely salt-and-pepper mane.

A voice came over an intercom. "Lunch is now served in the executive dining room."

Members of the group began to mutter to each other as they followed Chee from the security center. Burgess, Doyle, and Flynn lagged behind.

"So, what do we do, boss?" Burgess asked, voice low.

"Nothing right now. We'll talk with Pang and Neckar. Figure it all out, but I think this guy has to disappear."

33

The warehouse crew took a half-hour dinner break when Joe ordered in an extra-large pizza and a couple liters of soda for himself and his hardworking duo of Tito and Stella. Famished, the three hunkered down at a picnic table beneath the date palms on a rear patio outside the dock. Temperatures were still a sweltering ninety-seven degrees at 6:00 p.m., but a little breeze kicked up to make the dry air marginally tolerable. Wrens twittered around a feeder some nature lover had hung from the spindly arm of a nearby acacia tree. A roadrunner scurried behind a creosote bush in the distance.

Tito tried to keep up with the conversation—the weather, the billion-dollar football stadium, and the new Angel City women's soccer club that Stella was jazzed about. But all he could really focus on was how he was going to get a sample of the stuff they were off-loading from the shipping containers. He likely had less than two hours to make it happen. The product was well-wrapped in heavy-gauge plastic, not the flimsy garbage bag-like stuff the vitamin ingredients arrived in.

"Wish we could keep you with us permanently," Joe said. "Bring on one more person, and we'd have a real good crew."

It took a second for Tito to realize Joe was talking to him. "Yeah, it's a much nicer deal over here. Better everything."

Joe smiled, seeming to take the statement as a personal compliment. He reached for another piece of pizza.

"Sorry about the phone thing," Tito said.

"No big deal, all resolved."

"Flynn is an asshole," Stella chimed in. "And speaking of phones, I have to go check in with my kiddos. Make sure they're heading for homework and not giving grandma a hard time." She ambled back into the warehouse.

Joe turned to Tito. "Any word from the girlfriend?" He chuckled.

"All good. Just a little, uh, misunderstanding. Like I forgot our six-month anniversary."

"Oh, Lordy, Lordy." Joe laughed out loud. "Six-month anniversary. Wish I was back in the day when it was all that simple." He grabbed the empty pizza box. Tito picked up the cups and crumpled napkins. They deposited it all in a nearby trash bin.

Trailing Joe into the warehouse, Tito could feel himself color at the thought of Molly, those glossy lips and those long, trim legs. Since his were history, women's legs seemed to be a major theme of his erotic fantasies. What an idiot he was. She'd run for the hills when she saw his stumps—so fuckin' wrecked. They'd never have a six-month anniversary.

He gulped the last dregs of warm soda. Why was he thinking like this? *Stop the self-critical shit and the boo-hoo. Get your head on straight, man—you have to come home tonight with a sample.* That was what mattered.

"Back to work." Joe shuffled toward his desk in the far corner of the cavernous facility.

"Thanks for dinner, Joe." Tito thought the supervisor seemed like a decent guy. In another world, he might have enjoyed working here with Joe and Stella.

"No problem, Carlos. Long day. 'Preciate you hanging in there."

"Happy for the overtime." Tito wished he was actually getting a paycheck. Forklift operators made a helluva lot more than reporters.

Ten minutes later, back on his rig with a plan, he fingered the Swiss Army knife in his pocket. He'd make his move just before the end of shift so he didn't have to worry about the sample being on his person for long. What if it was fentanyl? Shit could kill you. He wiped his forehead again and jabbed the forklift tines into a pallet.

Loading and unloading, repetitious and mindless—he was in the zone like when he used to run every day before the IED explosion took that away forever. He checked his watch—it was 7:52, and he hadn't scored the sample. He couldn't let the opportunity slip away. His heart rate accelerated. It had to happen now.

Tito stuck his hand in his pocket and fingered the knife. Placing his current load carefully on a rack, he purposely knocked the twenty-four-ounce water bottle from his drink holder toward a huge stack of product. The bottle dropped to the ground between the rig and the pallets. The contents sprayed all over making a nice puddle. Perfect.

"Shit, uh-oh. Damn water bottle."

Stella whizzed by him and shook her head. Tito undid his safety belt and slid from his seat. He circled to the side of his rig, bent down to retrieve the fallen container, and pulled out his Swiss Army knife. He popped the Phillips head and rammed it into the side of a plastic-wrapped package. The screwdriver sprung back like a kid on a trampoline without piercing the skin of the casing. *Shit.*

Tito licked his dry lips. He drew back the implement, steadied himself against the forklift tire, and rammed for all he was worth. Bingo. Twisting the screwdriver to lodge contents in the blades, he quickly pulled it out, wrapped it in a napkin still greasy from pizza, and stuffed the sample into his pocket. He glanced over at the warehouse door. At the large windows was Flynn. *Shit, again.*

Between Tito's eyes, a low-grade headache intensified. A custodian with a mop shuffled slowly his way. Tito grabbed the empty bottle and scurried back to his seat, buckled up, then turned toward the loading dock to nab one more stack before the day was over. He raised a hand to thank the janitor.

Glancing at the door again, Flynn was gone.

—

Later, when Tito pulled into his space at the condo, Tonia Delgado's cruiser was parked in the adjoining spot. Leaning against her car and talking into her radio, she wore a gray Riverside County Sheriff Desert Rats Softball Team T-shirt and khaki cargo shorts. Her service revolver was holstered at her hip. She looked strong and kick-ass.

Tito slid out of his car and reached into his pocket. He approached Delgado and handed her the Swiss Army knife with the warehouse product lodged in the Phillips head screwdriver. She stashed her comms, opened the cruiser door, and pulled a baggie from a kit on her front console to secure the evidence.

"Impressive job, Tito."

"Thanks. I want that knife back," he said. "My father gave it to me."

Tonia turned and dropped it into a plastic box next to the computer. "I'll try. No guarantees."

She joined Tito as he walked toward the condo. He filled her in on the events of the day.

"I didn't recognize anybody except Flynn in that photo you texted, but hopefully, Pete and friends can ID at least some of them," she said.

Tito nodded, suddenly slowed by a wave of exhaustion. His balance wavered for an instant. His back was getting even for twelve hours in the truck. "Flynn's definitely moonlighting out there. He almost outed me. Tried hard enough."

"Dangerous bastard—he'd stab me in the back in a heartbeat," Delgado said.

"Yeah, I kind of figured that." Tito's gaze swept the street. He felt vulnerable and wanted to just grab his gear and tear-ass out of Thermal. He'd had it with the heat.

Tonia continued. "I just talked to Pete. He wants you safely back in LA tonight. Wants me on your tail until you cross out of Riverside County."

"Roger that, officer. I'm shovin' off in ten." He turned the key in the door lock and stepped into the entry hall. "Been great doing business with 'ya, by the way."

She smiled. "Got your six anytime, bro."

Tonia followed him into the living room. They both stopped short. What little Tito had in his temporary housing had been tossed like laundry in a washing machine.

"Oh, man." Tonia drew her Glock from its holster and quickly cleared the small apartment.

"I'll call this in, and crime scene can take it. You're going to have to leave everything here. Let's go. I'll follow 'til you get to the I-10 freeway."

Tito ignored her admonition to leave all and grabbed his laptop, his favorite Santana T-shirt, and his medical paraphernalia. Tonia frowned but didn't try to stop him.

He yanked open the drawer next to his bed. It was empty. His chest constricted. "My personal phone. It's gone." If whoever did this could hack his fingerprint passcode, they'd know about Molly. She was in danger. Even though Doyle was her father, Tito didn't trust the jerk. Ultimately, the asshole would see his daughter as expedient. He tried not to hyperventilate. "Let me keep the burner for now. I'll turn it in to Pete tomorrow."

"Okay, sounds good," Delgado said, holstering her gun. "*Let's vamonos.*" She led the way back to the parking lot, punching in Pete's number on her cellphone as they hurried.

34

"No way in hell!" Lucy shook her head in disbelief. "I've known David Lee since grade school. He's a total straight shooter."

Bea frowned. "Money, pressure, fame—it can do things to people—change them. Sometimes even the good ones."

"You're telling me he does contracts for this fool, Pang? No way." Lucy slapped her tablet closed, pushed back her chair, and scanned the questioning faces around the conference table—Bea, Pete, Dexter, and Aja. "I'm going over to the agency and talk to him right now, find out what the hell's going on. There's another answer to this, this misunderstanding."

"Whoa, Nellie," Pete growled. "Hold your horses."

"What does that mean?" Aja whispered to Dexter.

He murmured back, "Means chill. I think."

The detective stood and continued, hands on the table. His gold Saint Christopher medal swung from his neck as he leaned toward Lucy. "Listen, Lucy, and everybody, we need to keep this close to the vest until we find out more. We don't want to blow whatever advantage we might have."

Lucy headed for the door. "I'm sorry, but this is bullshit and it has to be sorted. Now." She took three big steps and grabbed the doorknob.

"Lucia María de la Vega." Bea's voice was dead calm and commanding. Lucy's head snapped toward her.

Bea leaned back in her chair and crossed her arms. "Yes you, the woman with all those pretty names. I love y'all dearly, but bless your heart, we both know you got a righteous, impulsive streak, so think hard before you fly off and tell Mister Lee what we know."

Whenever Bea addressed her with that awful Southern phrase, "bless your heart," Lucy knew she'd better pay attention. She still gripped the door handle but took a deep breath. "If he has betrayed me, if he's part of compromising medicines people depend on—"

"Luce," Pete said calmly. "If Mark Lee screwed with you and is in with Pang, we're going to nail him. If there's a good explanation, then he's exonerated. But for now, we need you to keep cool and hold off until we know what we're dealing with."

Lucy finally released the door handle. "If it's true about Mark, and I'm sure it's not, then Pang and his minions already know we're onto them."

"All the more reason to keep things between us for now," Pete said.

The room went quiet. Bea broke the silence. "Okay, folks, let's take a look at the images Tito sent to Pete around noon, see if we can ID anybody."

Lucy sighed, exasperated, and sat back down.

At the far end of the long mahogany table, a slightly blurry photo of a group of businesspeople in a warehouse came up on the big screen.

Bea leaned in, squinting. "Hot damn, some familiar suspects. We got Doyle and his bodyguard, Burgess, the bastard who slugged me. The chubby Asian man is Doctor Su Jin Pang with wifey Sandra Kellogg and Pine's fake fiancée, Claire Thompson."

"I think the skinny, young guy is Marshall Chee, Su Jin Pang's nephew," Aja said. "His picture was on some of their marketing materials, and he has a wide social media presence, a little too wide for a company wanting a low profile."

"I remember him," Lucy said, back in the game, "he was the quasi-tour guide when Bea and I were in Thermal. Nice clothes, high-strung, talked too much."

Pete tapped on a keyboard, and several faces were pulled into fuzzy but recognizable close-ups. "Don't know the security guard or the tall, Euro-looking guy."

Dexter asked, "Can you run these last two through your facial recognition software, or are the images not sharp enough?"

"I'll give it a try," Pete said. "In the meantime, Tito's got to get outta there. Burgess and Doyle might be able to ID him, and that, kiddies, could be lethal. A couple hours ago, I texted him to scram stat, but he said he wouldn't go until he got a sample of whatever they're off-loading from the containers."

"Shit," Bea mumbled and turned to Pete. "You think we could ask your friend Delgado to be on standby to make sure Tito actually leaves the facility tonight?"

"Already done. Called her the minute I got those photos."

"In the meantime," Bea continued, "Aja and Dexter, great job. And keep digging on social media regarding Chee."

"And let me see what more I can find on my friend Mark Lee," Lucy said. "Doubtful, but maybe I'm missing something."

Bea gave her a skeptical eye roll. "Girl, you're too involved—"

"I swear, I'll be totally discreet. I'll stand down for now. I promise."

"Then go for it," Pete said. "Need all the research power we can muster." He turned off the projector, and Dexter dialed the lights back up. They all stood and filed out of the room. Lucy and Bea were the stragglers.

Lucy slowly tucked her tablet under her arm. "Maybe there's another Mark Lee affiliated with the agency. Tons of people work there. It's a common name."

"I hope you're right, sister." Bea hustled out the door and called for Pete to wait up.

Lucy went to the big window overlooking Hollywood Boulevard. The evening lights were kindling their magic against a pale mauve sunset. The Walk of Fame, the Chinese Theater, and the Wax Museum all began to glitter. Traffic moved in small clots along the famous artery bisecting the town of dreams, illusions, and nightmares. Lucy turned her back to the scene and wondered if New York would be any different.

—

As the exits for San Bernardino and Claremont sped by, Tito felt his blood pressure begin to drop back into the normal range. He'd done it—survived the undercover assignment and scored the sample they needed. The cold fear that had lodged in his chest like shrapnel began to melt. He grabbed the burner from the center console and dialed Pete. Scared him shitless that Molly could be in danger once the assholes found out she and Tito were linked. And he was sure they'd find out. Likely, they'd already hacked his phone. Doyle would go ballistic.

Pete picked up immediately. "Tito, what's going on, man? You still in Thermal? It's late."

"On my way home, just passing through San Berdoo. Gave the sample to Tonia and booked ass outta there. Somebody trashed my so-called safe house this afternoon. They took my personal phone. Riverside sheriffs were sending in a crime scene investigator. Tonia'll fill you in. She's awesome."

"Just got a voice mail from her—haven't listened yet. Sounds like you were made."

"There's a cop named Flynn who moonlights as security at a second plant. Not the place Bea and Lucy were at. A new and renovated facility about a half mile further down the road, back in a palm grove. I was assigned there today to help with a big load they hadn't expected until next week." Tito put the phone on speaker, moving it from his aching shoulder back to the dashboard.

"That location wasn't on our radar. Good job."

"Thanks, and if my sample pans out, I'd say that's where the real shit is going down, not at the so-called vitamin plant. The downside—I think Flynn somehow figured out who I am." Tito explained about their conflict at the park and how Tonia had intervened.

"Damn."

"Yeah, and whoever trashed my condo and took my personal cell—

if they can hack the fingerprint ID, they'll know I'm a reporter and that I communicate regularly with Doyle's daughter."

Pete groaned. This could be worst-case scenario. "Not good at all. We'd better keep our eye on Molly."

"My thought, exactly."

"And if they might know who you are," Pete continued, "I don't want you going back to your place. Drop the loaner at the police impound yard, grab your car, and meet me at Bea's in Santa Monica. You know how to get there?"

"Yep. But sorry, man. I'm gonna stop for some groceries, then I'm going home. Gonna sleep in my own bed tonight. My building has good security, so no worries."

There was dead air for a moment. Then Pete said, "Okay, but seriously watch your back."

"Roger that, Sarge."

35

Molly backed up against the cool tile wall so she could see more of herself in the bathroom mirror. Daddy would be satisfied. Her two-carat diamond earrings were luxe but not over-the-top. Hair was tied back in a perky ponytail, and the navy linen sheath was snug but not trampy. She wore red heels to kick a little color into the simple ensemble.

"You look pretty," Mary said. She slouched against the doorjamb with moist eyes gazing at her daughter.

"Allergies, Mama? Or are you worrying again about me growing up too fast?"

Mary's smile was sad. "All of the above, plus not liking you going out on the campaign trail with your father."

"At least I'm not living with him anymore." Molly applied a bit more powdery blush to her already rosy cheeks. "I know you detest him. And I don't like him either, but he *is* my father, and I promised a year ago that I'd help out with the election stuff if I could. Did you know brain research shows that breaking promises actually registers in our minds, showing up as emotional conflict?"

Mary blew out a frustrated sigh. "No, I didn't know that. But Molly, sometimes promises ought to be broken because they require more than you should give." She turned and headed back into the living room.

Molly felt the truth in her mother's words. She picked up her phone from the edge of the sink and dialed Tito. She wanted to hear his opinion. He'd texted her last night that he was done with the undercover gig and was on his way home. Strangely, she hadn't heard from him since. Voicemail again. "Tito, I'm getting worried. Please call me. I don't do well with anxiety."

Her mother popped back into the bathroom. "The limo's here, sweetheart."

She announced the arrival with a light tone, obviously trying to sound upbeat. Molly appreciated the attempt. She kissed her mother, grabbed her bag, and headed for the door. Then, Molly stopped and turned, a concerned look on her lovely face.

"What are you doing today all by yourself, Mama?"

"Going over to Santa Monica Police Department to talk to an old buddy of grandpa's."

Molly's face lit up. "About a job?"

"No, honey, no job. Just a little career advising and mostly catching up with a dear friend."

"Ah, okay, then. Have fun. See you later this afternoon. Tito and I are going to dinner at *El Coyote* tonight to celebrate his being back in town."

"That's nice to look forward to."

"For sure." Molly hesitated for an instant. "And Mom, I think you may be right about that promise." She turned and hurried out the door and down the walk toward the shiny black limo. The young driver, dressed in black trousers, a white shirt, and a purple bow tie, opened the door for her and winked.

Molly slid in next to her father, across from Dr. Pang and Burgess. They all looked stressed—wrinkled foreheads and tightly pressed lips. The Woodford Reserve Bourbon was open. Her dad liked a hit of expensive whiskey before he went on stage. His minions never refused to share a drink.

"Hello, everyone." Molly would be Miss Sunshine in their obviously tense day. Polls called Doyle the strong leader, so she wasn't sure why they weren't more upbeat.

"Hi, darling. You look gorgeous." Her dad leaned in to give her a peck on the cheek.

She tried not to flinch. He smelled of peppermints, probably to cloak the odor of the alcohol. "Thanks, Daddy."

Burgess and Dr. Pang mumbled greetings. The limo pulled onto Main Street, then turned toward the entrance to the I-10 freeway.

"So, where are we off to today, gentlemen?" Molly asked. Her father rubbed his head and smiled at her.

"Thousand Oaks. Not far. Rally at the civic center—should be a good crowd."

"TO's a nice town." She turned to Burgess and Pang. "I have a friend who took courses at Cal Lutheran there. I overheard you say you got your GED, Mr. Burgess. Congratulations. It must be hard to go back after being out of school for so long."

She noticed his dull gray eyes brighten. "Yeah, was tough at first. I'm taking a class at Santa Monica College this summer. Online, criminal justice."

Doyle suppressed a groan. Molly looked at him and frowned. "You should be proud of Burgess, Daddy. He's improving himself."

"He's got all he can handle working for me. School will just dilute his focus."

"He's in love with a teacher. Has to keep up. Right?" She looked over at the bodyguard and smiled.

Burgess gave up the barest of nods and busied himself on his cell phone.

Molly could feel herself begin to get agitated. The ants that sometimes skittered in her skull were waking. The limo was getting claustrophobic. These three men, so controlled and soulless, seemed to eat up the air. What would happen if she threw a few fireworks into the mix? She tugged at the neckline of her dress; it was starting to strangle her.

"I'm going out to dinner with my new boyfriend tonight, Tito Luna. You met him, Daddy. You were very rude. He's a paraplegic vet, went back to school and got his journalism degree. You'd like him, Mr. Burgess."

The man gazed out the window at the passing cars zooming onto the freeway entry ramp. Pang dug into his jacket pocket and pulled out a brown plastic pill container.

"We'll talk about this another time," Doyle said. "You're still way too vulnerable to be thinking about dating."

"But that's all I think about. What did you think about when you were my age, Daddy?"

Burgess chuckled, then turned it into a feigned cough. He continued to find interesting sights out the window.

Dr. Pang leaned toward Molly, offering her the bottle of meds. "I can see you're getting upset and uncomfortable, Molly, sweetheart. Try these vitamins. One a day and you'll be delighted with the calm they bring. An ancient Chinese medicinal. All organic and natural. I take them myself, have for years. My mother took them, too—lived to be ninety-eight."

She shrunk from the offered container. "What's this? Lorazepam or something? I'm done with that stuff; I'm done with being sick."

"Vitamins are about wellness, my dear, not sickness." He rattled the contents and proffered the bottle to Molly again.

From the corner of her eye, she saw her father's deep frown. That was enough to propel Molly to take the damn vitamins. Anything he disapproved of was fast becoming her behavior of choice. "Thank you, Doctor Pang." She accepted the bottle and tapped a bright pink pill into her hand. Was this the pill Tito was looking for? She downed it dry, slumped back into her seat, and slipped the container into her purse. "And Daddy, I think this is the last time I'll be attending your rallies. I love you, but it isn't good for me."

He glowered, then raised his eyebrows in a beatific smile. "Ah, sweetheart, you're just having a down day. I'm sure you'll feel differently soon."

She looked at him, face grim. "No, Daddy, I won't."

—

Bea looked up into Dexter's serious eyes. The softness in his face was quickly disappearing, signaling the fleeting end of boyhood and the sharper angularity of maturity. At moments when this recognition hit hard, Bea had to reign in her urge to stroke her child's cheek and shed a tear or three at the swift passage of time.

"Mom, you're not listening to me." Dexter bounced on his feet, clearly frustrated. "Aja and I stopped by Tito's at lunch, and he wasn't there. His car was gone, too. I talked to him last night, and he said he'd meet us."

Bea pushed back her chair. "He might've just run out on a quick errand. Gas, toothpaste, ATM—who knows."

"Huh-uh. The vibes are bad. We looked in the windows, and the place seemed deserted."

"Pete talked with him before midnight, and all was fine." Bea checked her watch. "Let's give Tito a couple hours to show up, okay? He must be stressed and really tired. Maybe he forgot you were coming."

"No way. We were bringing barbecue from Baby Blues. He's a *big* fan." Dexter rubbed at his bristly chin. "I think you should give Pete a heads-up. Ask him to send out somebody to do a welfare check to make sure everything's good."

Bea leaned back in her chair. "Dexter..."

He crossed his arms on his chest. "Mom, I'm serious."

Removing her reading glasses, Bea sighed. "Before you get all freaked out, let me call Mary, see if Molly has heard anything."

Aja stepped into the office. "She hasn't heard anything. I just talked to her. They're supposed to go out for dinner tonight. She sent him a bunch of texts. Nothing."

Bea felt a niggling of concern begin to flicker. Maybe Dexter was right. "Okay, I'll call Pete. He'll get a cop to go over there."

—

As Doyle's guests arrived, he remained dressed in his signature sand-colored silk pajamas and robe, once again channeling Playboy magazine's deceased founder, Hugh Hefner. The rally in Thousand Oaks had gone well, and he was feeling good.

Dr. Pang, Neckar, Burgess, and this time, Flynn, filed into the living room. Engrossed in texting, Burgess lingered at his usual watch position near the door. Somehow it felt like Burgess was going soft, and they needed a new strong arm on the team. Flynn fit the bill. In khaki camo pants and a tight-fitting black T-shirt, the dude looked every inch a mercenary for hire. And Doyle paid top dollar.

The men took their customary seats, with Pang and the contents of his briefcase spreading across most of the big sofa. As always, he perched dead center near the tray of coffee and sweets. Doyle settled into a new, throne-like leather chair he'd just purchased. It was a good six inches higher than the couch. A big pitcher of Bloody Marys rested within easy reach. Fuck coffee and Danish.

The two women, Kellogg and Thompson, wanted nothing to do with the operations anymore. They were the chemistry geeks, rarely venturing out of the new state-of-the-art lab. Doyle had been told Claire Thompson was still smarting from her affair with Pine. She'd actually fallen for the fake news bastard. They'd have to watch her as a potentially weak link.

Chee was last to arrive, breathless and animated as usual. The only seating left was the footstool. He hesitated for an instant, then obediently sat down and pulled some notes from the breast pocket of his light-blue linen suit. The kid was beginning to dress more like Pang every day.

"Let's begin with a summary from each of you," Doyle said, keeping his voice somber as a priest's. He drained Bloody Mary number two and poured another.

Chee twitched and waved his notes like he was swatting flies. "I'll start." He cleared his throat. "The social media platform on the Dark Web is complete, including product info and ordering instructions. I hope you all enjoyed last night's demo. We already have over a thousand potential customers who're on a waiting list and will be contacted as soon as we go live on Monday."

Neckar leaned forward, knobby knees spreading wide. He

reminded Doyle of a praying mantis. "Accounting is all set up. Payments in cryptocurrency. And the offshore accounts are fully engaged. A big day coming up, gentlemen." The dour smile on the Kraut's face was the closest Doyle had seen the bastard get to an emotional outburst.

Doyle shifted his focus to Burgess, then Flynn. "So, the only fly in the ointment seems to be the punk reporter, Tito Luna. Thoughts? Anyone?" He already had the obvious answer.

Burgess hesitated and Flynn jumped in. "I'll take care of him, boss."

Doyle nodded. Pang bit into another sweet roll. Neckar flared his thin nostrils.

"Okay, then, Flynn. Make it happen. Tonight, yeah?"

Burgess eyeballed Flynn, then Doyle, and shrugged. "Fine by me."

"Okay, Flynn. Luna's at the storage unit in Pacoima. Burgess'll give you the details. After 10:00 p.m., the place is deserted. Get it done."

"Yes, sir, Mr. Doyle." The fake cop's eyes shone like shiny ball bearings. He was made for this shit.

36

"He's gone?" Bea was stunned. Her fingers grazed the yellow crime scene tape that surrounded Tito Luna's car and the immediate area.

She and Lucy stood with Pete in the parking lot of Vons Market on Sepulveda Boulevard in West LA. Groceries had spilled onto the pavement next to Tito's abandoned SUV. The smell of milk beginning to sour wafted from a broken carton, its contents curdled on the warm blacktop. A burrito had been stomped flat. While an LAPD crime scene tech snapped photos, a detective with short straight hair and dark skin joined the threesome.

Pete introduced him as Sanjay Bakshi from LAPD Vice. When Pete explained Lucy's and Bea's involvement in the investigation, Bakshi was welcoming, unlike a lot of cops the two women had dealt with over the years.

"An employee collecting shopping carts this morning thought these discarded groceries looked a little suspicious," he explained while perusing the area. "The manager came out around lunchtime and called it in." He turned to Pete. "Car's registered to your guy, Tito

Luna. I hear you just did a welfare visit at his place of residence."

Pete nodded. "He lives in LAPD's jurisdiction but was working an undercover assignment out in Thermal with the LA county sheriff, so we took the welfare call. Tito was fine around 11:30 last night when we spoke. He'd just arrived in from the desert. Was going to stop for groceries, then head to his condo. Appears he never made it."

"Did you find his phone?" Bea peered into the front of the car where the tech processed contents of the glove compartment.

Bakshi shook his head. "Nope."

"What about the surveillance cameras?" Lucy pointed at an overhead unit affixed to a light post.

"I was just about to go in and take a look at what they got," Bakshi said. "Come on, maybe you'll see someone you recognize."

Bea and Lucy followed the two cops through the upscale supermarket to a back stairway, past boxes of produce and massive freezing units, into the store manager's neat office. In a small adjoining room arrayed with monitors, security cameras watched the inside of the market, particularly the cash registers, along with four wide views of the parking lot. The operations manager, a man in his mid-fifties wearing a navy golf shirt with the Vons logo, had the previous night's recording queued up and ready to view. Pete, Sanjay, Lucy, and Bea crowded around the monitor as the manager pressed *play*.

"There he is." Bea pointed to a Jeep Wrangler driving onto the lot. It stopped next to the cart return nearest the store's entrance. Tito climbed out of the car, a little shaky on his legs. He went directly into the building without passing other customers. Nearly closing time, there was less than a dozen vehicles in the vicinity captured by the cameras.

The manager fast-forwarded the recording. "Here's the next activity."

Five minutes and seven seconds had elapsed on the digital readout when a light-colored, unmarked Dodge panel van pulled in next to Tito's ride.

Lucy squinted and leaned in close. "Damn, the license plates have been obscured with something."

Sanjay said, "I'll have the techs check the trash bins in case coverings were dumped when the abductors were out of camera range. They likely wouldn't risk being on the roads with concealed plates."

Bea's stomach felt increasingly queasy. Was he still alive? Was Tito suffering? She shouldn't have let Pete talk her into approving this high-risk assignment. The kid was too green. Now, how the hell were they going to find him in a metropolitan area of more than ten million people?

The manager fast-forwarded again. The next action happened fast. Tito went to his car, a bag of groceries in his left hand. He pulled the fob from his pocket and beeped open the car. He reached for the door handle just as a large man dressed in black with a balaclava hiding his face hopped from inside the van and grabbed him. Tito dropped the groceries and struggled. He hit the dude with a solid right hook, but the perpetrator landed a brutal kick across Tito's prosthetic knees. The kid went down hard.

"What assholes," Lucy said. "They were totally aware of his vulnerability."

"Tito was made before he even left Thermal." Pete's cell phone buzzed but he ignored it.

The security recording continued as the attacker dragged Tito into the van. A second person, likely the driver, seemed to stab Tito in the neck. The vehicle's sliding side door shut.

"Drugged?" Lucy asked.

"A safe bet," Sanjay said. "Your man is hauled inside the van and subdued, the door shuts, and off they go. Thirty seconds from attack to exit. Very slick. They've done this kind of thing before."

Pete's phone sounded again. He huffed and pulled it from his pocket, took a look, and frowned. "The report on the substance Tito collected is in. The toxicologist from the narcotics analysis unit wants to meet with me in person. He's on his way to my office with somebody from the DEA. Gotta run."

"He say anything about what it is?" Lucy asked.

"Nope. Nada. Wants an in-person with me in thirty minutes. I'll keep you posted. And Bakshi, thanks. We'll talk later tonight."

The man nodded. "Sounds good. I'll put out an APB, finish up the crime scene analysis, and have his car towed to forensics. This friend of yours could be in some pretty hot water."

—

Bea and Lucy stood together leaning against Bea's silver Beemer. The Vons lot was now full of shoppers stopping for groceries on their way home from work. The sun had dropped behind the building, and shadows grew long.

Bea felt drained and full of guilt for letting Tito take the assignment. She was responsible. He disappeared on her watch.

Lucy put a comforting arm around Bea's shoulder. "So, what's our plan, girlfriend?"

"I'm going to fill Mary in." Bea checked her phone. "She's texted me about ten times. Dexter has, too. And I'll be biting my nails, waiting to hear from Pete on the tox report. An in-person meeting spells serious shit."

Lucy nodded. "And I'm going over to talk to Mark Lee and find out what the hell is going on with the contracts and his relationship to Pang. Can't wait another minute on that. Sorry."

Bea shrugged off Lucy's arm. "Lucia, you have to wait until we can get you some backup. I'm afraid for your safety, girlfriend. If he's involved with Pang and Doyle, anything could happen."

"Lee would never hurt me."

"People can do really nasty, unconscionable things when their backs are against the wall. If his business and his job are in jeopardy, who knows what his reaction will be?"

"I'll take my chances. If he's in this mess with Pang, we have to know." Lucy turned toward her car. "Later, Beebs."

Bea nabbed her friend by the shirtsleeve. "At least wait until we've heard back from Pete. If all we have are more vitamins, then y'all got nada to hang on Lee or anybody else."

Scowling, Lucy pulled away toward her ride.

Bea followed her. "Okay, are we agreed? You wait? I can't let you do this. And you know I can take you if I have to."

Lucy rolled her eyes. "I dunno, you've been pretty slack at your workouts lately."

Bea flexed her neck in a dance move. "We gonna have us a girl fight here in the Vons parking lot? That'll make it two brawls we've been in over the last week."

Lucy stopped and laughed out loud. "Okay, let's not push our luck. I'll wait. But only until we get the word from Pete."

"Deal. And I don't think you're faster. I'm very fast. NCAA Division I women's b-ball fast."

"Ancient history. I'm faster. Been doing some serious training since the baby was born." Lucy dashed toward her car.

Bea feigned a move after Lucy but stopped to pull her ringing phone out of her pocket. She took a quick glance, then ran full blast as her friend backed out of a parking space.

"Luce! Wait!" Bea waved her arms.

Lucy stopped the car and rolled down her window. "What's happening?"

Breathless, Bea leaned in. "Aja has dinner for us and found something interesting. Meet me at your condo in fifteen, 'kay? Everybody's there."

Lucy nodded. An impatient horn honked behind them.

—

An hour later, Bea, Lucy, Mary, Aja, and Dexter were gathered in Santa Monica at Lucy's dining room table amid half-finished Panera salads, trolling for some new, helpful evidence.

"So, what do we have?" Lucy stood and grabbed a pitcher of iced tea from the kitchen island. Anxious and needing to move, she rounded the table filling half-empty glasses and picking up used plates and utensils.

Aja bit into a hunk of crusty bread and tapped on her laptop keyboard, ignoring the crumbs that dropped between the buttons. "Just a sec, let me show you something."

"Is Molly okay?" Dexter asked Mary. The girl hadn't joined the group and was holed up in her darkened bedroom.

Mary sighed. "She was with her dad campaigning today. Didn't go too well between them. And then Tito's disappearance. She's pretty depressed."

"Should I go talk to her?" Dexter pushed back his chair.

"No, but thanks, honey," Mary said. "I think she's finally sleeping, which is good."

He nodded, not appearing completely convinced.

Aja jumped in, eyes glued to her screen. "Okay, here we go. This may have no relevance to anything, but I discovered that Doyle owns two storage units. One in West LA and one in Pacoima. The one in West LA is in his own name. The one in Pacoima is under that Keeter Doyle business you mentioned a while ago, Mary. Something with his uncle back East."

"Good find, Aja." Bea smiled at her young protégé. "Doyle's had some long-term dealings with Uncle Keeter."

Mary's eyes narrowed. "I knew about the local unit, but not about anything in Pacoima. That's way far out in the valley. Why would he have a unit there? And under Keeter's name?"

Lucy caught Bea's eye. "Tito?"

The room went silent. Molly stood in the bedroom doorway, her coppery hair a mess. "You think Tito might be there? You think my own father—" She began to shake and gurgle. Her eyes rolled up into her head. Dexter flew out of his seat. His chair toppled over. He grabbed Molly before she hit the floor. The girl spasmed in his arms.

Mary screamed and ran to her child.

Bea dialed 911.

Lucy rushed into Molly's bedroom and turned on the light. She scanned the room. The girl's purse was thrown onto a chair. Lucy rifled thought it. Nothing. She rushed into the adjoining bathroom. On the counter next to the sink was a bottle of fuckin' pink pills.

37

Lucy joined Bea at the window into Molly's hospital room. She handed Bea a latte from a nearby coffee machine. The scent overlaid the hospital's fearsome, medicinal stench.

Mary and Aja sat at Molly's side. Dexter leaned against the wall behind them watching his unconscious friend. Monitors beeped. At the station down the hall, nurses and techs laughed.

The sound of cheer stung Lucy's sensibilities. "Anything new on her condition?"

"The seizure was a bad one. And damn. I still haven't heard from Pete on the substance from the plant and what the hell it is. Called him a bunch of times." Bea began to pace. "It would help the docs to know if those pink 'vitamins' triggered Molly's condition. I guess maybe we'll understand more when her bloodwork comes back from the lab." She stopped pacing, her eyes probing Lucy's. "How are you and yours doing?"

Lucy took a hefty gulp of bitter caffeine. "I just talked to Michael. He and Elsa and the baby are doing fine. It's good for him to change some diapers, get puked and peed on, and bond with his son. The little dude just went down for the count. He's been sleeping through the night. Praise the Lord."

"Ah, so glad to hear it. Parental sleep deprivation is an absolute killer."

"Speaking of killer, I'm going to go crazy here, Bea. There's nothing we can do but stare at Molly and pray. I think we should check out Pacoima."

"It's late." Bea glanced at the pizza-sized clock on the wall above the nurse's station that read 10:08 p.m. She held the warm cup of coffee in her hands and contemplated it for a moment. "Maybe you should head home to your family, Luce."

"I'll be leaving for New York in four days, and then I'll be home with Henry twenty-four seven in a city I don't know. You and I may never have a chance to work together again, and this story is a big one. I'm staying with it." Tears welled in her stormy blue eyes.

"We will always find a way to work together. We're partners." Bea gave Lucy a long hug, then sighed. "Okay, let's go to Pacoima. I'll leave Pete a message that we're on our way out there. He'll be pissed, but that's what you get when you ignore your lady friend's phone calls, right?"

"Definitely. Let's take my Jeep. We'll fade into the background if we need to. Your Beemer's too fancy."

"It is fancy, isn't it? I love fancy. Let me get my Glock from the glove box."

"Is that the Glock 19 your brother gave you for your birthday a couple years ago? The very firearm you swore you had no use for?"

"Yep, the very one. And I guess I've found it handier than I'd imagined. You never know in this line of business, right?"

Those words chilled Lucy to the bone.

—

Tito felt as if he was actually dying of thirst, like his skin and bones were shriveling up and he'd soon become mummified. Maybe that was their plan.

The air was tepid in the dark storage unit. He smelled moldering cardboard boxes, old motor oil, and his own stink. His wrists were zip-tied to the rear bumper of an old Chevy truck. They'd removed his prosthetics and tossed them into a dark corner. Every muscle ached. A ball-peen hammer banged at his skull.

Duct tape and a sour-tasting sock sealed Tito's mouth shut. He could hardly breathe. This was it. This was where his story ended—no opportunity for life, love, kids, the house on a hill. He sniffed away a tear. Fuck. He listened to too much country music.

Tito hadn't heard any movement besides his own scuffling and the dull thrum of the ventilation system in a while. He knew he'd slept but had no idea how long. He was beginning to doze again when he heard fumbling with the padlock to the roll-up door of the unit he was stashed in. Panic blew through his chest. *Mierda*. What now?

The steel door rolled up. A bright fluorescent light from the hallway outside the unit burned his retinas. He flinched.

Flynn stood in the doorway, his stance dark and predatory.

Tito swallowed hard. This meeting was not going to be pleasant. His eye caught the shape of a pistol on the man's hip. Looked like a semiautomatic. Was it going to be a quick shot to the head? Or torture. Electricity? Near drowning? He was scared shitless but also feeling a surge of fury.

The asshole ambled to a far corner of the unit and returned, tossing the prosthetics next to Tito. Flynn pulled a box cutter from his pocket and leaned down. Tito squeezed his eyes shut. Fuck, was the dude going to run that blade across his carotid?

Hesitating for an instant, Flynn sliced the zip ties holding Tito's wrists. He ripped off the duct tape and pulled the sock from Tito's mouth. The young reporter gagged, ran his tongue over his battered lips and tasted blood.

Flynn sneered. "Put those sticks on. I'm not gonna carry you outta here. You're gonna walk."

Despite hands that he could barely move, Tito experienced a glimmer of relief as he awkwardly crawled across the floor and grabbed the old friends who helped him rise up every day. With them, he might have a prayer. He flexed his fingers until a prickle of feeling returned to his phalanges, then lifted his pant legs and awkwardly attached his prosthetics. His stubs were sore and angry. He moved slowly, buying time, then grimaced and struggled to stand.

Flynn offered a hand. Tito croaked out a laugh. He would've spit on the bastard for that demeaning offer of help, but there was no saliva left in his mouth.

Unholstering his gun, the dirty cop waved it toward the hallway.

"You're a piece of work, Flynn," Tito rasped. He stepped into the light and spotted a security camera. He thought about a quick move, then felt the hard tip of a muzzle against his backbone. They passed eight units with padlocked roll-up doors, then took a side exit out of the building. The fresh air on his skin was bracing.

A single pole light illuminated the empty parking lot. Tito wanted to make a run for it but knew he was too weak. He'd end up making a crawl for it, and that wouldn't get him anywhere but closer to death with a mouth full of gravel. The van was directly beneath the lamp. Flynn opened the sliding door and herded Tito into the vehicle.

Tito sat on the floor across from the door. Pale light filtered through the windshield. "So, now what? You taking me to the desert to shoot me and dump me in a shallow grave?"

"Nope." Flynn handed Tito a bottle of water.

Grabbing it with shaking hands, he unscrewed the cap and guzzled down the contents, spilling half of it down his shirt. Flynn offered another bottle which Tito wanted but ignored. "Fuck you, asshole."

His thoughts went to Molly, and he wanted to cry. After surviving multiple deployments, injuries that almost took his life, years of rehab—and now on the brink of a real life, it was done.

Flynn's face was slashed by dark shadows. "You're not gonna die, Carlos Hernandez, or whatever the hell your name is. I'm here to help you."

Tito coughed out laughter. "Yeah, right. Help me right into the ground."

Flynn pulled a shiny metallic item from his waistband. It was not a gun. The box cutter again? A screwdriver? Flynn pushed the object toward him.

Tito froze. "Are you shitting me?" He felt wildly light-headed. What was going on? Could this be real?

38

Driving though the aging, poorly illuminated industrial park on the northern edge of the San Fernando Valley, Lucy spotted the self-storage facility just ahead on the left. She began to slow.

"Keep going!" Bea admonished. "We don't want to look like we're casing the place."

Lucy stepped back on the gas and cruised by the dark Valley Vu U-Store-It warehouses. An aging, dirty panel van was a hulking shadow at the edge of the lot. "Look, Bea." A shot of adrenaline tightened her chest.

Bea craned her neck for a better view. "Shit, I think it's the one from Vons. Looks empty."

"They must be in the warehouse." Lucy doused the headlights and turned into the parking area of an auto glass replacement shop several buildings down. Despite being closed, a neon OPEN sign still burned orange in the window. A single truck with side racks for hauling windshields was parked in the lot.

Bea fished the Glock from her purse and stuffed it into her denim jacket pocket. "We gotta get to Tito before they bring him out in a rolled-up carpet or something horrific."

"*If* he's in there." Lucy pointed to the glove compartment. "Hand me my gun."

"When did y'all start carrying?"

"*Moi*? I don't carry."

"Uh-huh." Bea raised her chin in the way she usually did before passing judgement. "Got a permit?"

"Of course." Lucy rolled her eyes. "Could be pushing the expiration date a little bit, though."

"A couple months?"

"Maybe a couple years." Lucy snickered.

Bea reached into the glove box, hesitated, then grabbed the dull, black grip. "Shit. What is this? A damn cannon?"

"My uncle's. Was the only handgun he had in the house. I'm a dead-on shot with a rifle. This is kind of in-between." Lucy snickered again.

Bea pulled out a Smith & Wesson .44 Magnum. She hefted it over to Lucy. "Okay, Dirty Harriet Follow my lead. Try not to drop that sucker—I don't want to get blown away."

They pressed tight against the building, hunched low, and scurried across a weed-choked alley next to an auto detailing shop. Several smashed windshields leaned against the stucco wall. Lucy pointed out a security camera above the door. Trying to stay out of its field of view, they skittered along a narrow sidewalk toward a three-foot hedge of spindly oleander bushes. Beyond that was the Valley Vu U-Store-It parking lot.

"Let's get to the van." Bea took a deep breath. "Then, we'll move to the dumpster next to the gate and into the place."

"Roger that." Lucy rolled her neck and adjusted her grip on the .44. God willing, she wouldn't have to fire it. The recoil was brutal, and the damage it could do to a human being was chilling. She hoped the intimidation factor alone would be enough to slow down any asshole who looked into its long, black barrel.

Just as they reached the van, Tito emerged from the warehouse. A man walked tight behind him holding a gun. The dude was dressed in dark clothes and a baseball cap. He holstered his piece in a shoulder harness. Was he trying to take Tito somewhere else and murder him? Heart pounding so loudly she thought it would give her away, Lucy watched from behind the rear bumper.

Bea moved from the driver's side and crouched next to Lucy at the rear of the vehicle. "On the count of five," she whispered, "I'll approach from here. You get to the front and cover me with the peashooter." Immediately, she started the silent count on her fingers.

One, two... Lucy's hurried steps were muted by the grating metallic sound of the vehicle's door sliding open. She reached the front on *five*. Tito crawled inside, exchanging muffled words with his captor.

Simultaneously, Bea made her move. She sprung forward on her basketball player legs, ducking and weaving.

"Hands up, motherfucker!"

"What the hell?" Flynn's mouth fell open. He hesitated for an instant.

"Now!" Bea's serious-as-shit voice even scared Lucy.

Flynn's hands rose.

"Get his gun," Bea barked. Lucy came up fast behind him.

"Shit! Black Widow and Wonder Woman." Tito broke into hysterical laughter. He crawled out of the van and teetered over beside Bea.

Lucy stepped up directly behind the perpetrator. "Hands on the roof," she growled. "Spread your legs."

The guy hesitated again.

Lucy took aim. "On the roof. Now, asshole."

He eyed Lucy's .44 and obeyed. "Wait, you got this wrong. I'm a cop."

Bea widened her stance. "And I'm Beyoncé."

Lucy quickly patted him down. Pulling a pistol from its nylon holster, she noticed that the barrel was threaded to accommodate a silencer. She stuck the gun into the back of her jeans. She frisked him one more time. "We're clear."

Bea kept her Glock aimed at Flynn's center mass. She grabbed the phone from her pocket and handed it to Tito. "Call Pete."

Trembling, he took the phone and began to dial. "This dude's okay, Bea. He's not who we thought he was."

"Huh-uh. He's the fake Thermal cop and the frickin' security guard at the pill mill. He was gonna murder you, Tito."

"No, he saved me. Really. Check his creds."

"What?" Bea lowered her gun, just a bit, then raised it again.

"Truth, man." Flynn's fingers tapped on the roof of the van. His eyes skipped to Lucy's .44, then back to Bea.

Lucy grabbed a wallet-looking item from his hand and moved quickly away again. She tilted the wallet toward the pale light. "Holy shit. This looks legit."

"It is legit," Flynn snarled.

"What's going on?" Bea vibrated with nervous energy.

Lucy cleared her throat. "We have with us here Officer Christopher Flynn. Drug Enforcement Agency, Washington, DC."

Before any more could be said, an LA county sheriff's cruiser tore into the lot, lights flashing. It skidded to a stop next to the van, gravel spraying.

Pete jumped out of the passenger side. "What the fuck?"

"He's comin' in hot," Lucy whispered.

Bea went rigid.

"Drop the damn gun, Bea." Pete's voice was steely, like he was giving an armed felon his last chance before a tactical squad moved in. "He's one of ours."

Slowly, she holstered her weapon. "Okay, I just found out."

Pete's eyes turned to Lucy. Her stomach lurched.

"And what the hell is that, Vega?"

Lucy flinched. He'd never called her Vega. The .44 dangled from her hand. She shrugged, and with no place to stash the big gun, she set it on the ground.

Pete's hands were fisted. He paced like a madman. "What the fuck are you two doing out here?"

Bea snapped out of the shock she seemed to be in. "Tito's life was in danger. And I tried calling you a bunch of times, left messages. You never—"

"You're *not* fuckin' cops. You're reporters. You report, you take pictures and write stories." He scowled. "You do not *become* the news—like, two dead women found murdered at Santa Clarita warehouse."

Lucy had never seen Pete so upset. Bea stepped back. Tito slumped against the van.

A tall, white-haired African-American man finished up a radio call and slid from the cruiser's driver's seat. He wore a cliché navy-blue DEA windbreaker.

"I'm Special Agent-in-Charge Ron Gold, out of the Southwest Field Office." He aimed the announcement at Bea, Lucy, and Tito. Stepping forward, he slapped Flynn's shoulder. "All okay here, agent?"

"Sorry about this, boss." Flynn scowled at the group as if they were gum wads on his shoe. "Shit news media."

"Watch your mouth," Lucy growled.

Usually fast with a slap-down to anyone dissing the fourth estate, Bea barely responded. Shaking, she said to Pete, "You coulda told me about this."

He strode toward her again, then veered away. "I don't have to tell you everything I'm working on. In fact, I tell you too damn much, way too much, and that's gonna stop. We're *not* partners."

Lucy winced. Bea looked as if she'd been slapped.

Gold stepped up and rested a hand on Pete's shoulder. "Calm down, Detective. We'll sort this out."

Pete punched the air. Lucy could feel his need to slam a fist into something.

The special agent's phone chirped. He raised a finger, then turned to take the call.

Flynn glared at Lucy and held out his hand. It was square and calloused. "My service weapon."

Pulling the firearm from her waistband, she felt there was something off about the guy, but she couldn't identify the trigger. She'd seen him before, and not just on the security tape. Handing him the weapon, he inspected the thing as if being in her possession had somehow corrupted it. They evil-eyed each other.

"So, did you finally find out what the pink pill was?" Bea asked Pete.

"As you know, we've been waiting to hear. Molly's still hospitalized."

He pretended to ignore her.

Tito gasped. "Molly's sick? Again? What's going on? I need to get to her. Now!"

Lucy patted his shoulder. "Soon. We'll be on our way soon. She's okay."

Pete planted his feet and crossed his arms on his chest like a recalcitrant kid. Lucy rolled her eyes.

"Don't be an asshole, Detective," Bea said, her hurt turning to anger. "What are we dealing with here?" She glanced at Flynn and Gold.

Looking ready to flee what was beginning to seem more like a domestic than a run-of-the-mill turf war, Flynn moved to the van and slid the side door closed. He rounded the hood, then climbed into the driver's seat and switched on the ignition. "Check in with you later, boss," he called to Gold through the open windows.

Back on the phone, the special agent nodded acknowledgment. Flynn pulled onto the dark road that would take him to the freeway.

Bea's anger and frustration were growing. "Pete. You need to talk to me."

"No, I don't." He paced through the shadows, shaking his head like a stubborn horse. Then he stopped, took a deep breath, and seemed to rein himself in. "Okay." He cleared his throat. "It's similar to benzodiazepine, like Xanax or Valium. It's a tranquilizer, not an opioid like we first thought. It's something new."

Agent Gold, now off the cellphone, stepped up next to Pete. "Unfortunately, stage three trials were never completed in this country, and those done in China are suspect. They were conducted by our Doctor Pang whose Wuhan area pharmaceutical lab was shut down for lack of regulation. Two years later, he turned up with a postdoc fellowship at Berkeley."

"We know about the Berkeley connection." Bea chewed at her lip.

Gold took a deep breath and checked his phone again. "Detective Anthony has assured me that we can trust you and that all this is off the record for now."

Bea nodded. "Of course."

Lucy shook her head in accord.

Pete continued. "So, about this drug—in a significant number of people, this shit can cause convulsions and perhaps even permanent brain damage."

Tito moaned. "Fuck. Her father gave her poison to shut her up."

"We don't know that," Pete said. He redirected the conversation. "So, man, what do you remember about your abduction from Vons last night?"

"They hit me fast and hard when I was dead tired and had let down my guard." Tito wiped tears and grime from his face. "I was on my home turf, know what I mean? Been in that store a thousand times. Stupid. So careless. All I remember was that I was in the same van that Flynn's driving now. Smells like old takeout and gasoline. I woke up in the storage unit here, maybe an hour ago. My prosthetics were gone, and I was zip-tied to a car bumper. Flynn showed up, and I thought I was dead meat 'til he showed me his badge."

Tito looked to Lucy like he was about to pass out.

"Go home and get some rest," Pete said, his voice finally calm. "We'll need a full statement from you, as well as a debrief on your assignment in Thermal. Can you get to the station tomorrow around lunchtime?"

"Yeah, sure."

Gold turned to Pete. "That call was headquarters. The federal search warrants are all in order for the morning. At or near 5:00 a.m., Pang, Chee, Doyle, Kellogg, Thompson, and Burgess are gonna feel the heat. The accountant, Neckar, has disappeared. Flynn's been our man undercover in the desert for three and a half months, so he and his team will hit the labs in Thermal. They're coordinating with the FBI and the Riverside sheriffs."

"You think Burgess or Doyle killed David Pine?" Lucy asked the special agent. The warrants were critical, but she wasn't sure if any of this was getting them closer to fingering the murderer.

"We think it's Burgess, Doyle's enforcer, but we got shit to prove it," Gold said.

"I'm going to check Pine's condo one last time," Lucy said, almost to herself.

"It's been done, Lucy, so stay out of it," Pete said. "And Burgess is mine. Gonna drill him down in front of his sweet little schoolteacher until he gives us everything he's got."

Special Agent Gold nodded approval.

A large, dark-blue truck with the county logo on the side pulled off the road and bounced across the gravel in their direction.

"Crime scene's here." Gold directed the vehicle up toward the warehouse entrance. Two techs in full PPE exited the vehicle. He turned again to Pete. "Let's go, Detective."

"Five in the morning?" Bea said. "You're doing the raid just before dawn?"

Pete's eyes narrowed to slits in the gloom. "Yeah, and if I see you anywhere in the vicinity, I'll arrest you for obstruction. Understand?"

Tito nodded. "Yeah, sure." He appeared to curl into himself like a beaten animal.

The charged atmosphere seemed to lose its shimmer as Pete disappeared into the storage facility with the DEA special agent and the crime techs, leaving Bea, Lucy, and Tito alone in the darkness.

39

Lucy kept her arm around Tito as he limped to the Jeep. She settled him in the backseat, wrapped him in a slightly grungy but warm beach blanket, and handed him a fresh bottle of water. Then, she dialed the hospital.

Bea tossed Tito a couple peanut butter Clif bars scavenged from the bottom of her purse. "We can do an In-N-Out Burger drive-through on the way back. You need some calories."

Tito adjusted his prosthetics. "Thanks, but what I really need—"

Lucy passed her phone to Tito. "It's Mary, she's with Molly at the hospital."

"Oh, my God, thank you." He seized it like a fast shortstop diving for a grounder.

"Hello, Mary. Yeah. Is she okay? Can she talk?"

Mary must have first demanded an update on everybody's condition at the warehouse, because Tito grudgingly rushed through the lowdown. Then there was a pause, and the tone dropped to quiet and intimate. Had to be Molly now on the line. He lay down and covered himself with the blanket.

Lucy started the car and drove out onto the road, heading toward the freeway. In her passenger side mirror, a tech was putting up lights next to the CSI truck.

Bea set the radio to a late-night country station where crooners warbled about lost love, hot nights, and cold beer. "I only listen to this stuff on remote back roads or lonely freeways late at night," she said in explanation.

Lucy glanced over at her friend in the greenish glow from the dash. Tears streamed down Bea's face. Pete had been a real prick.

"So, what's up with your man?" Lucy asked. "Never seen him so seriously upset."

"I know. Maybe this is the end." Bea pushed hard on the pressure point between her eyes. "Ah, shit. I do know we love each other, but bottom line, he wants a traditional wife and family. That's who he is. I'm always gonna be riding the edge. Never gonna be baking brownies."

"He adores you," Lucy said.

"Yeah, but as you've reminded me many times—that may not be enough to make things work." Bea dabbed her eyes with a tissue. "He's the sweetest lover I've ever had. Will kill me to see him with somebody else." She forced a laugh, but it caught in her throat. "Now, you're leaving me, too."

Lucy reached across and squeezed Bea's hand for a moment. The strangling emptiness of loss, the glass with the eternal hole in the bottom that would never hold water, was in both their sorry grasps. She sighed and offered Bea bullshit words of comfort. "Relationships suck. Leaving sucks. It all sucks." Now they were both leaking cups of tears. Lucy blinked away the evidence.

The Jeep sped down the ramp onto the freeway and joined the artery of speeding white headlights. Six Flags Magic Mountain amusement park sparkled across the road.

Tito moaned from the backseat. "Molly sounds so weak." He sat up and fastened his seat belt. "What's our ETA?"

Lucy caught his gaze in the rearview, relieved to change the focus from her pain to his. "Thirty minutes, kiddo. What did she say?"

"She'll be in the hospital overnight, but she's doing much better.

Doyle—that motherfucker."

Bea took a long gulp from a commuter cup. "We're gonna nail his ass, Tito. Tomorrow could be the day."

"Maybe. But these people are smart. And Molly said she doesn't think Burgess murdered David Pine."

That caught Lucy by surprise. "No?"

"She thinks Burgess is pulling away from Doyle and trying to straighten out his own life. Doyle's really pissed about it, and that's how Flynn was able to wormhole into their organization. He's a master opportunist."

"That's why he's so good at his undercover job," Lucy said. *Too good, weirdly good.*

Bea blew her nose. Took another swig from her cup and coughed. "We'll see what Pete ferrets out of Burgess in the morning. So, who does she think killed Pine?"

Tito hesitated. "She thinks it's Flynn."

Lucy's head spun. "But he's DEA undercover. Pete and Gold vouched for him."

He shrugged. "I know it sounds kinda bizarro, but the guy seems to live his life in perpetual lies. A fake Thermal cop, a fake security goon, a kidnapper—who knows what else. And DEA or not, he's got a pure evil steak a mile wide."

Tito's comment kick-started Lucy into thinking more about Flynn. She conjured him in her mind and tried to identify the funky, skin-crawling aura he oozed.

"Is it possible," Bea said, "that he's a double agent?"

"If he's actually working for Doyle and Pang, he could score a hell of a lot more bank than what he gets as a federal narc," Tito added.

Then it dawned. Lucy banged the steering wheel. "I remember where I first saw Flynn."

"Where?" Tito leaned forward.

"At Pine's funeral. It was him. Snuck up behind me when I was trying to keep a low profile in a grove of trees, shooting pics of the mourners. He showed up just as Pine's boss at the Daily, Pine's supposed girlfriend, Claire Thompson, along with her BFF Sandra

Kellogg, all arrived in a limo."

"We know Kellogg and Thompson are chemists at the plant," Bea said. "But what're they doing with Lance Ludlow, the LA Daily News chief?" She chewed her thumbnail for a moment. "Wait, there's a tie-in between the Doyle-Pang cartel and the media. I didn't make the connection. Mary discovered that Doyle, through Keeter Enterprises again, bought a major share in the newspaper a few months ago. Shit."

Lucy nodded. "I remember that. And at the cemetery, Flynn tried to bully me into not taking photos, called me a paparazzi. But his phone rang, he turned away, and I bolted downhill. I didn't see him at the funeral service or later at the gravesite."

"You never got a picture of the bastard?" Tito asked.

"No, damn. Pete got ID badge copies of the cemetery staffers from their HR Department, and Flynn wasn't in the mix."

"Maybe he was working on the Pang-Doyle payroll as part of his undercover gig at that point," Tito said.

"Maybe. Felt really ominous," Lucy said. "My hackles were seriously standing at attention. Like you said, Tito, there was something pure evil about his presence."

"Here's a good picture of him from the Thermal warehouse." Tito passed his cell to Bea. She studied it, then held it up for Lucy who took a quick glance.

Bea peered over her shoulder at Tito and handed the phone back. "That's the creep. When he showed you his badge back there in the van, did you get the feeling Flynn was on your side?"

"I dunno. Could be he was just trying to get me to chill. I was pretty amped." He texted the photos to the women.

There was a long silence in the Jeep. Then Bea said, "All we have are gut feelings."

Lucy rubbed at her neck, agitated. "Tomorrow, I'm going back to David Pine's condo. I don't care if Pete thinks they covered it all or not. With the zip drive he sent to you, the guy obviously felt information had to be hidden to protect himself and his story. Maybe there's something still stashed. And I also want to show Flynn's picture around the complex. I'm sure that was never done because he wasn't on anybody's radar, but he is now."

Bea checked her phone's calendar. "I've gotta be in the office tomorrow late morning for a staff meeting, but I can meet you up there later. Like, two-ish?"

Lucy nodded. "I may go earlier, do some canvassing, but I'll see you there."

"Y'all need to be careful, Luce." Bea put her hand on Lucy's shoulder.

Lucy smiled and shrugged it off. "Flynn'll be out in Thermal directing the lab raid. Doyle and the rest of the assholes should be in custody by midmorning. I'll be fine. Safest day ever."

Her phone rang again. It was Molly for Tito. He retired back to his beach blanket and whispered words.

40

In the desert darkness, Christopher Flynn sat in the panel van smoking a cigarette. The barest flush of day was beginning to brighten the horizon. Stars still glimmered in the sky, and the dusky sweet smell of creosote and sagebrush scented the cool pre-dawn air. On the far side of the arroyo above the newest Riverside Pharma warehouse, his team gathered near their tactical truck awaiting his final guidance and direction before descending on the facility like a flash flood in a Sonoran rainstorm.

He and the German accountant, Neckar, had secured the accounts and the drug formulary data that they'd use to jump-start a deal somewhere else. All he had to do now was oversee the raid until his people had the action in hand, and then he'd disappear. No more bullshit government job, no more ex-wife bleeding him dry and kids who couldn't stand him. Doyle and friends would be left holding the proverbial bag of shit. They deserved it. They were it.

The only loose end he still worried about was Pine. The guy was a sneaky bastard even in death. He had the whole story, whether he realized it or not. And the Vega and Middleton bitches were rabid dire wolves. They knew more than they'd disclosed and were just waiting to screw him to the wall. He'd overheard one of them say she wanted to check out Pine's condo tomorrow, which was now today. He'd be there to make sure whatever they might discover was shut down hard.

"Cap. We're ready to roll," one of his men called, excitement in his voice. A slit of morning sky just at the horizon had turned a bloody orange. Flynn stubbed out his cig and grabbed his automatic. Adrenaline spiked. He was back in Afghanistan rushing across the arroyo to his team.

—

Bea tossed restlessly under the sheets. Her bedroom was dark as a closed closet except for the gleam of the LED clock on her dresser. It read 3:47 a.m. The raids would start just before sunrise, an hour away. Pete had warned her off showing up when law enforcement teams served the warrants and commenced their searches. He'd be leading the Burgess confrontation in Sylmar, Flynn would be supervising out in the desert, and likely the guy they'd met at the storage facility parking lot, DEA Special Agent Ron Gold, would descend on Doyle. The others, she didn't know about—likely DEA and FBI working with LA county sheriffs. Agent Gold's last words to her: *no press.*

Despite Pete's admonition and Gold's likely resistance, there would be press, at least at Doyle's hacienda. Bea couldn't suppress a wave of guilt for end-running Pete but also couldn't wait to see the asshole, Doyle, standing barefoot in his driveway in pretty pajamas whining at the top of his lungs as the feds executed their papers and ripped into every part of his ugly life.

She switched on the table lamp and tossed off a cotton blanket. Crawling out of the seductive warmth of her bed, she stood up tall, did a short routine of sun sign yoga stretches to get the blood flowing, then pulled on black running tights, a dark-gray T-shirt, and a hoodie. In the sweat socks she'd worn to bed, Bea tiptoed quietly into her bathroom across the hall, splashed cold water on her face in the glow of the nightlight, and pulled her hair into a ponytail.

Heading for the stairs, she peeked into Dexter's bedroom. He was dead out, long feet hanging off the end of the too-short double bed she'd bought for him in junior high. Hayes was sound asleep as well. Splayed across a beanbag chair, comic books and a spilled bowl of Doritos littered the floor at his side. She closed the door.

Grabbing her fanny pack and running shoes, Bea crossed the kitchen to the Keurig machine, made herself a double hit of espresso in a commuter cup, entered the attached garage, and slid into her silver BMW. In ten minutes, she was on San Vicente heading to Doyle's place in Brentwood just a few miles away. Passing high-end retail shops and restaurants, she turned onto Rockingham and motored north into the hills at the foot of the Santa Monica mountains. The exclusive community was made famous, or perhaps notorious, by the OJ Simpson fiasco. A million and a half would buy you a starter home, and you might see Gwyneth Paltrow, LeBron James, or Taylor Swift pulling out of a gated drive in a shiny Land Rover or pricey eCar. Street-side parking was only by permit, which Bea realized might be a problem.

As she navigated the narrow two-lane road higher into the hills, streetlights disappeared, and darkness was kept at bay only by custom residential lighting. Although a pale slip of day was beginning to brush the eastern prospect, it was still a nighttime sky. The end of Doyle's peaceful slumber was counting down.

Bea snugged her car up close to a thicket of oleander, white petals hovered like ghostly starfish in the gloom at the edge of the road. She doused her headlights. Looking out over Doyle's estate, she had about a three-block jog downhill through the quiet neighborhood.

Exiting her Beemer and stepping onto the pavement, Bea stuffed her phone into the fanny pack. Her press ID hung on a lanyard around her neck. She tucked it into her T-shirt, wanting to be identified only if necessary. She planned on discreetly watching it all go down from a hedge she'd scoped out across the street.

The muted thump of someone running sounded from the shadows around a curve. A second later, a black man with dreadlocks, dressed in basketball shorts and a Clippers T-shirt, jogged into view. He looked familiar, but Bea, not wanting to be recognized, glanced away and pretended to tie a lace. Her reporter face was not unfamiliar in LA. He passed her with a "g'morning." She raised her hand in acknowledgement as he cut to a dirt trail between two properties and continued his early jog up the steep incline.

A coyote howled in the distance. The dry, cool air smelled of dust and lingering night-blooming jasmine. Bea took several deep breaths and began to trot downhill, hoping to look like a random early morning fitness enthusiast to anyone who might glance her way. She usually put in about three miles every other day, but this run was going to be short and furtive.

Rounding a hairpin curve, her footfalls smacked the pavement. As the road straightened and descended sharply, Doyle's house, several blocks ahead, blazed with light. *Damn, looks like the raid is already well underway So much for rolling at dawn.*

Doyle's Mediterranean-style mansion was gated but not set far back from the street, allowing a clear view of the portico where action was playing out. As she approached, several unmarked cars and a crime scene van were parked in the driveway. Brandon Doyle himself stood on his front steps in a white T-shirt and white silky pants, giving hell to Special Agent Ron Gold. Two scantily clad teenaged girls pressed behind him. Bea knew they'd better be eighteen, or Doyle would be immediately off to the slammer on sex crimes along with any federal drug trafficking charges.

A young blond male agent in a DEA T-shirt, black military-style pants, and boots with his service revolver in a mesh shoulder holster, approached her. "Ma'am," he said. "This is official police business. Move along, please."

Bea clearly did not make it to the hedge she had aimed for, and now here she was, just where Pete didn't want her to be. She stepped away from the agent but still heard Doyle braying from his front porch.

"I told you, dickwads, I have nothing to hide. This whole witch hunt is purely political. You found nada, right? You incompetent fools. And when I'm senator, don't think I won't remember which agency trashed my house."

Bea felt sweat begin to dampen her armpits. They hadn't found anything? No way. That was the moment she realized she knew something Gold needed to be aware of. She knew about a safe room. Did he?

She turned to the agent blocking her way. "Sir, I have to talk with Ron Gold right now. I'm Beatrice Middleton from Network News, and I have some information he needs." She pulled out her lanyard and pushed her ID toward the young man. Her pulse was racing. Gold and his team couldn't leave empty-handed.

He took a quick glance. "I'm sorry, ma'am, but my orders are no media."

Across the lawn, Doyle continued to dance around and talk trash to Gold.

"Please move on, ma'am, or I'll have to detain you." The man was serious as the grave, but Bea had to talk with Gold.

She stepped back from the DEA guy and edged toward the wrought iron fence. "Special Agent Gold! Ron Gold!" she yelled.

He turned her way.

"Awww shit," Doyle cursed. The girls were now huddled together being escorted to a police cruiser. "It's Bea goddamn Middleton, one of my ex-wife's gal pals from TV news. Spreading lies about me. Fake news. Totally fake news. Arrest the ball-busting bitch!"

Bea raised her voice. "Agent Gold, please, I've got some information you need to know about. It could be pivotal."

He turned, eyes squinting her way. "What are you talking about..."

"Did you speak with Doyle's daughter? About the safe room?"

Gold moved toward Bea. She stepped closer to the fence. Was he was going to listen?

Doyle pounded his fist against a concrete porch column and winced. "Middleton is full of shit, just looking for a story. Those women want to ruin me. They got an agenda. Trying to turn my own beloved, brain-damaged daughter against me, too." He paced and scowled. "Arrest her ass. What are you waiting for, Gold, you pussy?"

Heat rose in Bea's face. "Nice jammies and sweet little girlfriends, Brandon. Are they in high school yet?" She shook her head in disgust.

"Shut the fuck up, bitch." He lurched in Bea's direction, but one of the agents grabbed him and pushed him down on a bench next to the front door.

"Let the woman through," Gold said to the young blond agent. The kid stepped aside with a frown.

"What is it, Ms. Middleton? This had better be worth my while, or as your friend Detective Anthony said last night, we'll take you in for interfering with a federal investigation. And I'm not bullshitting you. Hear me?"

"Okay, I hear you, but did you talk with Molly Doyle?"

An Asian-looking woman with short hair in her early thirties moved to Gold's side. Her nameplate said Ito. "I spoke with her in the hospital last night," she said.

"Did Molly tell you about the safe room where Doyle keeps his cameras and secret files, his piles of porn and God knows what else?" Bea asked.

Gold turned to his colleague with a questioning look on his face.

Ito shrugged. "Miss Doyle never mentioned anything about a safe room, but she was still pretty heavily sedated. We've got his security camera footage already downloaded."

"There may be another system." Bea felt the time was right to push her luck. Gold would either give her the benefit of the doubt or lock her up. "Molly told my friend Lucy Vega about a hidden room with big-screen TVs and additional computers. You met Lucy at the storage warehouse last night, Special Agent Gold. Come on. I think I know where it is. It might just be the nerve center."

Gold pursed his lips for an instant, then sighed. "Okay, show us what you think you got." He lowered his voice and caught Bea's eye. "This had better be good."

"This is bullshit," Doyle screamed, leaping up from his assigned bench. "I don't have a goddamn safe room. You bastards already confiscated everything I have, and you're not going to find anything that will incriminate me. This is outrageous."

Bea couldn't help but smirk at the look of panic on his face.

"Sit down, Mister Doyle," Gold ordered.

Doyle's voice changed from outraged victim to petulant teen. He wailed, "I want my phone! You can't do this!"

Gold turned to Doyle and growled, "You're a lawyer, sir. You read the warrant and know we have the right to seize all of your electronic devices, including phones." Gold then nodded at Bea.

Heart pounding, Bea hoped to heaven she could find the room, which was either a library or a study, and get the magic door to open before the feds called her bluff and arrested her. Molly had mentioned something about a button on a bookshelf. She had said her dad ran his house security from there. Supposedly, only he and Burgess had access.

Bea needed to talk to Molly. Hurriedly, she texted the girl and prayed she'd respond before Bea lost credibility by leading Gold randomly through the house. Were the contents of this room a figment of an injured girl's imagination, or was there something solid? Bea licked her dry lips. She was putting more than just her reputation on the line based on Molly's possibly unreliable information.

To Bea's relief, her phone chimed with a text back from Molly. Surreptitiously, she glanced at the message.

"It's in his office—white bookshelves. First floor, right-hand side. The button that opens the door is behind an antique brown leather King James Bible. LOL."

Gold opened the front door to the house and motioned Bea through. "Okay, Ms. Middleton. It's showtime. I hope you're right about this."

Me, too. Bea stepped into the foyer. It held the funereal scent of daylilies just past their prime. Orange pollen and withering stamens littered the white marble floor.

She had never been in Doyle's home. Taking a second to get acclimated, the soft light from open French doors pulled her toward what seemed to be the great room. White walls, leather couches, pricey artwork—all right out of *Architectural Digest*. As she stood in the center of the room, off to her right was an arched doorway revealing wall-to-wall, white bookcases below thick crown molding. *Bingo.*

"That's his office," Gold said, sounding irritated. "We've searched it top to bottom."

"Maybe there's more. The entry to the safe room is in there. The latching mechanism is behind an antique Bible." Bea led the way. There had to be over a thousand books on the shelves. Where to begin?

Doyle was yelling again, this time the obnoxious voice grated from the foyer. Then he was in the office, having thrown off two agents trying to contain him. He flew in front of a section of the bookcase featuring a row of vintage Chinese porcelain.

"Move, Brandon," Bea said. Was he standing in the way of the entry point, trying to shift their focus to another part of the room? She played a hunch. "Agents, could you remove Mister Doyle? He's blocking our access to the family Bible."

Gold nodded, and several of his people grabbed Doyle and hauled him out of the room. "This is sacrilege!" he squealed. "Don't you dare touch my family Bible. My great-grandfather brought it from Ireland."

Keeter, the pharmacist with the creepy, long fingers? Bea moved forward and touched the rare vases. They were held tightly in place with museum wax. One shelf down from the vases was a stack of three antique Bibles. The one on top seemed to be a King James version, favored by Catholics. She pulled it carefully from the shelf and opened the book. Latin. Bea's fingers then probed behind the other heavy tomes.

There it was, as Molly had said. She pushed a lever and stepped back, heart pounding as the case swung open. What would they find? Enough to put Doyle and his cartel away?

The secret door opened onto a broad console with a dozen big screens and five computer terminals. Fine leather office chairs, a viewing-and-editing station, and enough electronics to make full-on feature films—let alone maintain state-of-the-art security—were on display. On the center screen, what appeared to be a freeze-frame image, time-stamped 4:45 a.m., caught Doyle hopping midair from the sheets accompanied by the two waifish and naked girls.

Gold turned to Bea. "Thank you, Miss Middleton. You can be sure you'll be the first to get the story when we're ready to go with it." He pulled out his radio. "Delaney, send in the digital team. We got a lot of work to do."

41

Lucy woke up late to find the jogging stroller, that was usually just outside the kitchen door, missing. Next to the coffee maker and a cold blueberry pancake was a note: *Guys day out, off to Zuma Beach. Love you. M & H*

Michael knew she needed these last few days on the story before leaving it all behind for NYC. He was thrilled they were moving as a family, but Lucy sensed a twinge of guilt on his part as well. His needs were in the forefront, and Lucy was giving him that for now. It was the only way they'd have a chance.

She poured herself a cup of coffee from the carafe and sipped it, then finished off the pancake at the kitchen sink. It was wonderfully sticky with maple syrup.

The day was already unseasonably hot. Climate change had done a number on what used to be temperate summer mornings near the ocean. A decade ago, they rarely needed air-conditioning.

After the hit of caffeine and sugar, she took a quick shower, then ponytailed her hair and dressed in a loose-fitting, blue chambray shorts and a tank top. Lacing up trainers she used for trail running, she grabbed her camera and purse and was on her way to confront David Lee. She'd promised Bea she'd wait, but things were moving too slowly. She had to act. Had he betrayed her and somehow hooked into Doyle, Pang, and their cronies? Impossible. Right? She texted him that she was on her way.

—

The cluster of high-rise office buildings in Century City rose like heat-seeking missiles into the unconvincingly cool blue sky. Lucy parked in the underground lot and took the elevator to the marble atrium, where a pair of humorless guards at the security desk monitored entry to the upper floors.

Her sandals, flip-flopping across the hard floor, sounded like dull castanets. Ignoring the guards' disapproving faces, she leaned against the counter and almost swooned at the feel of the chill stone against her skin. "Lucy Vega, here for Mark Lee at Creative Talent Associates International."

She didn't know if Lee had received her text and was afraid she might have a hassle at security, but in moments, she was cleared to take the chrome-and-mirror elevator up to the top floor. Chester met her as the door to the penthouse slid open. Fresh orchids graced the reception foyer where a black-clad woman with spiky blue hair signed for a thick envelope and flirted with the handsome UPS driver. The dude flashed a disarming grin, then slipped her his resume and head shot—a wannabe actor. Delivery was his day job. Nothing like getting to know the gatekeepers at C-TAI.

Chester was not as friendly as during her last visit. This time, dressed in a lilac shirt, purple plaid kilt, and black patent leather Doc Martens, he led her down a windowless hall lit by overhead can lights. They illuminated an impressive array of Chinese landscape paintings. Lucy's stomach roiled, and she could feel her heartbeat begin to pound in her ears as she followed him past the pricey artwork. How would Mark receive her? To even vaguely suggest to a trusted friend that you might suspect their involvement in an international drug ring, like she was about to do, was literally making her sick.

The door to Mark's office was open. Chester motioned her in and then disappeared. Mark sat at his desk and looked up from a pile of file folders. Opposite floor-to-ceiling windows that overlooked the city, two big screens displaying his client's music videos played soundlessly. Lee had scored the proverbial corner office. He frowned at his longtime gal pal.

"Your text was very terse, Lucy, not like you. And what's the deal about me being part of some pharmaceutical scam? Are you insane?"

He didn't invite her to sit down, but she did so anyway. The cushy chair was made of buttery white leather that looked welcoming but stuck to the bare skin of her legs like her great-grandma's plastic couch cover. Where was Chester's former offer of the booze of her choice?

"Listen, Mark, I know you're not involved in this shit, but we have a murder investigation and have to find out if there's a tie-in to you. Maybe you're being set up—I don't know. But if I don't figure this out, the cops are going to come banging on your door with zero concern for you and your company's reputation. I'm sure you'd rather talk to me."

He scowled. "I never should have said yes to you."

Lucy winced. "No, you did the right thing. We can't let these people walk. So, help me here, okay?"

"Helping you is a dangerous act." He slumped back in his chair and sighed. "Okay, fill me in."

Lucy tried to move to the edge of her seat, but the leather was like Velcro. She grimaced.

Mark chuckled. "I know they look better than they feel, but I keep them so people won't get too comfy."

Lucy rolled her eyes. "All right, here's the deal. Your uncle was at Berkeley the same time as all of our suspects and was known to them. And we have evidence that you, Mark Lee, handled contracts for these people. Your name is on the documents, and the address is this building." Lucy tried to be cool and business-like, but she shredded a Kleenex in her hands.

"Have you ever seen a legal document prepared by me?"

"Yes, of course. I have examples right here in this file." She pulled a manila folder from her purse and presented him with several contracts he'd supposedly prepared. She placed them on the desk and sat back in the chair from hell. "Your name is on these, from your Century City office. And you went to Berkeley for your MBA, Stanford Law. So, it seemed logical to at least consider—"

"If you had ever seen a legal doc prepared by me, you'd know that I use my legal name, Ming Chao Lee, on all my work. Or 'shining journey,' as my dear mother would say."

He took a quick look at the contracts in her file, frowned, then pushed the papers back across the desk to Lucy, just out of her reach. "Those are not mine." He slapped down a black folder with the agency logo on the front. "These are. Read the signature lines."

Miserably uncomfortable, Lucy stashed the ruined tissue in her pocket and rose to pick up the papers. Sure enough, this was not the Mark Lee of Pang and cronies. The name was indeed Ming Chao, and the signature wasn't even close. Along with embarrassment, she felt an immense wave of relief.

"Great, this is good. I think this will completely exonerate you. I'm sorry, Mark, sorry that you had to go through this."

He crossed his arms over his chest and glowered. "I can't believe you didn't trust me."

"But I did, and still do, trust you completely." His face was so grim. Had she lost his valued friendship forever? "I just had to make sure the evidence agreed. I know you understand how these kinds of things work."

"Okay, I'm just pissed that I have to deal with this crap. I have so much on my plate these days." He unfolded his arms and leaned her way. "But I can understand how you could think it was me."

"You can?" A glimmer of hope that he might not see her as a total traitor kindled a tiny flame in her heart.

He continued, "For a while, I routinely got mail for a Mark Lee who is a property manager and real estate developer or something like that. The business moved out several months ago. His office is, or was, the same address, different floor. He's also of Chinese heritage, but no relation. Mark Lee's a common name. And I think I digitized his card." He scrolled his computer screen, then tapped several keys. "The building administrator may know where he's gone." Mark's printer groaned out a page with a card in the center. He handed it to Lucy.

She stood up and cleared her throat. "I hope you can forgive me, Mark. I had to follow up on the lead. Please don't take this personally—I had to do due diligence and all that. And I want you to know that your initial translations helped us tons, got us focused. The whole nasty organization is being served with subpoenas and warrants today. They've been poisoning people, and you've helped in getting them off the street. You've saved lives, literally."

A meager smile struggled to his lips. "Well, at least that's good to hear."

His phone rang. He checked the caller ID, then stood. "I have to take this, Lucy."

"Of course, sure. Again, I'm so sorry to have added to your bad day, Mark, Ming Chao." Truly a man on a shining journey. She wanted to give him a hug but didn't think it would be appreciated this time.

On the way out, she stopped by the building management office and asked about the other Mark Lee. They had no forwarding information and had heard the company closed permanently. Lucy texted Bea about the Lee situation and suggested Aja or Dexter go through public records to see if there was any tie-in between the MIA real estate company and properties involved with Doyle, Pang, and their cartel.

Trudging back to the parking lot, Lucy glanced at her watch—it was almost noon. Time to head up to Pine's condo in Valencia. She raced to her car, pressed start, and dialed up the air. Steering toward the exit, she swiped her credit card to pay the parking fee, winced at the ridiculous charge, then turned onto Boulevard of the Stars.

A dingy white panel van pulled out of the underground lot just behind her. A ragged splinter of fear poked Lucy hard. But a middle-aged woman was behind the wheel, not Flynn or Burgess. Another dusty, light-colored van of similar make appeared in line behind the woman. Lucy knew she had to chill. The upsetting meeting with Lee had rattled her nerves, and now she was seeing Flynn and scary white vans everywhere.

If Century City was a furnace today, Valencia in the northern metro was even hotter. Lucy's car thermometer read 108 outside as she turned into Pine's condo community. The parking lot was mostly empty—evidently the pandemic aftermath had not kept these workers home. She found a space just down from the manager's office, grabbed her gear, and got out. She recalled the man's name was McTavish.

When she knocked on the manager's door, yapping commenced. What was the name of his little dog? Gigi? Fifi? She hoped to hell the guy would give her the key to Pine's condo. Out of desperation, she'd purchased a lock-picking kit online and had watched YouTube instructional videos, but she didn't have much faith that she could make the magic happen.

The manager's door opened and the septuagenarian McTavish greeted her. Clad in tight, black, knee-length leggings and a black undershirt with a Gold's Gym logo. His dog was tucked under his skinny arm.

"May I help you, young lady?"

"Yes, hello, Mr. McTavish and little Fifi, right?"

"Why, yes." His affect brightened.

"I'm Lucy Vega. My associate Bea Middleton and I were here the week before last. We're friends of the late David Pine and your former tenant, Claire Thompson."

"Poor David. And Claire's friends…" He hesitated for a moment, then recognition dawned. "Ah yes, your colleague was the beautiful African-American woman."

"That's her, Beatrice Middleton. Definitely a stunner." *And I'm chopped liver?* "She's on her way to meet me right now. We wanted to get permission from you to see David's apartment one last time. Looks like it's still unoccupied."

"New folks move in tomorrow, actually. Locks get changed first thing in the morning. You came just in time."

Lucy smiled with relief. He was going to give her the key.

"By the way, we found Claire," Lucy said. "She's living with a friend in Van Nuys for now. Still extremely upset. Not sure you ever recover from something like that."

"Yes, I was afraid it would keep the apartment off the market. The law says I have to disclose that a death happened in a residence, but so far, so good. The applicants were cool with it. Wait just a minute, and I'll get you the key."

Offended by his cavalier attitude, Lucy wondered how any prospective tenant could be cool with murder. Maybe she was being overly sensitive. Death is everywhere, and everyone needs a place to live.

He stepped back into his apartment and rummaged in a metal tackle box on his kitchen island, then returned to the doorway and handed Lucy the key. "Any word on the killer?"

"The police have a couple leads, but nothing yet."

"What a shame." He shrugged. "Please give Miss Thompson my best. And Miss Middleton, too."

"Will do."

"And just leave the key in the drop box when you're done. Fifi and I are heading down to the weight room to pump iron." He chuckled. "Too hot to exercise outdoors."

"Miserable!" Lucy smiled and wiped a hand across her forehead. "Thank you, sir. Have a nice workout."

She turned and hurried toward Building A without passing anyone. Tennis balls bouncing on a distant court echoed from down the arroyo. Up the cement stairway, she found Pine's unit and let herself in. The place smelled of fresh paint and disinfectant. The living room rug where David Pine's blood had spilled appeared to have been replaced. This was where their friend and colleague had lived and breathed—a fine man and an outstanding journalist with homicidal information.

Sadness turned to anger, burning in her chest. Would the murderer walk away? It was looking likely. But the chance of finding some resolution, however meager, to life's many intolerable injustices was what kept Lucy hooked into photography and journalism.

Reaching into her large purse, she pulled out an electric screwdriver and a plastic case containing an array of bits. After one last perusal of cupboards, drawers—tops, bottoms, and sides—and toilet tanks, she would remove the covers from every vent in the place. If Pine had left one scrap of information behind, Lucy was going to find it.

42

Bea sat at her desk inputting notes and observations from the morning raid while finishing off a leftover carton of mu shu pork. She was beginning to outline the story and was wildly anxious to know what Gold had uncovered in Doyle's clandestine safe room. She'd tried to hang around, but they'd thrown her out even though she was the one who led them to the goodies.

A wave of exhaustion suddenly hit her hard, but the day was still early. The clock on the corner of her screen indicated time to head up to Valencia and meet Lucy for a final search of Pine's condo. She didn't have high hopes but also didn't want to miss turning over every single rock and pebble of possibility.

She pressed the Save button and powered down her laptop, tossed the empty food carton in the trash, and hustled through the cube farm to the stairs. Her cellphone rang with an *Unknown Caller*. Life insurance? Act now or miss out on something big. She disconnected.

Avoiding the elevator in favor of the exercise she hadn't gotten this morning, Bea ignored the phone ringing again. As she entered the stairwell, she was immediately struck by its unwashed gymnasium aroma. Why did building stairwells always smell so rank? Her phone sounded yet again—*Unknown Caller. Give me a break.* Boom. *Adios.*

Descending the stairs at a healthy pace, the phone rang once more as she stepped outside into the parking lot. Persistent sucker. What was going on? She hit *Accept Call.* "Hello."

There was a long hesitation on the line and then a scratchy voice. "Bea Middleton?"

"Yes. Who's this?" Bea squeezed the key fob and unlocked her car door. She slid onto the hot driver's seat, opened the windows, and immediately turned on the air.

"It's Claire Thompson."

Bea froze. *What the...* "Uh, hello, Claire."

Had the woman been swept up in one of the morning's raids? Then, Bea remembered Pete saying that if anyone might fold and be willing to negotiate a deal, it would either be Burgess, who was trying to make a better life for himself, or Thompson, who might have actually been in love with Pine.

"Claire, where are you?"

The woman uttered a peal of laughter that rang with a definite note of hysteria. "I'm out of the country, somewhere I can't be extradited or found by Pang and his monsters." She began to cry.

"Pang and Doyle—they were picked up early this morning on a DEA warrant. It's over," Bea said.

"You don't understand."

"What don't I understand? Tell me. I'm on your side, Claire. I know you loved David."

There was a heartrending sob and labored breathing. Thompson was clearly struggling for control.

Bea checked the backup camera and moved out of her parking spot. "Can we get together and talk? I'll meet you anywhere."

Bea had an app allowing her to record calls. She'd never used it before and fumbled, dropping her phone. She stretched down and snatched it from the floor, hoping she'd engaged the appropriate prompts.

Bea could hear Claire laugh and then cry again. "It's not over."

"What do you mean?" She pressed the button on the steering column to engage her Bluetooth and zoomed up the freeway on-ramp.

There was a long pause with Claire sniffling and hiccuping. Then, silence.

Bea began to sweat and not from the temperature. She pulled into the near lane and kept to the speed limit. "Claire? You still there? Talk to me."

"You haven't caught David's murderer."

"You mean Price Burgess?"

"God, no, not Burgess. He's muscle but not a cold-blooded killer. I saw who did it, and now he's after me."

"Who are you talking about, Claire? Who killed David? We'll get the son of a bitch. I promise you."

Claire's voice dropped to a near whisper. "It was Christopher Flynn."

"Pang and Doyle's security guy?"

"Yes," she said. "He's a DEA agent, gone rogue."

"Oh, my God." Bea almost changed lanes on top of a semi. Its deep diesel horn blasted. "Are you certain of this?"

"I saw him do it. I started screaming and he ran."

"Will you testify to this in court?"

"No way, I'm gone. But I wanted somebody who could maybe do something to know."

In the background, Bea heard a garbled announcement over a public address system. Was it from an airport? The language was not English. "We could talk to the police about witness protection..."

Claire laughed out loud again, then blew her nose. "I'll send you a link from my burner phone. Explains everything. Please don't try to find me."

"But Claire..."

The line went dead.

Traffic had suddenly thinned, so she floored it. The Beemer could move. She dialed Pete, but he didn't pick up. *Damn him.* She left a voice message.

"Pete! I just talked to Claire Thompson. Said she saw Flynn

murder David Pine. I recorded her phone call, but she's permanently MIA—like, out of the country. Lucy's up at Pine's condo. I'm on the way. Flynn could be tailing her. Damn it, get back to me."

Two minutes later, Pete returned her call. No greeting—straight to business.

"We had a solid raid this morning. Fill you in later. Flynn headed the team taking down the labs in Thermal, but I heard from one of his people that the dude was only there for the first half hour, then disappeared."

"Going where?"

"I dunno, but if he shows up at that condo, he must be scared shitless there's something there that'll incriminate him."

Bea's BMW shot past a Maserati. "Where are you?"

"On the 210, almost to the 5—twenty out."

"Me, too. I'll give Lucy a heads-up. She has no idea that Flynn disappeared from the Thermal raid."

"Roger that. I'll call for support, just in case. Tell your girlfriend to lock herself in if she's gonna stay at Pine's. Or better yet, get the hell outta there. But she won't go for that." He paused. "Later." His police radio crackled. Bea heard his siren activate.

He was gone.

Fingers slick with perspiration, Bea dialed Lucy. No answer. She left a voicemail.

"Flynn murdered Pine. Lock the doors, and call me back ASAP. Pete's on his way."

Cursing as she came upon a slow clot of traffic, Bea prayed that her friend got the message.

43

Lucy commenced her scan for possible hidden info at the top of the kitchen cabinets. She hoisted herself onto the marble counter. Pine was not particularly athletic and would probably never have climbed this high, but she planned to cover every inch. She checked the cupboards for leftover detritus, for weak sides that could be popped open, or loose molding that could be pried off.

Nothing.

Clambering down, Lucy did the same with every lower cupboard and drawer. Again, nothing. The kitchen was clear.

She pulled on blue nitrile gloves and performed the same routine in the two bathrooms. False bottoms to drawers, the toilet tanks, suspicious floor tiles—all was copacetic.

Walking the edges of the carpet, she looked for places it could have been pulled up, with items hidden below. Nothing.

She counted seven HVAC vents—one in the kitchen, two in the living and dining room, one in each bathroom, and one in each bedroom—all floor-level. Pulling out her flashlight and electric screwdriver, she placed a Phillips head in the chuck, torqued it tightly, and began in the kitchen with the first vent.

The work went smoothly. She pried off the cover and peered carefully into the dark cavity, ran her gloved hand up the duct, and only felt cool metal. Nothing stashed in this one.

She repeated the task in each room but came up empty. Her last chance was the vent in the second, smaller bedroom, which also could have been Pine's study.

Her phone rang on the kitchen counter. She'd respond when she was done with this last vent. Probably Bea calling to say she was on her way. Looked like a wasted trip.

Lucy knelt down on the rug and removed the vent screws. They were so loose that they practically fell out onto the carpet. She lifted off the cover, turned on her flashlight, and looked inside. *Shit.* A shot of excitement iced her very bones.

An old-school, handheld mini-recorder had been pushed back into the corner. She ran her hand up into the ductwork. Nothing more. This was it.

She thought she heard a quiet thump or a door closing nearby.

"Hello? Bea? That you?" No reply.

Lucy stilled to listen, then scolded herself. Probably just something outside or in a neighboring condo, or maybe from those tennis courts. When she got this amped-up, she became overly sensitive and hypervigilant. On airplanes, Lucy couldn't stop herself from listening through her flying phobia haze for an engine to shut down or a hydraulic hose to burst. She laughed at her paranoia and proceeded to remove the recorder and slip it into the pocket of her shorts. Carefully, Lucy replaced the vent cover, stood up, and headed back to the kitchen.

She put the electric drill on the counter next to the sink. Peeling off her gloves, Lucy pulled out the recorder for a moment, then hit *Play*.

It was David Pine's voice, no question.

"Bea—it's David here. I'll be putting this recording in the FedEx for you first thing in the morning." *The morning he never lived to see.* "Sorry to be sending you all this stuff, but I need backup in case something happens. It's about Christopher Flynn, a DEA agent currently undercover with the Riverside sheriffs in Thermal. He's moonlighting as security head for Riverside Pharma. I have a witness that says he's a double agent on Doyle and Pang's payroll…"

Lucy sensed movement behind her, but not soon enough.

"Look at me, bitch." The voice was low and malevolent.

The voice—she'd heard it in the eucalyptus grove at Pine's funeral. Flynn.

Slowly, Lucy turned and found herself staring down the tight, black hole of a silencer screwed tight to the Glock 17 she'd taken from him at the storage facility. The same gun he'd probably used in Pine's murder. Electrons began to buzz in her brain, raising the hairs on her arms like before a storm-loaded sky closed in and lightning rent the air. She could almost smell the ozone. Or was it sulfur emanating from his evil soul?

"I personally warned you at the funeral, and you didn't listen." He moved in closer, like he had in the grove. This time no Ray-Bans, just hard, smoldering coals assessing her like she was pond scum. "You've really fucked up this time. But I got a place for you in the desert. I was gonna use it for Tito Luna, but you'll fit real fine. Then I'm gone."

This guy was insane. "Where are you, uh, going?" Could she keep him talking, buy some time?

"Setting up shop somewhere there's nothing but opportunity and no oversight." He laughed out loud but without emotion.

"You won't get away with this. You don't double- or triple-cross the DEA, the Riverside cops, and Doyle's organization and walk away free and clear."

Lucy noticed a large, dark-colored duffel bag next to the door behind him. Her heart hammered in her ears. Was he going to stuff her dead body into that thing? No way in hell. *I have a baby. He needs his mother. I will not let Henry grow up to be an orphan like I was.*

"You're not dumping me in a shallow grave in the desert or anywhere else, Flynn, you piece of shit." Her eyes darted to the door. Could she beat him to it before getting shot? Not likely.

His eyes narrowed to slits, and he spit on the new rug. "You stupid cunt. You are nothing. A skinny girl who takes fucking pictures. You'll do what I say. Give me that recorder you found."

Lucy hesitated an instant too long.

He sneered and seized her arm. Violently, the homicidal bully shoved her against the kitchen counter and wrenched the tape recorder out of her fingers. The granite corner cut painfully into her lower back. He jammed the gun against her temple so hard she was momentarily stunned. It only served to amp up her adrenaline and desperation. Close combat made a perp with a firearm vulnerable.

Lucy snarled and, fast as a cat, grabbed the suppressor. She shoved the barrel down and aside with all her might. The gun fired. The sound was a muffled *pop*.

Ducking, Lucy wrenched herself from Flynn's grasp and raked her boot down his shin. He yelped and fired again. She felt a hot burn to her neck and collapsed onto the counter by the sink.

The electric screwdriver sat inches away.

Lucy snatched it, spun around, and drilled the bit into Flynn's eye.

Blinded, he screamed and dropped his gun. It skittered behind a garbage can. His eyeball hung from its socket.

Lucy's face flushed with determination and rage. "Feel *that* from a skinny girl who takes pictures," she rasped. Her throat was too constricted with panic to scream.

The driver whined like a dentist's instrument in Lucy's grasp. Flynn was disoriented. They struggled for the tool. Lucy kicked, bit, and scratched, finally breaking free. She went for the other eye. The screwdriver made contact beneath his eyebrow. Blood flowed like he was weeping crimson tears.

Flynn's right hook came up out of nowhere, slamming into Lucy's ribs. She heard a crack. She gasped and fell to her knees. The drill flew from her hand, and blackness threatened. In that moment, Flynn managed to regain possession of his gun.

—

Brakes screaming into the turn, Bea followed Pete's car to the condo parking lot. They leaped out of their vehicles almost in tandem. Hesitating for an instant, then, unspoken, they set aside their personal issues and sealed their partnership on this strike.

Bea led the way toward Pine's condo. "There's her Jeep." Bea's heart banged in her chest.

They jogged quickly down the sidewalk, almost running over a scrawny, older man in black leggings carrying a chihuahua.

"Oh, Miss Middleton, isn't it?" His face was alight in recognition. "I'm McTavish, the complex manager. Your friend is up in David's condo."

"That's where we're headed."

"Lucy, that's her name, she wanted one last look-see. I gave her the key."

"Yes, thank you, you're very kind." Bea turned toward the stairs to the second floor, beginning to run.

McTavish called after them, "I talked to the guy, David's other friend, too. Gave him a key as well. The locks will be changed tomorrow anyway."

"Fuck." Pete drew his gun. They took the steps two at a time.

Bea saw the panel van in her peripheral vision. "He's here."

—

Scrambling away on her hands and knees, Lucy's breath came hard. Flynn grabbed her by the hair and jerked her up onto her feet. She gritted her teeth, twisted, and lunged at Flynn again, her boot making direct contact with his groin. He lurched and slipped on the slick, bloody kitchen floor. Losing his balance like a malevolent Bambi on ice, he fell hard. His head crunched on the stove's edge.

Eyes a blinded, bloody mess, Flynn shot at Lucy and missed.

She fell back against a lower cupboard. Another *pfft*. A slug burned her thigh.

Flynn pulled himself off the floor, lunged, and kicked. His foot hammered Lucy's chest. The broken ribs shrieked in agony.

She rolled away, sucking for oxygen. Was a lung punctured?

He fired again, but the shot went wide. How many more rounds did he have? The Glock 17 carried fifteen and one in the chamber. It was over for her.

Footsteps hammered outside in the breezeway. Somebody called her name. Or was she hallucinating?

Face red as the devil himself, Flynn aimed his Glock at Lucy's center mass.

The condo's door slammed open. Pete bellowed, "Drop the fuckin' gun, Flynn."

The asshole spun around, weapon waving wildly at the detective. Lucy scrabbled to the side, out of the way.

Pete fired once, twice.

Flynn dropped in place, his ruined eyes staring at nothing.

Bea rushed to Lucy.

44

In the backyard of Bea's Santa Monica bungalow, the aqua pool sparkled, hummingbirds hummed, and bougainvillea's fuchsia poms glowed as the sun settled into a sweet, pink sky. The lovely summer evening offered a sense of perfection only California at its best could conjure. Bea slid an arm around Lucy's shoulders. Despite the warm night, she felt her friend shiver.

Lucy exhaled a quick breath. "Doc said another millimeter lower and it would have been my jugular that got nicked." Her voice was weak and ragged. She picked at the stark white gauze bandage on her neck as if it were a scab she was trying to dislodge. "I still can't believe this happened. I could've bled out right there in Pine's condo on top of Flynn, that wretched excuse for a human being." Her fingers on the wound folded into a tight, angry fist. "Baby Henry almost lost his mother. I feel like my whole life is a spinning top and I'm trying not to fall off."

Bea followed Lucy's gaze to Alyssa on the far side of the pool with Henry on her hip. She was showing off big-sister skills with Hayes trailing along attentively.

Bea sighed, reached into the cooler for a couple beers, and handed one to Lucy. "Life ain't nothin' if not a balancing act on chronically unsure terrain. Sometimes we deal with an itty-bitty earthshaker, sometimes it's a jolt off the frickin' Richter chart. You dodged a bullet, literally, sweet pea. But it simply wasn't your time to leave this planet. The Big Apple's calling. Now, you must go forth and continue your precious life. *Carpe diem*, right?"

Lucy nodded, but the stunned look remained.

"By the way," Bea said, "the Mark Lee who was the property management and real estate guy we initially mistook for *your* Mark Lee the talent agent turns out to have brokered the sale of the Thermal warehouses to Pang and crew, along with similar setups in Arkansas, Louisiana, and West Virginia. He also facilitated Pang's clinic and Doyle's mansion, plus a bunch of other related stuff." Bea squeezed Lucy's hand. "The feds nabbed him and are auditing his business records with a fine-tooth comb."

"So relieved my dear friend wasn't part of it. I knew he wasn't." Lucy blinked away tears that welled in her eyes. "Made no sense." She took a distracted sip of her beer.

"Hey, girl, enough shoptalk. Let's go get a bowl of that jambalaya Pete's been cooking up. Hardly worth dating a Cajun man without enjoying the cuisine."

Lucy nodded. As they headed inside, she asked, "You two all right?"

"Talk about shifting ground. I love the man and he loves me, but as much as Pete says he's into my so-called independent free spirit, he hates it. Know what I mean?"

"You know I do." Lucy sighed and touched the bandage on her neck again and limped toward the house. "Anyway, let's focus on the positive tonight, shall we? Like food."

"And Dexter says he has some kind of big surprise for me tonight. Very tight-lipped about it. I think he may have ordered one of those cheesecake variety plates from the New York Deli and had it shipped in."

Lucy smiled. "Yum, I hope you're right."

They moved through open French doors into the kitchen where the crowd was growing. A huge pot bubbled atop Bea's stove. The spicy, bold fragrance was swoon-worthy. Aja joined Bea and Lucy.

"Do you know what's in the jambalaya?" she asked. "I've never had it before."

"Get ready for a treat." Bea tossed the ingredients question to Pete who waxed enthusiastic about his Louisiana family recipe.

Aja fired up a zydeco playlist on her iPhone.

Pete winked at her, picked up a wooden spoon, and held it as though he was about to conduct an orchestra, waving it to the tune. "First, we got the basics—onion, celery, and bell peppers. Then the meat—smoked sausage, usually andouille, but as a nod to my other half, I use sweet Italian sausage."

Bea remembered the very first time she and Pete met and how they bantered about whether Georgia or Louisiana had the best barbecue. Food had always been an item of enjoyment between them. Was it possible that this might be the last of the man's cooking she'd ever savor? A bitter taste rose in her mouth.

"Then I pile in the shrimp and chicken. Once the meat and vegetables have cooked, tomatoes, stock, and rice are added to the pot. The spices I use are red pepper flakes, cayenne, garlic powder, and black pepper, finished with my long-deceased *Tante* Marie's secret ingredient. Beyond that, I improvise."

A big green salad and two pans of cornbread sat in the center of the island amid open bottles of Italian red wine.

"So, grab your bowls," Pete invited all, "and *bon appétit, mes amis!*"

Bea sensed their eyes skittering over each other, too fearful to connect and see a relationship slipping away.

As Pete was finishing his spiel, Dexter and Aja grabbed bowls and were first in line, with Hayes and Alyssa next. Michael Burleson now had baby Henry. They were still enjoying time by the pool where the kiddo had discovered the cornhole game set and was reaching his chubby arms into the opening.

Mary O'Hanlon came from the back porch and stood with Lucy and

Bea, watching the young people dig in and moan at the deliciousness.

"You okay, Mary?" Bea asked.

She nodded, a tired smile on her lips. "Knowing that Brandon Doyle no longer has control over our lives is, well, a dream come true from the nightmare that Molly and I have been living in over the past years! I will be eternally grateful to you both."

They hugged and clinked glasses in toast.

The doorbell rang. "Come in!" Bea yelled.

Tito and Molly, faces flushed with happy exertion, joined the group. Bea leaned over to Mary. "As Queen Elizabeth said in the movie *Shakespeare in Love*, 'She's been plucked since I saw her last, a woman knows.'"

Mary winced and shook her head.

"She couldn't have been plucked by a sweeter William," Lucy whispered.

"Come on, ladies, get some grub before it disappears," Pete called out to the three mothers. With enthusiasm, they moved in for bowls and spoons.

Dexter laughed and hooted with someone at the front door.

"I wonder what's going on out there," Bea said.

In seconds, the cause was known.

Bea's brother Luther, Mary's lover and sheriff of Shellman County in South Georgia, stepped into the kitchen and up to the island. The bodies parted to make way for the big man. Trailing Luther, as he had all his life, was Rio Deakins, her brother's best friend and a man who'd joined the Middleton family when he was an abandoned eight-year-old boy. The two had been her irritating big brothers since she was five.

Bea felt her mouth drop open. She thought her heart would burst with surprise and delight. "Oh, my Lord! What in the world?" She grinned, shaking an admonishing finger. "You two bad boys!"

She turned to her son who was smiling ear-to-ear. "So, this is the surprise you've been so cagey about?"

"Uh-huh. Uncle Luther wanted to keep it on the down-low," Dexter said. "So amazing that they're here."

"I thought you were ordering in cheesecake."

"We be cheesecake!" Luther declared, flexing a bicep.

Mary laughed out loud. In a flash, she was in Luther's arms.

And then there was Rio. Tall, black, and gorgeous, he was Dexter's mentor and father figure, as well as an Emory professor and Special Forces vet with an expertise in PTSD. Not to mention, the man was the secret and unattainable love of Bea's life—the man she could never have because he was married to another woman who was smart, beautiful, and he loved her.

"Bring it here, Beazly girl. I haven't seen you for ages. Just that ugly son of yours." He hugged her tight and spun her around, laughing.

When Rio finally let her go, Bea's eyes slid to Pete. This time they connected. He knew Bea's history with Rio and could probably feel her popping pheromones. He backed away.

Bea didn't follow him.

"My God, what are you two *doing* here?" Mary's face was wet with happy tears. "Okay, fess up. How did this happen?"

Luther laughed and kissed her again. "Rio got a last-minute invite to a UCLA conference."

"Their keynote speaker bailed," Rio said.

"They were desperate," Luther teased, "but it was all-expenses-paid with a plus-one."

"My wife's in New York, so I talked Luther into taking a couple vacation days. The good Lord knows, he must have hundreds saved up. Anyhow, here we are!" Rio slapped a big box of pralines onto the countertop. "To celebrate Lucy and her family's big move. Straight from River Street Sweets in Savannah, Georgia."

The crowd appreciatively *ahhhed* and dug in. Introductions were made all around. More hugs and hand slaps.

A half hour in, Pete made his excuses—had to pick up the kids, it was his weekend. Bea didn't think it was his weekend, but she walked him to the front door with promises that they would talk soon.

With a sad, heavy heart, she watched him drive away. He didn't look back. Strains of *New York, New York* drifted out from the kitchen. Despite her attempts to be upbeat for Lucy's sake about the

East Coast move, the loss of Detective Pete Anthony triggered feelings of desolation. An empty nest, no lover, a fantasy lover she couldn't have, her best friend soon thousands of miles away, and Mary and Luther returning to Savannah—it was overwhelming.

She shut the front door behind her to block out the happy sounds inside. Struggling for composure, Bea sat for a moment next to a potted geranium on a wrought iron bench she'd bought at a yard sale.

She must focus on the positive. Doyle, Pang, and his cronies were in custody. Burgess had turned state's witness and was singing like a bird. Claire was on the lam, but likely no other folks would be poisoned or denied the medications they needed to survive in this hard world. And David Pine's murderer was dead. Her journalistic work had meaning. That's where she would return and find comfort.

Bea's phone chirped. She took a quick look. Her boss, Winfrey Chambers, had left a text message.

"The Daily News is for sale. Maybe we should gather some friends, pool our pesos, and give it a shot. Thoughts? Talk Monday."

Something stirred deep inside of Bea. Intrigue? Dread? Hope? Monday was only a day away.

Acknowledgments

Deep appreciation to the Rocky Mountain Fiction Writers amazing Littleton critique group led by Mike Hope and Mindy McIntyre. All stellar writers, teachers, and colleague--this crew is the best!!

Thank you to authors Rosemary Gibson and Janardan Prasad Singh for their exemplary work, China Rx: Exposing the Risks of America's Dependence on China for Medicine. This work helped spur the root idea for The Rx for Murder.

Thank you to my insightful beta readers Marlene Simon, Carolyn Olson Adams, and Karen Sackler Novick for finding the issues and helping me fix them.

Special shout out to the supportive Colorado writing community including my friends at Rocky Mountain Mystery Writers of America, Sisters in Crime-Colorado, the Colorado Author's League and Rocky Mountain Fiction Writers.

Sincere gratitude to Susan Brooks, publisher extraordinaire at indie press, Literary Wanderlust. It's a privilege to be part of this great team.

And finally, props to my family—Alan, Lacey, Michael, and my new twin granddaughters Paige and Lillian. Love you all so much.

Biography

Voted Rocky Mountain Fiction Writers Writer of the Year for 2021-22, Sue Hinkin was raised in Chicago and is a former college administrator, TV news photographer, and NBC-TV art department manager. She was also a Cinematography Fellow at the American Film Institute. Her debut novel, DEADLY FOCUS, a thriller featuring Los Angeles TV news journalist Bea Jackson and her BFF, photographer Lucia Vega, was a 2018 International Book Award finalist. The second book in the series, a Reader's Choice winner and Silver Falchion short-lister, LOW COUNTRY BLOOD, is set in Savannah, GA where Hinkin was a Dean at Savannah College of Art and Design. THE BURN PATIENT was released mid-pandemic and recently won the Foreword Indies award for best mystery from an independent publisher and the Colorado Humanities Center for the Book Award for Best Thriller of 2020. THE MERMAID BROKER was released April 1, 2021 to strong reviews. Book 5 in the series, THE Rx FOR MURDER, will be released in July 2022. See more at www.suehinkin.com. Sue Hinkin now lives in Littleton, Colorado where she is the new grandmother of twin girls who already love a good book.